Also by Sar

Eyes on Me

SARA CATE

sourcebooks
casablanca

Published by Sourcebooks Casablanca, an imprint of Sourcebooks
P.O. Box 4410, Naperville, Illinois 60567–4410
(630) 961-3900
sourcebooks.com

Originally self-published in 2022 by Sara Cate.

Cataloging-in-Publication Data is on file with the Library of Congress.

Printed and bound in the United States of America.
SB 10 9 8

Trigger Warning

Dear Reader,

Your safety and well-being are important to me. Please be aware before embarking on this story that there are themes and first-person experiences that may be triggering to some readers. This book deals with topics of **depression, anxiety**, and **attempted suicide**.

I promise you there is a happy ending involving a body-confident camgirl and a very vulgar voyeur with bad jokes and a filthy mouth.

Prologue

Seven Years Ago
Garrett

"So I had a fistful of her hair in my hand, and we were both in the moment when I looked her right in the eye and said, 'Suck my cock like a good little girl.' The next thing I knew, she reared back her fist and clocked me right in the face," Emerson says with a groan.

"Oh shit!" I shout with a grimace.

"Damn!" Hunter replies with a laugh.

Poor Maggie is staring at Emerson with wide eyes and a look of horror on her face. "I don't think she liked that."

I can't help but laugh as I watch my best friend wince, holding his beer against his cheek to soothe the giant purple bruise he's sporting. I would have paid good money to see that play out. I can just imagine him at that moment, the big man that he is, thinking he had a pliable woman in his hands, only for her to sock him right in the face.

It's a pity that they couldn't have a little fun, that they didn't know going into it that they were *not* on the same page sex-wise.

"I mean…I thought we were getting along great," he says. "She seemed kinky enough, and she definitely appeared into it, but I guess I was wrong. Not a fan of a little sexy degradation, apparently."

Yeah, I know the feeling. The last time I brought a girl back home and tried anything outside of vanilla, it didn't go well to say the least. I tried to record the sex—nope. I asked another girl to masturbate and let me watch—nope. I tried to finger a woman at the bar in public, where no one could clearly see what we were doing—nope.

It made me feel like a creep. Like there was something wrong with me because I wanted to try shit outside of the "norm." Just like I'm sure Emerson feels about his little degradation kink.

How many of us have felt comfortable enough in the moment to really ask for what we want only to be rejected and treated like a freak? So yeah…I get it.

That's probably why it's been so long since I've been between the sheets with a woman.

"Fuck, man." I let the words slip through my lips, and all my friends glance my way. "It's bullshit that there isn't a way to match people up by the kinky shit they like to do in the bedroom."

They all laugh. Naturally, they think I'm joking, and I guess, most of the time, I am. But not this time.

"I'm fucking serious," I say, breaking through the laughter. "How nice would it be if you could meet up with someone who likes the same twisted shit you do? You wouldn't have to hide it or be embarrassed by the kinks that get your panties wet."

"You're fucking crazy, Garrett," Hunter says, but I slam my beer down.

"I am not. Who here doesn't have some freaky bedroom desires you've always wanted to do but are too afraid to ask? I mean, obviously, Emerson isn't afraid to ask."

They laugh again.

"Come on. I'm serious," I say. They can joke all they want, but I have heard their dirty stories. I know my friends have some freaky kinks they're not owning up to. "Out of all the shit you've done, what is the one thing you wish you could ask for? You know you have something. So let's hear it."

"You first," Maggie replies with a mischievous grin.

"Fine." I straighten my spine and finish my beer, letting the liquid courage seep into my veins. "I like to watch."

"Watch what?" Hunter asks with a look of skepticism.

I shrug. "Anything, I guess."

"So you'd rather watch people having sex than have it yourself?"

I never really thought about it like that, but yeah, I guess so. I nod.

"You're a voyeur," Emerson adds, and I glance over at him. He doesn't sound surprised. I've never really tried that word on to see how it feels, but I don't hate it. It makes sense, and I guess that's what I am.

"Is that really so weird?" I ask. "I'm talking completely consensual. I'm not going around and peeping into people's windows or anything, but if I could find a girl who wouldn't mind letting me watch her alone...or her with someone else, I don't know...the thought gets me hot. Why should I be ashamed of that?"

"You shouldn't," Emerson replies, and I can tell he's taking me seriously now. In fact, he has a willful expression on his face that I know means he's brewing an idea.

And that's exactly what I need.

To be honest, the past couple years have been rough. I'm hanging on by a thread with this company, and if it weren't for the friends I've made, I think I would have jumped ship months ago. The work is soul sucking; we're constantly trying to fulfill someone else's dreams, but the events we plan flop. Then the money gets sucked away instead of being invested back into the company.

I love working in entertainment. I love parties and people and the excitement of the planning process, but lately, I've had zero motivation to get out of bed, let alone show up for work. I need something to wake up for. I need a purpose.

So I hope like hell that idea forming behind Emerson's eyes is a good one—because I fucking need it.

———————

I'm still in bed the next morning when I get the call. It's Emerson who breaks the news to me—the company we work for is filing for bankruptcy, and the last four years have just been flushed down the toilet.

But before a shadow can be cast over my future, he says, "Would you be interested in starting our own business?"

"Umm…" I rub the sleep out of my eyes and glance at the clock. It's almost eleven. "Yeah. Definitely. Why?"

"What if it was a dating service?"

A *dating* service? My brow furrows as I wait for him to elaborate.

"You got me thinking last night. All that talk about compatibility and kinks. I think it's a great idea."

With bated breath, I wait for him to say something enticing and not just a weak idea or half a plan. I'm counting on Emerson to say the word and make this happen because if he doesn't, I don't know what I'll do next. Thankfully, my best friend doesn't do shit half-assed. When he's passionate, he makes it happen.

"I say we do it. I want it to start as an app, like a dating service, but not a cheap hookup site. I want this to be prestigious. Membership tiers with VIP status and services people actually want. Then, down the road, I'm thinking about a real club."

"A nightclub?" *Please say no.* I don't think I have the energy to deal with another soulless nightclub.

"A sex club, Garrett. Exclusive. Someplace people can be free to pursue their wildest desires. No judgment. No shame."

Fuck yes. I sit straight up in my bed and glance around my messy apartment. "What do you need me to do?"

"You're good with people. I need you to be the face of the company, and I want all of your ideas. I know you have them."

"Okay, I'm in."

"Good."

Hopping out of bed, I keep my phone on speaker as I brew my coffee and get myself ready for the day. Emerson rattles off more ideas, and I volley back with my own. Anxiety still nags at my consciousness, the fear that I don't have what it takes to pull this off, but I'm too fired up to let it stop me.

Emerson Grant has faith in me, and I'm not going to let him down. Which means I can't let those inner voices win. Can't let them control me. This is going to be great. Our club is going to be great. It has to be.

"Hey, Emerson," I say before we hang up.

"Yeah?"

"Thanks," I say, hoping I don't sound too cheesy or lame.

"No need to thank me, Garrett. This was your idea."

And that may be true, but it's his drive and leadership I needed. Like I said, these past few years have been low, and I'm tired of being low. I don't think he'll ever understand just how much this company means to me.

Because Salacious Players' Club saved my life.

PART I

The Lake House

Rule #1: Don't check text messages from your mom at the sex club.

Garrett

THERE ARE ONLY THREE THINGS I TAKE SERIOUSLY—RUNNING, A well-tailored suit, and sex.

I *have* to be serious about that last one; it's my job. Not *having* sex, of course, but knowing everything about it in order to curate an enjoyable and arousing experience for those both doing it and those who want to watch others doing it. I have to know the minute details that turn people on, that make them feel safe, and that keep them coming back for more. The fine line between hot and creepy. Catering an encounter for men *and women* alike.

Being an expert of the ins and outs, if you will.

And right now, I have my eyes on a delicious little couple in room seven, who are doing everything perfectly. The woman is cuffed to the bed, her golden skin catching the dim red light as the man behind her pounds at a perfect rhythm to make her go wild. The angle is sublime, but I make a mental note to pull the bed to the right about ten more degrees, so the spectators can see her face better. Believe it or not, that's what the people really want to see anyway…her face. The look of need and hunger in her slightly pained and wanton expression.

I made a good choice in inviting these two back. I watched them together a few weeks ago, and it was my idea to incentivize the couples who draw a crowd into renting the voyeur rooms again. A little discount on their membership, a few added VIP perks, and in return, I offer them time together in the red-light room where, for one hour, she can feel like a first-class prostitute, selling her pleasure, and he can be the highest bidder.

They put on a hot show. He came strolling in, in an expensive-looking suit, and gave her a devilish smile, while she tried to appear unaffected. It was impressive, and the crowd was into it. Completely.

Well, crowd is a bit of an overstatement. It's only a handful of people. The curtain is drawn around the viewing area, creating an intimacy among the small group currently gathered. We can't exactly let a mob back into the voyeur hall; it sort of ruins the experience if you're trying to observe something private in the company of a hundred others, who are also trying to experience something private. This is a classy place, after all. Can't have a horde of horny men stroking it in a crowd like it's some sleazy backroom peep show in a dirty porn store.

And that's where I come in. Knowing exactly what to regulate and how to let it all happen so nothing gets out of control. It needs to appear natural, even though I'm covertly controlling everything behind the scenes.

So far, so good tonight. There's one woman watching alone near the window, biting her lip as she witnesses the woman on the bed climax *again*. There's a couple standing so close to each other that I can't tell if her hand is down his pants or his hand is up her short dress or both. Which means it's just dark enough in here; although I might have them turn down the red light just a hair… It seems to be giving off a glare on all the metal in the room, and it's distracting.

All in all, the energy in the room is spot-on.

My phone buzzes in my pocket, but I don't pull it out right away; it's against the rules to have phones in here or any private areas of the club, even if I am one of the owners.

The red-light couple are wrapping up anyway, so I quietly slink out of the voyeur hall, through the private service door, and head toward the office. Once I'm safely in the brightly lit staff hallway, I fish out my phone.

The notification reads: *You have a new message from Mom.*

Oh, lovely. A message from my mother after watching people fuck like heathens. I'm willing to bet my left testicle this is yet another invitation to join her and my stepdad at the lake house this week.

You should come up. The weather is beautiful this week.

Ha. I was right.

Every year, she and my stepdad stay at their lake house three hours away, and every year, they invite me to come with them. I'd be more inclined to say yes if his twenty-three-year-old brat of a daughter wasn't going too. So every year, I disappoint my mother with a *thanks, but no thanks* response, and this year is no different.

Mia is the bane of my existence. The apple of not only her father's eye but my mother's too; she's spent the last fifteen years soaking up every ounce of their attention and being a serious pain in my ass, and while I'm far too old to complain about sibling rivalries now, I'm perfectly content just pretending she doesn't exist.

"Who are you talking to?" Hunter asks over my shoulder as I linger by the door, staring down at my phone.

"My mom."

He winces as he walks by. "Gross, dude. I can still hear people fucking behind this wall."

"What? Is that weird?" I reply with a laugh.

"Not for you. Tell her I said hi," he says as he disappears down the long hallway, turning toward the office.

"I can't tell if you're being nice or dirty," I shout, my voice carrying down the corridor, and in the distance, I hear Hunter laugh.

The banter between me and the three people I run this company with is half the reason I love this job so damn much. We get along great. It's always fun, sometimes a little stressful, but never too heavy or too serious.

Just how I like it.

I almost forget I'm in the middle of a conversation via text with my mother, but the buzzing of my phone in my hand reminds me.

You haven't been up to the lake in years.

The sting of guilt actually gets me for a second, as I think about disappointing her once again. But I really am busy with work, and it's not that easy for me to just leave the club for several days at a time. I risk losing my momentum, the energy I need to keep everything running smoothly. The fresh ideas, the creative projects, the new events, the incoming clients, and the all-important VIP incentives. There's a lot on my shoulders, and I can't risk letting anything fall. Not for a second.

I'll think about it, I reply to my mom.

You should come. Mia is bored up here without you.

Looking down at my phone, I laugh. The last thing my stepsister is, is bored without me. At peace, maybe. Soaking up the undivided attention from our parents without me around, definitely. But the last thing she is, is bored.

Tempting, I respond. But if I wanted to be hissed at every ten seconds, I'd get a cat.

Be nice.

Ha. Nice? Mia and I haven't been *nice* to each other since the day we met a decade and a half ago, when she was only eight. I was in my early twenties. We really shouldn't have had a problem with each other, considering the thirteen years between us, but as

Mia grew up, she found ways of getting on every last nerve I had. She's been nothing but an entitled brat who isn't content unless her presence is a constant source of torture for me.

Luckily, I can dish it out just as much as she can. And she's not eight years old anymore.

Besides, I know Paul really wants to see you.

Dammit. She's going to play the Paul card. My stepdad has been in and out of treatment for bladder cancer for the past couple of years. One minute he's doing great, and the next...she says stuff like this. And it makes me worry. I should go over there more and stay in the loop, so they know I care, but life just gets in the way.

"Meet you at the bar?" Hunter asks when he comes back around, pulling my attention away from my phone. "It's Maggie's turn to watch the club this week."

"Ahh...and be the only single guy in the group again? Sounds fun. I assume Drake is bringing his flavor of the week."

"Not sure he has one this week," Hunter throws back. "So you'll have him."

I tilt my head back and raise my brows, forcing a tight-lipped smile. Hunter's best friend, and the head of construction for the club, Drake, is a known ladies' man and won't be at our table more than five minutes before he declares open season on the single girls at the bar.

Thursday night drinks have been a decade-long tradition for us, but I really don't have the energy for another couples' night with the team. I hate to cancel on them again. It's just...the dynamics have changed so much. It was fine when Hunter and Isabel got married because I still had Emerson. But now, he's blissfully entangled, which is great. I'm happy for him.

I am.

But when I pull open the door of the bar we frequent every

Thursday night and the first thing I see is the man I have looked up to and idolized for nearly a decade sucking face with a twenty-one-year-old like they're in the last row of a movie theater, the bitterness starts to creep in.

"That's enough," I groan as I approach the table to find my best friend and his new, very young girlfriend consuming more of each other's mouths than they are the drinks in front of them.

Charlotte blushes as she turns away from Emerson.

"Oh, I'm sorry," he says, picking up his drink. "I thought you liked to watch."

I roll my eyes. "I like to watch sex," I clarify. "Not whatever romantic canoodling that was."

Charlotte's eyes widen as she leans forward. "Wait, is that your…thing?"

"My thing?" I ask.

"Yeah…your kink."

A lighthearted chuckle erupts from my chest. A bit simplistic if you ask me, but I'll humor her. "I guess you could say that. I'm a voyeur, but I thought you already knew that."

She shrugs. "I just wanted to hear you say it." She lifts up her hazy IPA and takes a sip, and I watch her for a second. Charlotte is one of those girls who doesn't hold back. If she has a filter, I'm not sure she knows how to use it, which isn't something I thought my best friend would be into, but he's currently looking at her with the most smitten expression I've ever seen on that smug face of his.

It's hard to take this shit seriously. In fact, I don't. Call me cynical, but falling in love has to be the most delusional thing a person can do. Emerson looks happy, I'll give him that, but honestly, how long does he think this will last? Enjoy the sex and companionship now, friend, because a few years from now, she'll probably resent him for the way he chews and he'll be wishing he could still prowl the club with me.

I just don't believe that once you see the deeper, darker side of a person, you can still spout this romantic bullshit. People are flawed as fuck, and relationships are better kept short—or in my case, not at all.

And no, for the record, I am not *jealous*. I'm perfectly fine keeping my head on straight and not throwing it all away for some young pair of tits and a bright smile. Just because my best friend has been hoodwinked doesn't mean I ever will be.

When Charlotte puts her drink down, she squints her eyes at me. "So does that mean you want to watch us?"

Emerson laughs, but I do my best not to react. "You're the first one of my friends' girls to ask me that. I'm still waiting for Isabel and Hunter to offer," I joke.

"Answer the question." Her arms rest on the table, giving me a challenging expression.

I consider it for a moment. It's not about seeing my friend naked or fucking his girl. I do it for the interaction. Seeing the way people express themselves during sex, the way they move, the way they sound, the way they come. Sex is never the same, no matter who's doing it. And porn doesn't count. It's too scripted and controlled. So, yeah, I like to watch because it's about the most interesting thing you can watch two (or more) humans do.

"I wouldn't turn down the invitation. *Is* this an invitation?"

"No," Emerson interjects, and I laugh.

"It's okay. I only have to catch you on the right night in the club," I reply, and he can't seem to hide the hint of a smile that creeps onto his face.

"True," Charlotte replies.

Late as usual, Hunter, Drake, and Isabel enter the bar. As the five of them greet each other and fall into a steady rhythm of conversation, I feel myself pulling away. Again.

I've been doing this a lot lately, and I'm sure they've noticed.

Truth is, I'd rather be at home, where I can bask in my loneliness, instead of a crowded bar under the scrutinizing gazes of my closest friends. I find myself pulling my phone out, looking for emails and text messages that don't come. Almost wishing something would come up at the club so I'd have something else to focus on.

The good sport I am, I stay for another round and try my best to laugh at all the jokes, even telling a few myself. But I'm home by eleven, trading my Tom Ford suit for cheap flannel pajamas and lying in bed, where I actually consider subscribing to one of those online Chat with Hot Young Girls services. I mean…I'm not above it. I've done it before…for research, of course.

But it's not real. Nothing feels real anymore.

Rule #2: If you happen to fall in love with your stepbrother, never let it show. Never.

Mia

"AND WHAT EXACTLY WOULD YOU DO IF YOU WERE HERE WITH ME right now?"

The gray-haired man on the screen chuckles, deep and gravelly. "Oh, darlin', I'd make you feel so good."

"Oh yeah?" I ask. "How? Tell me exactly how you'd do it."

"And you'll touch yourself for me while I do?" he asks, a small tremble in his voice giving away his nerves.

"If you want me to," I reply. I'm lying on the blue, crushed-velvet couch, the one in the basement of my parents' lake cabin. It's not actually comfortable, but it's great for the camera angle, and the color contrasts perfectly against my light skin. My long silvery-blond hair is fanned out around me, and I'm in nothing but the black lace panty set this particular client likes most. He's offered to buy me an entire closet full, but I turn him down every time. I don't like taking gifts from patrons because then it feels like I owe them something in return.

ChiefG1963, who told me his real name is Gregg, clears his throat. He's nervous. He always gets timid around this part, but

I know this is what he likes. He has a flair for dirty talk, and he'd rather spell it all out for me than have me tell him what I like, because every time I've tried in the past, he cuts me off.

"Well, I'd start by licking those perfect pink nipples you got there, baby girl."

"These?" I ask, slipping the edges of my bra down to give him a good view of my full breasts.

"Oh yeah." He growls. "Then, I'd—" There's a knock on the door of his office, and I hear a man in the background. Gregg looks up at whoever it is. I wait, slipping my bra back over my breasts, so whoever just walked into Gregg's office doesn't get a show he didn't pay for.

Gregg turns back toward me with an apologetic expression. "Baby girl, we have to cut it short today."

I pout for the screen. "But we were just getting to the good part."

"I know, but I've got investors to tend to, and money doesn't wait, sweetheart."

Trying to look as reluctant as possible, I sit up and stare down at the camera of my laptop. "Are we still on for tomorrow?"

"I wouldn't miss it," he replies. "That beautiful smile is the highlight of my day."

For that comment, I reward him with a bright one, full dimples, and a lip bite, because sadly, I know he's being honest. Gregg is one of my regulars, and he may be loaded, but I can tell by the way he spends the majority of our time on these chats, telling me about his day and his work, that I'm probably the only person in his life who actually listens.

We always spend the first half of the hour chatting and he tells me all the places he *wishes* he could take me or all the things he would do with me. And I give him my complete attention. Then we normally get to the sexy stuff, if work doesn't get in the way.

And that's how most of my clients are—equal parts genuine conversation and erotic amusement. They're mostly all starved for attention, desperate for connection, and craving something a little dirty.

I've honed my actual skills from being provocative on-screen to just sounding like I care.

Okay, that sounded heartless. I *do* sort of care. Or rather, I get paid to care.

After I hang up with Gregg, I consider turning my cam back on to try and find another VIP request in the live stream chats, but I somehow let the next hour go by surfing Tumblr on my phone.

My dad and stepmom are currently out on the boat with their friends, so I'm left alone in the house, which makes it easy for me to work.

We come up to the lake every summer, and even though I'm twenty-three, plenty old enough to get my own place, I enjoy coming up here each year. I realize I'm probably supposed to be partying in Cancun or Vegas with other twentysomething-year-olds, but that's really not my style. I'm really more of a comfortable-where-I-am kind of girl.

My parents live like they're already empty nesters, regardless of the fact that I haven't exactly left the nest yet. It just means they're gone a lot, don't worry about me, and give me all the privacy and Wi-Fi service I need.

The camgirl thing is a fairly new gig. I stumbled upon it last fall when a friend of mine from cosmetology school—which I had recently dropped out of—told me about the money she was making, without even having to leave the house. I'm a people person, and being a tease was always my strong suit, so I figured it would be perfect for me.

It was awkward at first, flirting with strange men, especially since I used to be so self-conscious about my body. I always thought this sort of thing was for super fit, toned girls who had the confidence to strut around in string bikinis. But there's no thigh gap between these legs, and my tits might be full and squishy, but so is my ass.

Then, I quickly learned, some guys like it that way. Some of them *really* like it that way.

Soon, getting naked for men—and doing stuff to myself for them—made me a little more confident in the shape of my body. It's funny to think about my first session, when I was so nervous I could barely show the tiniest glimpse of pussy, and now I'm perfectly comfortable spreading it for the camera.

Sure, I get the big tips that way. But I also really fucking love the way it feels, even though I cannot explain why.

Now, this is my job. I flirt, do a little strip tease, touch myself, and on a good day, I might actually get an orgasm out of it. Then I get paid. I mean…who could complain?

After tossing on something more decent than the black lingerie I had on, I head upstairs. I'm halfway through making an iced coffee in the kitchen, with my five-year-old black cat, Betty, weaving around my legs, when my phone rings. Glancing down, I see my stepbrother's name on the incoming video call, and I freeze.

Why the hell is Garrett trying to video call me?

Out of pure curiosity, I answer, propping my phone up against the backsplash, so he can see me while I continue putting together my caramel caffeine concoction.

"Don't hang up," he says as soon as it connects.

"Okay…" Glancing down at the phone, I see that he's shirtless and sweating, his cheeks red and his hair wet. A white towel hangs around his neck, but I force myself to look away. "What's up?" I ask, trying to remain cordial, even though Garrett has literally never been nice to me in my entire life. Why would he when he could torture me instead?

My dad couldn't have married someone with a nice son? Preferably an ugly one too. Why did my luck just happen to land me with a stepbrother who is the complete opposite of those two things?

"How's your dad?"

Well, that question throws me off. He knows my dad has

been battling cancer for two years now, but it's never inspired him to reach out or even come over, so why now?

"Umm...the same, I guess."

"What are you drinking?" he asks, suddenly changing the subject.

"An iced coffee," I reply with my lips around the metal straw.

"I'm not sure you need more energy."

"Did you call me just to judge my lifestyle?" I bite back.

I pick up my phone and carry it, facing me, up to the third-floor balcony. The sun is about to set, and it's breathtaking from here. Something I refuse to miss each evening. Sometimes I even bring my cam out here and let my viewers watch me prop my feet up on the balcony and sip my coffee while the sun sets over the lake. It's usually when the creepers drop into my inbox to tell me they want to slap my tits or bend me over the railing or something else super vulgar, but I ignore them. No one ruins this moment for me.

Setting my phone up against the planter on my patio table, I let my stepbrother watch me instead. The only difference here is that I can see him, and as I glance over, I notice that he has his phone propped up too and is currently stretching, giving me a full-screen view of his long, lean muscles, under perfect sun-kissed skin, with a trail of dark body hair leading down his chiseled abs, disappearing into his shorts—

"Are you listening to me?"

"Yes," I lie.

"Then what did I just say?"

"Something about...running another marathon or something?"

He scoffs and rolls his eyes. "I asked how your summer is going at the lake with Mom and Dad."

"Boring," I reply.

"Aren't you a little old to be spending your summers with our parents?" he argues casually.

"Don't be jealous because I work from my computer and can spend my summers here for free. Besides, they're never around anyway. They're either at the casino or on the boat with their friends or doing God knows what else."

"Still doing data entry?" he asks in a teasing tone.

"Yep," I reply. Clearly, I don't go around advertising the fact that I make my money flashing my goods to men on the internet. There's a whole lot of stigma attached to it.

Not to mention, Garrett would give me endless shit for it. If he found out, he would use it as ammunition to belittle me. It's hard enough being a sex worker without my ass of a stepbrother making me feel like shit for it.

But I do wonder how he'd react. If anything, Garrett is the only person I wish I could tell about my job. Because if I did, he might actually start looking at me as a woman rather than a bratty little sister. Not that a rich, fit, and gorgeous guy like my stepbrother would ever go for someone like me, but I almost wish he'd see what I do on camera. The very thought of Garrett watching me spread my legs in front of my phone screen has me blushing. That would change his perception of me for sure.

I only hope he'd be more turned on than disgusted.

"So, are you coming?" I ask casually. Did that sound too needy? I glance over to the screen to see his reaction, but he's still stretching.

"We just opened the club three months ago. I can't take a week off already to come up to the lake."

"So come up for a weekend. It's only a couple hours."

"Why do you want me to come up there so badly? I thought you hated it when I was there. Don't you like having that lake house to yourself while they're gone?"

Garrett and I have never really gotten along. We're both competitive, have a cynical sense of humor, and take almost nothing seriously. It doesn't help that our parents got married when I was eight and he was twenty-one, and the only thing I could do to get his attention was to get on his nerves.

He used to come to the lake with us every summer, but then

one summer, about ten years ago...he just stopped. I can only assume it was because of me.

"Whatever. I don't care," I snap with a little too much sass.

"Damn. What crawled up your ass?"

"I was just asking. Come or don't come. It doesn't matter to me. I just thought you'd like to see Dad before it gets worse."

"Oh really? This is about Dad? Because a second ago, it sounded like you just wanted to see me."

"I don't," I reply stubbornly.

"Are you sure? Because hitting on your stepbrother is a little desperate. Is it that hard to find guys who will date you?" There's a playful smirk on his face, the same one I hate because he uses it to drive me crazy.

"I'm going to hang up on you. Why are you such a jerk?"

He laughs. "I like how worked up it gets you. That's what big brothers do."

Hiding the way that phrase triggers not-so-deeply hidden feelings, I quickly look away from him. Garrett is *not* my big brother. He's never been my big brother, but he's put on this whole brother act since our parents got married, as if reminding himself and me that, blood or not, we are related.

So I bite my tongue because I can't say what I really want to. I can't tell him that I really *do* want him to come up here and spend time with me. I can't say how I really feel about him because everything is a joke to Garrett. *I* am a joke to him. And if he ever knew how I really felt, he would never let me live down the day I admitted that I am ridiculously in love with him.

So I cover it up with sarcasm and superficial hate.

"Bye, Garrett," I mutter before hitting End Call.

But I don't get up right away. Even after the sun has disappeared behind the trees, I sit here and let this feeling of loneliness settle in. I'm really no better than any of my clients.

I'll get over him someday. I have to. Because at the end of the day, Garrett sees me as his little sister, while I see him as the love of my life.

Rule #3: Don't drink and download apps.

Garrett

FlirtyGirl: Hot Babes 24/7
SkankView: The dirtiest girls on the web
BabeWatch: Real women ready for you

I SUPPRESS A GROAN AS I SCROLL THROUGH THE VARIOUS AVAILable sites. This is embarrassing…and I'm nearly drunk, hence why I've swallowed my pride and pulled up this search in the first place. I briefly considered grabbing a ride and going to the club to see if anything exciting was happening in the voyeur hall, but it's not really couples and sex I want to see right now.

"Fuck, I'm pathetic," I mutter to myself before clicking on the first, least sleazy site. I've been on it before, when I was browsing for inspiration for the club. It wasn't long before I shut down the idea, but for a moment, I wondered how one of these *performances* would translate to a live experience for our members, but the idea never really fleshed out correctly in my head. How would that even work? Put girls onstage with a bunch of vibrators and dildos and line up the audience like in a theater?

No, that sounds terrible. I'm sure someone else could make it work, but that person is not me.

Unlike last time, logging in today is for shameless entertainment and, hopefully, a hint of a human connection.

The app is more tasteful than I thought at first. It's sleek and inviting. Not like some of those in-your-face, vulgar porn sites. In fact, it looks more like a regular social media app. Scrolling through the girls live online now, I click through a few different ones.

The first is a beautiful Asian woman in a gaming chair with large headphones around her ears and what looks like a video game controller in her hands. I can't help but laugh. She has over ten thousand active viewers, and she's fully clothed, playing video games.

Okay, next.

A busty redhead is cooking in her kitchen. This one is a bit sexier with the camera angle coming from somewhere low and a crisp HD view of her pushed-up tits hanging out of the front of her low-cut tank. She makes small talk with the viewers while she cooks, periodically responding to posted questions and comments.

It's appealing to observe her for a moment, lost in the delicate ministrations of her long, manicured nails as she dices vegetables and flicks her hair behind her shoulder.

But it loses its luster after a few minutes.

I'm cracking open my fifth beer of the night when I click onto a live profile, WickedKitten214. I drop back onto my couch as the video feed cuts to a close view of cute pink toes on a tile floor and a girl's voice in the background.

"I like this shade more than the last one. What do you think?"

I pause with my drink halfway to my lips. *That voice.* It's oddly familiar.

The camera view changes as the girl sets the phone down against something, giving me and seventeen thousand other people a view of her body—a yellow crop top and a black skirt with a span of soft, pale white flesh in between.

My eyes catch up before my brain does, but that's probably

because of the beer. I can't tear my gaze away from what I'm seeing right now. A *very* familiar outfit on a *very* familiar body with a *very* familiar voice.

"What..." I manage to mutter before long, white hair drops into view followed by her face. *That face.* A cute dimpled chin, round cheeks that nearly swallow up her big blue eyes when she smiles, and supple bow-shaped lips currently covered in some coffee-colored lipstick.

My beer lands in my lap, splashing cold, carbonated liquid all over my bare chest and flannel pajama pants.

"Fuck!" I bark, dropping my phone, grabbing the can from my couch and setting it on the coffee table. I run to the kitchen to grab a towel, drying myself off while gaping at my phone still playing from the floor and my fucking stepsister's voice filling the room.

Mia? No.

Ignoring the mess seeping into the fabric of my sofa, I go back over to the phone on the floor, carefully glancing at the screen, as if she can see me, which she can't, and waiting for my eyes to correct themselves because they *must* be wrong.

It's just a woman who looks eerily similar to Mia.

But then she hangs her head back and laughs, a full cackle that always comes out just a little bit deeper than her speaking voice.

Yep, that's Mia all right.

Finally gathering the courage to pick up my phone, I lift it from the floor and stare at my sister on the screen.

She's not your sister, asshole.

I mean...what do I care if she's flaunting her shit online? She's a brat anyway, and it's certainly none of my business.

Quickly, I click out of the live feed and scroll a few other camgirl options, but the nagging reminder that my twenty-three-year-old stepsister is putting herself on display in front of all those creeps, who are probably thinking and saying some pretty deplorable stuff to her, bothers me enough to click right back into her broadcast.

Mia is screwing on the cap of her soft pink nail polish while going on and on about how she considers herself more of a homebody than a club girl. Then she shows us the spiked seltzer she's drinking and asks viewers to comment with what they're drinking.

I cannot tear my eyes away. It's her…but it's just a few shades off from being the real Mia. I just got off the phone with her a couple hours ago, and I try to remember how she sounded when she was talking to me compared to how she sounds now. With me, she was a little more agitated, defensive, and she chewed on the inside corner of her mouth when she wasn't speaking.

The girl on the phone screen now isn't quite Mia.

I see her bedroom in the lake house in the background. Where the hell are my mother and stepdad? She wouldn't do this with them at home, would she?

Fuck! What the fuck is Mia doing on a webcam app?

Maybe she just does these live streams for fun. To make a little side-hustle cash. It can't be any more than that. She definitely doesn't take her clothes off on camera or do any of the nasty, depraved things I'm sure these seventeen—nope, now twenty-one—thousand people want her to do.

At the bottom of the screen, the comments from other users scroll, and most of them are tame enough. They probably have filters in place to keep men from being predatory in the comments. There's a space for me to leave one of my own, but I don't. Along the side are more buttons, one to message her, for a fee, of course, and another to request a private video chat.

It's just a default setting. Mia doesn't do that.

No, no, no, no, no.

My drunk conscience is warring with this feeling of overprotectiveness because that's my little sister. But there's something else taking up space in my head too…something that doesn't have a name, but it echoes in an unfamiliar cadence: *mine, mine, mine.*

It's that nameless shade of testosterone-fueled possessiveness that drives me to punch my thumb against the *Request a Private Room* button.

What...am I doing?

A pop-up notification appears over Mia's video, informing me that her private room rate is $450 an hour, and I barely blink an eye before hitting the green *Proceed* button.

The pop-up goes away, and I watch as Mia's eyes on the camera slant down to the bottom of her screen, as if she's reading a notification. A moment later, she addresses her viewers.

"All right guys, this polish is dried, so I'm gonna head to bed. Have a great night, babes! And don't drink too much!"

A second later, my screen goes black.

WickedKitten214 accepted your private room invitation.
Would you like to give camera access?

Give camera access? No.

Would you like to give microphone access?

I really didn't think this through. No. Mia can't hear or see me. I don't even know what I'm going to say, but I think when I requested this room, I did it thinking I could confront her about this. But is that what I want to do? Or do I want to see just how far she's willing to go in these private chats?

Microphone access...no.

A moment later, she's on the screen again, but instead of displaying the huge number of viewers in the top corner, it looks more like a regular video call. My username appears in the corner: Player428.

"Hello there," she says in a flirty drawl. "Oh...you're going to be shy, huh? That's okay. Just send me messages in the chat box. I'll get you to open up eventually. These private rooms can be intimidating at first."

She's carrying the phone through her bedroom, but I can't see much more than her face and the top of her chest. For a minute, I just stare at her round cheeks and the contrast of her white teeth against her dark-stained lips. Why have I never noticed how flawless Mia's skin is? Or how full her lips are?

"Why don't you start by telling me your name?"

I hesitate with my fingers over the text box. What should I say? For some reason, the only other person I could see doing this, flirting with women so openly, comes to mind...

Drake

I watch her eyes read the message and a smirk pulls at her lips. "I like that name. Okay, Drake...it's Friday night and you're here chatting with me. Are you drinking anything?"

Beer.

But I spilled it all over myself when I saw your face.

Fuck, that was lame. She laughs anyway, not the full-belly laugh I'm used to, but a simplified version that still manages to make me smile.

God, Mia...what the fuck are you doing? This can't be real.

"No, you didn't," she replies playfully. She crawls into bed and puts her phone into some sort of holder, so she no longer has to keep it upright with her hands. This new position gives me a perfect view of her body nestled against crisp white pillows and a rustic wooden headboard.

That's her fucking bed. I've seen it a hundred times from our summers at the lake.

My cock twitches in my pants. *No. You shut the fuck up.*

I haven't seen Mia in person in six months. But even then, I never really noticed how grown-up she's gotten. There's no denying that the bratty little kid I once knew grew into a beautiful woman, even if I've never bothered to look at her that way. She has exquisite curves and the confidence of someone comfortable in her own skin. Stepsister or not, that's fucking sexy.

"Drake, I think I'm going to slip into my pj's. Do you want

me to go off camera or stay where you can see me?" She bites her lower lip and gives me a flirty raised-brow expression.

My cock practically jumps this time.

Type off camera, *asshole. Type it now.*

And maybe if I wasn't a little drunk, I would. But I tell myself I'm just doing this to test her, to make sure she's not really getting naked for strangers on the internet.

But it feels just a little too satisfying to type out the words:

Show me.

Goddammit. Goddamn me. Goddamn my stupid cock and my fucking mom for marrying someone with such a stubborn, beautiful brat of a daughter and goddamn Mia for doing this to me. And goddamn the world's longest dry spell I'm currently in.

The camera must be on some sort of swiveling attachment because she rotates it around a bit, letting me watch her climb across the bed, crawling in such a way that I'm given a sneak peek of her cute ass beneath that black, pleated skirt.

God, I just looked at Mia's ass.

I groan.

I've managed to contain the shameless monster in my pants to a minor chub up until this point, but when Mia smiles at the camera as she slips her skirt down, revealing a black thong and an ample, round ass, I really do try to look away.

I *try.*

"I hope you're still there," she says, turning around while she digs in her drawers for her pajamas. "Because I can't see my messages from here."

She pulls her yellow top over her head, and my gaze catches on the softness of her belly and the supple curves of her hips. And that gross big-brother brain kicks in with some sick satisfaction that she looks better than she did a few years ago when she was on that gymnastics team, and I was hounding her about her terrible eating habits and lack of nutritious calories. God, she got so mad at me for that, but she was too skinny, and her arguments about how skinny-shaming were the same as fat-shaming had little effect on me. I just wanted to see more flesh on her bones, and fuck me…she looks…better now.

"The blue or the red?" she asks, holding up two different silk pajama sets, both lacy and sexy, but I'm too busy staring at the cute dimples in her ass to care about color.

Neither.

She leans forward to read the screen from across the room. Then her eyebrows shoot upward as she takes in my response.

"Oh. Want me to stay in this?" She models her lacy black thong and see-through bra for me.

Chubby no more, my cock is starting to strain against my boxers. This feels wrong.

Okay…no, it doesn't. But it fucking *should*. Because it *is* wrong.

Mia has no idea it's me on the other end of this call. This is a major invasion of her privacy, and I'm crossing about a hundred bright, bold lines, surrounded by sirens and caution tape and *Do Not Enter* signs, but I ignore every single one of them. I can't help it.

"Or would you like to see me in less?" she asks so quietly I almost don't hear her. Stepping closer to the camera, she leans down and gives me a full view of her cleavage. As she stares into the lens, it almost feels as if, for a split second, she can actually see me and that, somehow, I've been caught, and she knows it's her stepbrother watching.

"Okay, Drake. In order for you to see more of me, you're going to have to show me more."

My first thought is to swipe away right now.

Instead, I type:

How much can I show you?

She reads my message and smiles. "Rules say you have to keep *your* clothes on. But you don't have to show me your face if you don't want to."

I can't.

"I understand." She gives me a sympathetic look while

thinking for a moment. It's strange to have Mia look at me without a disdainful expression. So this is what it's like to speak to her when she doesn't hate you.

And I don't miss the way she seems so much more human and relatable now than in the live stream. As if she's really trying to connect to the man on the other end of the call. Knowing that it's me she's talking to feels good, but the reminder that it's often other men she's trying to relate to makes me want to hurt someone.

I don't have a shirt on.

"Oh," she replies, "are you in bed right now?"

I practically leap off the couch and run to my room. Dropping onto the mattress, I quickly type my response.

I am now.

"Show me your bed, and I'll show you something."

Deep breaths. Deep breaths. When I hit the video button at the top corner of the screen, my finger is shaking. I angle the phone down, so only my bare chest and the top of my pajama bottoms are showing. The only light in the room is coming through the open door, so she gets a blurry, dark view of my abdomen on my black linen sheets.

I watch her expression change from anticipation to surprise. Her lips part just a hair and her eyes lose a little of their focus.

"Oh...Drake," she whispers, "you have a great body."

Thank you, I type, sticking to the text messages instead of talking.

Now what are you going to show me?

She smiles. "What would you like to see?"

Your tits.

Her head tilts to the side. "So predictable, Drake."

I laugh because it's her and it sounds like her giving me shit like she always does.

Fine. No tits then.

Her eyebrows rise. "Okay, then what's it gonna be?"

My brain and all of its rational, appropriate functions are

gone. They haven't been running this show for a while, and if my cock could type, it would. Instead, I'm left to do all the typing for it.

Turn around and touch your toes. I want to see your ass.

Peel off that thong and show me everything.

Her gaze loses more of its focus.

"Everything? You really went for it."

I don't want to be too predictable for you.

She laughs. "I think I'm going to need a little more for that view, Drake."

More money?

With a bite of her bottom lip, she replies, "No. More of you."

I thought that was against the rules.

"I lied."

That mischievous grin I know so well comes into view, and I falter, almost accidentally letting my camera pan up to my face. Instead, I pull my arm a little farther away, showing her my full body, still clothed from the waist down. The dim light makes the bulge in my pants hard to see, so I dip my hand under the waistband and take a hold of my cock.

The warm, tight grip of my hand makes my spine light up with sensation, and my chest sucks in a desperate breath.

"Whatcha got there to show me, Drake?" she asks in a breathy plea.

Still holding my cock in one hand and the phone in the other, I awkwardly work my erection out of its confines and angle the camera so she can see it. Just knowing Mia is staring at my swollen dick has my heart pounding in my chest.

"Oh, God…" She moans, and I have to bite my lip. It doesn't sound porn-star fake. It sounds completely fucking real. "You've earned this."

Keeping the camera angled toward my cock, I watch as she does as I said. Turning around, she hinges at the hips and bends slowly, giving me a delicious view of her ass. The black fabric of her bra and panties contrast against her pale flesh as she slides her thong down her legs.

My hand strokes my cock on its own as I stare at the perfection of her tight, puckered hole, just above the glistening skin of her moist folds. She's wet. Does she always get wet on these calls?

Nope. *It's for me*, I chant in my head as my stroking picks up speed.

"Drake, you better not come without letting me watch," she says sweetly.

Typing with one hand isn't easy, but I manage a reply—thanks to autocorrect.

Then get on your bed and play with your clit.

You come first.

She hums in delight. Standing upright, she sits on her bed and turns the phone to face her again. "I'm going to need something from you then."

Whatever you want.

"Turn on your audio. I want to hear the sounds you make when you come."

Fuck, I could come right now. Just the filthy words coming out of her mouth have me ready to spill.

Okay.

She unclasps her bra from somewhere between her breasts and they spring free. Suddenly, my feisty stepsister is splayed out on her pretty white bed, naked and perfect, all for me. I drink up the sight as I will myself *not* to blow. Not yet.

"I'm waiting, Drake…" she teases as she casually strokes her cunt.

Oh, what the fuck… Without another thought, I hit the microphone button and stay silent, letting the smacking of my flesh as I stroke myself be the only sound heard through the line.

"Much better," she replies. With a slight angle of her phone, she aims it toward the apex of her thighs as she moves her middle finger in tight circles around her clit. God, she's good at this. The camera angles and dirty talk. Too fucking good at this.

On one hand, I cannot fucking believe she does this.

And yet, here I am…really fucking enjoying it.

"Now, let me hear you, Drake." She moans as she watches the screen and keeps up her circular stroking.

I let out a heavy grunt, a few octaves deeper, trying to mask the sound of my voice.

"Yes," she pants. She's watching me beat my cock like it's the hottest thing she's ever seen, and maybe it's what all men tell themselves when they watch her do this, but I swear she's actually enjoying it. Her cheeks are turning pink and her legs are fidgeting, and the pleasurable sounds seeping through her lips sound genuine. And I should know. It's literally my job to know what sounds real and what sounds fake, and fuck me…this is real.

Another one of my grunts echoes through my empty room, and she answers with her own breathy cry. "I'm gonna come," she says, her voice strained. "Stroke harder, Drake."

And I do. I'm handling my cock so hard, I'm surprised it doesn't break.

"Finger yourself," I tell her, and she gasps for a minute at the sound of my voice.

Oh fuck, fuck, fuck.

My own words replay in my head as I try to decide if that really sounded like me or if it was just strained enough to pass for someone else.

"I wish you were here to do it for me," she replies, clearly not recognizing my voice, but even as she says that, one of her fingers curls between her folds, disappearing inside her as she cries out. Then she looks back at the phone and pumps at the same rhythm that I am.

"Come with me, Drake." She moans loudly.

"I'm coming," I whisper in a deep raspy voice.

Her eyes don't leave the screen as I unload all over my own

chest. Her attention is rapt on the seed I'm spilling, and then a moment later, I watch her abs contract, her eyes squeeze shut, and her thighs close around her hand as she lets out a cry of pleasure that makes me want to come again.

The only sound for a few long minutes is our heavy breathing, the camera still focused on the pools of cum on my chest.

When Mia does finally open her eyes, she looks momentarily affected, as if this was as strange for her as it was for me.

"Wow, Drake…that was…a good way to end my day."

As she sits up, I can see her attempt to reclaim her composure. A feeling of intense shame washes over me, practically knocking the wind out of me. *What the fuck have I just done?* Before I can even give myself a chance to reply, I swipe the app closed.

Rule #4: If you find yourself getting off to your stepsister, it's a sign you probably need a break.

Garrett

"MIA? YOUR LITTLE SISTER?"

"Will you please stop saying it like that?" I have my head in my hands as Emerson stares at me with a look of shock on his face. I didn't hesitate to open up to my best friend, especially since he has no room to judge. He's currently screwing his son's ex-girlfriend like it's an Olympic sport and he's going for gold.

"Wow," he mumbles.

"Yeah, wow."

"So what are you going to do now?"

That's the question, isn't it? I can't seem to let this go.

Something happened last night. Something I never saw coming. Obviously, she had no idea it was me on the line, but it doesn't change the fact that I felt things for Mia I never have before. That was the single hottest moment of my life and I need to figure out *why*.

With any luck, I'll get up to the lake house and realize there is absolutely *no* physical chemistry between us and that last night was a total fluke. Then I'll go back to being the almost-brother she can't stand, and we can resume our lives as normal.

"Well, that's where you come in," I say, glancing up at my friend and business partner.

"Me?" He looks a little nervous.

"Yeah. I know it's asking a lot, but would you mind if I take a week off to go up to my parents' lake house? She's up there, and maybe if I spend some time with her, I can—"

He puts up a hand. "Garrett, go."

"Really?" That was easier than I thought.

"Yeah. To be honest, I was hoping you'd go up there anyway. Launching the club has been stressful as fuck, but the hard part is over. You need a break. You've been working too hard, stretching yourself too thin. Go up there, spend some time with your family, maybe fuck your stepsister if you want. You could probably use a good lay anyway."

My face stiffens in a tight-lipped expression. "I'm not sleeping with her."

He laughs, and I grimace in return.

"First of all, we don't get along at all. Second of all, I get laid plenty, thank you." It's a lie, but he doesn't need to know that. "I don't need to go chasing twenty-three-year-old pussy, least of all my stepsister's." I stand up, giving him a pointed glare. "And I have absolutely no intention of getting caught up in some romantic hostage situation like you've gotten yourself entangled in, at the mercy of a woman who refuses to let you go."

Leaning back in his office chair, a slow, lazy grin stretches across his face. "Oh yeah…it's terrible," he replies sarcastically.

Damn, the asshole *is* wearing a grin like he just got his dick sucked, and for all I know, maybe he did. Charlie is probably hiding under his desk at this very minute, and he's making this whole relationship thing look pretty damn enticing.

Oh well, it will never last. They'll have their little fling, have lots of sex, and then it will crash and burn like all relationships do eventually. No thanks. Definitely not something I want or need.

"Okay, seriously, I'll have good cell service up there. Keep me updated on everything down here. I'll be back before the end of the quarter. And I'll brainstorm some incentives—"

"Garrett," Emerson barks. When I force my shoulders down away from my ears, he continues, "Go relax for a week. The club will be fine. Like I said, you need a break."

I know he's right. I do need some time off, but that little voice inside my head keeps nagging me, telling me I can't stop, can't rest. That I must keep working and pray the club doesn't fall apart while I'm gone.

But then if it *doesn't* fall apart without me, it means I was never really needed in the first place, right?

"All right. Thanks, Emerson. Seriously, though. If you need me, just call."

"Have a good time."

And with that, I leave his office, walk through the empty hallway toward the front of the club, and wonder how the hell I'm supposed to function for the next week without this place.

———

As I pull up to the lake house, I wave to my mom and stepdad, who are sitting on the front porch. It's been almost six months since I've seen them, which is a disgrace, considering they only live twenty minutes from me.

"Hey, stranger!" my mother says, standing from her rocking chair and jogging down the steps. When she wraps her arms around me, I'm immediately wrapped in comfort. And assaulted by guilt. "I missed you," she whispers against my cheek before kissing it.

"I missed you too, Mom. Sorry I haven't been around much."

When she releases me, I turn toward Paul, who hauls me into an equally strong hug. As he pulls away, I notice his face is a little more gaunt than I remember, and he's probably about twenty pounds lighter, but all things considered, it's not as bad as

I feared. He's still wearing that wide smile and sporting the same deep dimples that Mia inherited.

My mom and Paul got married when I was twenty-one, and since my dad has always been more of a send-a-check-on-my-birthday and forget-my-middle-name kind of dad, I've seen Paul as a father figure for most of my adult life. His first wife died of a heart condition when Mia was a baby.

"Hey, bud," he says with that hearty laugh of his. "Glad you could make it this year."

"Yeah…thanks for having me."

"Oh, stop. You're family." His giant hand lands on my shoulder with a thud, making my knees wobble. I glance around the yard toward the lake, my eyes scanning for that familiar mop of silvery-blond hair.

"Where's Mia?"

When I hear the screen door slam, I spin around and stare up at the girl standing on the porch, leaning against the banister in a string bikini and denim shorts so small I can make out the curve of her ass hanging out of the bottom.

Something about seeing her in person after last night has me unsettled. Is this the first time I'm seeing Mia as a real woman and not the little girl I've always seen her as? Last night I sure didn't see her as a little girl, not at all.

She's looking at me with a mirrored expression of uncertainty—or is that disgust? "What are you doing here?" she asks, and not in an *I'm so excited to see you* way.

"Mia," her dad replies in a scolding tone.

"Lovely as usual," I say in response.

"Be nice," my mother mutters under her breath.

"Our video chat yesterday must have been pretty convincing," Mia says, and my eyes nearly bulge out of my head. But thankfully, my mind quickly catches up, and I realize she's referring to the actual video chat we had yesterday before I put back an entire six-pack and downloaded a camgirl app.

I clear my throat. "It was. I realized I haven't been up here in a while, so I decided to take a week off. Apparently, Emerson said I looked like I needed it."

"Well, I'm glad you're here," my mother says, putting her arm around my shoulder and squeezing me hard into a side hug.

"Me too, Mom."

Mia's flip-flops slap against each step as she walks down toward me, and I have to force my eyes to remain on her face instead of the subtle bounce of her breasts barely covered by that bikini.

When she's standing a foot away from me, I see her hesitation, and I know regular siblings would hug at this point, but Mia and I have never been normal. And after last night, I don't even remember how we used to be, but somehow, I find myself pulling her in for a hug, which is a dead giveaway that she's rattled my sense of reality. She stiffens against me, obviously surprised by my actions—as am I.

I really shouldn't be noticing the fullness of her breasts against my chest or how good her coconut-scented shampoo smells next to my nose. But I am.

Fuck. Why is this happening to me? Why out of all the people in the world, am I feeling myself drawn toward this *one*? The worst possible person for me to suddenly be attracted to. But I can't ignore the way my body is reacting to her presence because of last night.

Maybe it's just her boobs. I'm a guy, and it's not like my sex drive can tell the difference between the boobs of a nice girl and the boobs of a snotty bitch who hates me.

As she pulls away, her gaze lingers for a split second on my mouth before looking toward the lake.

"Well, I'm going for a walk," she says, and I notice her phone in her hand. "You guys have fun catching up. I'll be back before dinner."

It dawns on me at that moment that she could be signing on to her little live stream on her walk. Will she get naked and masturbate for strangers in the woods? Probably not. But I'm here to figure out if this attraction toward Mia is real, so I might as well start now.

"I'll come with you," I announce, and everyone goes silent while they look at me like I've grown a set of tits on my face. Mia and I do not spend alone time together, so I get how bizarre it must look to everyone that I'm suddenly offering to do so now. But I'm here on a mission, and I don't like to waste time.

"That's a great idea!" My mom suddenly jumps in, clearly excited that we might finally be burying the hatchet and getting along. "You two go. Paul and I will be inside making dinner. You guys need to catch up anyway! You haven't seen each other since Thanksgiving."

Oh, if she only knew.

"Um…" Mia replies, obviously at a loss for words.

"If you don't mind, of course." Our eyes meet briefly, and I notice a hint of hesitation in her expression. Then I remember what it was like being able to talk to her last night without her hating me, even if she had no idea it was me she was talking to.

"Sure…I guess," she mutters before turning around and walking down the drive toward the road. With an uneasy smile back at my mom and Paul, I quickly follow behind her.

The next thing I know, I'm on a forest trail around the lake with a scantily clad Mia. My dick and my brain are both in shock at how strange this is.

It's awkwardly quiet for a while, and I know this would be the perfect opportunity to get Mia to talk about her secret job. There's so much I don't know about her, which is mostly my fault. I never took the time to get to know Mia, and now I only have a few days to figure out why she's suddenly the only thing I can think about. Maybe getting her to open up about being a camgirl will help me understand it.

Either way, I know that I cannot leave this trip until I know why the hell I'm suddenly hot for my stepsister.

Rule #5: Sadists and masochists are not the same thing.

Mia

WHAT THE HELL IS HE UP TO?

I glance over at Garrett on our walk, in his tight black T-shirt and gray athletic shorts that give me a view of his muscled thighs and his tight ass. And it's almost enough to distract me from whatever the hell he's doing here.

At first, I assumed he's just at the lake to see my dad, but then he suddenly volunteered to take a walk with me...which was strange. So my guard is definitely up.

Not to mention how his arrival hinders my plans to work while I'm here. If he's staying in the basement, there goes my time on the blue couch with my regulars.

"So..." he says, walking a little faster than me, so I keep having to pick up speed to catch up to him. I normally bring my phone on these walks, chatting with my viewers while I work up a sweat. But now my phone sits silently in my pocket.

"So..." I echo. "You were able to get away from your precious nightclub, I see."

"Yeah...I mentioned it to Emerson. He seemed to think I needed it."

"Do you?"

"Do I what?"

"Need it?"

His eyes scan my face as he swallows. "Yeah. I think I needed a break. I need to be around my family."

"All of a sudden?"

"What?" he asks, turning toward me with his eyebrows pinched together.

"You live twenty minutes away from us. It just seems a little random that you all of a sudden want to spend time with your family."

"You know I'm busy running a company. I don't have the luxury to see my parents all the time like you do. I don't still live with them," he snaps back, and my jaw hangs open from that insult.

I freeze and throw my hands up. A few steps past me, he stops and turns toward me.

"Is this why you came on the walk with me? To be an asshole and tease me about living in my dad's basement?" I ask.

"You—" he starts, but stops himself. Taking a deep breath, he composes himself before continuing. "I didn't mean to insult you, Mia. I just…I used to love coming to the lake, and the way Mom spoke on the phone yesterday, she seemed to think Paul would appreciate me coming this year too."

My stomach drops. "Why would she say it like that? He's fine."

"I'm sure he is," he replies with a sympathetic expression. "I just think she was saying anything she could to get me to come."

For a moment, we stare at each other, and I wish that Garrett could just be real with me. It would be nice to have someone to talk to about this who didn't constantly dismiss me or mock me. But that's not who we are to each other.

"Come on," he says, gesturing for me to keep walking with him. When I finally fall into step next to him, we're quiet again. I still can't shake the feeling that Garrett knows something he's not telling me. But I don't push it.

After a while, he asks, "So, what the hell do you do up here all week?"

"Relax," I reply. "You should try it sometime."

"I know how to relax."

"Oh yeah? So tell me…how do you relax?"

He contemplates for a moment, one strong brow arched in thought. "I run."

"Running is not relaxing."

"It is to me."

"And that's what makes you a sadist," I say, teasing him. "That's like saying sex is relaxing."

He reacts with surprise. "Sex *is* relaxing."

"If you think sex is relaxing, then you're doing it wrong." I laugh.

"Oh yeah? You're a sex expert now?" he asks, and I notice the way his brow creases as he glances at me, something unsettled and almost *angry* on his face.

"I'm not a sex expert at all, but I just think sex is supposed to be fun, not relaxing."

Suddenly he stops and turns toward me, taking a step in my direction, closing the distance between us. I almost forget to breathe as he starts to speak.

"You know why I consider running relaxing? It's because of how I feel when I'm done. The same goes for sex. You can't call it relaxing because you've never been fully satisfied in bed. Letting go of every thought in your head and only focusing on the sensations in your body and not what you're thinking. Working up a sweat and being so in tune with someone that you can experience their pleasure as if it's your own. And then coming hard enough to see stars, now that's what I call relaxing. If you find someone who can do that, then you'll know what I mean."

"Oh, someone like you?" The words slip out of my mouth and hover in the few inches of space between us as I stare up at him. It's certainly the closest we've ever stood to each other, and suddenly we're talking about sex. What is happening?

My heart is pounding, my temperature spiking as I stare into his eyes, feeling the weight of this conversation. And now... imagining *that* kind of sex with him.

"Very funny," he mumbles as he turns away.

"All the girls at the dance club you own must be very lucky," I say, teasing him. Garrett's been working in nightclubs for as long as I can remember, and I can only imagine how much pussy he must be raking in daily.

"I don't sleep with the girls at my club," he replies as we continue our walk.

I laugh, glancing over at him. "You're kidding."

"No, I'm not. It might shock you, but I'm a professional. And I enjoy my job. I don't do it to pick up chicks."

I don't reply, but I stare at him skeptically for a moment. I have to admit that Garrett does strike me as different compared to most men, but if I know anything about men—and I've met enough through the app to have a pretty good idea—it's that they only want one thing. And they are willing to do just about anything to get it.

That's why I'm happy with my job. I only give what I'm willing to give. No one can touch me or use me. And at the end of the day, I get a paycheck. I don't have to worry about slimeballs who want too much.

It's the one place where I hold the power.

Our walk grows quiet for a while as we try to beat the sunset back to the house. Finally, he breaks the silence as he mutters quietly, "Masochist."

"What?" I ask.

"Earlier you called me a sadist for loving to run, but the correct word is masochist—someone who enjoys inflicting pain on themselves."

"Oh."

There's a twinkle of mischief in his eyes as we continue walking, like I've brought up a topic he's interested in talking about. "So what's a sadist?"

"A sadist is someone who likes to inflict pain on someone else."

"Hmm," I reply, before quickly adding, "like inviting yourself on my walk just to watch me suffer."

This time his smile is full, and I don't miss the way it creates wrinkles around his eyes. Then, he turns that warm, sexy grin on me as he replies, "Exactly."

Rule #6: Sexy pet names are always a good idea.

Garrett

ONCE WE GET BACK TO THE LAKE HOUSE, OUR PARENTS ARE ON the porch, my mom with a glass of rosé in her hand and my stepdad manning the grill. The aroma of charring hamburgers fills the air as Mia and I bound up the steps.

"Got yours well done, Mia," her dad says. She peeks over his shoulder to see the crispy, black edges of the last burger on the grill. I've eaten with Mia enough to know that if she spots even the slightest pink in her burger, she loses her mind.

"Thanks, Dad," she says, giving him a peck on the cheek.

"That should be a crime," I tell her. "Paul, you're an accessory to burger murder."

He laughs, but she rolls her eyes at me.

"I've been telling her the same thing since she was a kid," Paul adds.

"You two, stop picking on her," my mother says, putting an arm around Mia, who leans into her. Seeing them together…I'm reminded of the fact that Mia was just a kid when my mother came into the picture. Having lost her own mother at such a young age, she clung right onto mine when they met.

My mother had me at only eighteen, and Mia's dad had her at thirty-two, which meant when the two forty-year-olds met and fell in love, they brought together children who were thirteen years apart. But I think my mother relished the opportunity to start over with another child, finally having the daughter she always wanted. After my dad left, she had devoted her life to me. She rarely dated; in fact, she never had much of a social life at all. I was a full-grown adult just as her life seemed to begin again.

And then I'm suddenly reminded that the girl my mother sees as her daughter is the same girl I saw naked yesterday, and I haven't stopped picturing her naked since.

"I need a drink," I mutter to myself as I head inside. I go straight to the fridge in the kitchen, pulling out a light beer and setting it on the counter as I fish my phone out of my pocket. I've only been gone for a few hours, and I'm already itching to check my work email for any messages from the team.

There's nothing new in my email and not a single text from anyone.

"What's that face for?" Mia asks as she leans over the counter and watches me. With the way she's bent forward at the hips, she's practically pushing her breasts out.

Does she know what a tease she's being or is she really that naive?

"Nothing," I say, cracking open my beer. "I was just asking myself how I'm going to survive this week without doing some sort of work."

She rounds the kitchen counter, standing right next to me before she hops up onto the surface so that now, instead of having to face her overflowing cleavage across the island, I have a close-up view. Her knees fall apart as she leans back on her hands.

If I didn't know any better, I'd say she's fucking with me, teasing me on purpose just to drive me crazy.

"Looks like you're stuck with me. Unless you're thinking about going back," she says playfully.

I can't tell if she's being sarcastic or serious; there's something almost flirtatious in her demeanor that's throwing me off. Mia has never once been the least bit flirty with me, so I assume it's sarcasm.

But after last night, I can personally think of about a hundred things we could do to make these next seven days downright sublime.

No. Stop it.

My dick has somehow grown a brain of its own, and it doesn't care about the multitude of reasons I should avoid thinking about Mia this way.

"You're not getting rid of me that easily," I reply.

There's a twinkle of trouble in her eye. Then she snatches the beer out of my hand and raises it to her lips. Just watching the way her throat works as she swallows the liquid down, I realize I'm in big, big trouble.

After dinner, I get myself settled in my basement bedroom. The lake house is three floors, and the finished basement is usually reserved for guests, with a large cozy living room, a private bathroom, bedroom, and a door that leads to the hot tub out back. All in all, it has me wondering why I haven't been taking advantage of this vacation home more.

Pulling out my phone, I check my email *again*, but still... there's nothing.

Then, I feel my thumb drifting toward the new camgirl app. The one I just downloaded last night.

She wouldn't be online right now, would she? She's somewhere upstairs, two floors up, but our parents are home. Would she really be so bold as to go live with them just two doors down?

My question is answered when I open the app and see her name at the top.

WickedKitten214 is live.

Dammit, Mia.

When I click on her live stream, the video opens up showing her on her bed again, fully clothed, thank God, and drawing something in an open journal. She's on her stomach with her knees bent, her feet crossed, nonchalantly chatting while drawing.

"I used to want to be an artist when I was a kid," she says. "My parents took me on a trip to Venice when I was ten, and I remember these artists on the street that could paint a whole portrait in like fifteen minutes. And I remember thinking...I want to do that when I grow up."

Then she lifts the notebook to reveal the drawing on the page, and I let out a loud cackle when I see the horrific sketch of her cat, Betty, with a lopsided head and crooked eyes.

She giggles as she says, "But as you can see, I'm no artist. My parents put me in gymnastics instead, which was fun, I guess. I was better at that."

I find myself reclining on the blue couch, propping my feet on the coffee table as I watch her. She has a sort of charisma that's perfect for the camera; she's able to keep the broadcast entertaining without feeling awkward or letting the moment drag on.

How did I never notice how charming she is?

My eye keeps tracking down to the private room request button, but it would be pretty stupid to pay $450 to chat with someone that I can walk up two flights of stairs, in the same house, to see for free. But then again, I don't make smart decisions.

I punch my finger against the button and agree to the fee again, trying not to think too much about it. It's research, I tell myself. I need to see this through. There has to be some reason I'm suddenly finding myself attracted to a girl I've known for fifteen years.

Seriously, why her? Why not any of the hundreds of girls that have crossed my path in the same amount of time? Hundreds of girls that I felt *nothing* for. But now, for some reason, I'm drawn to this one.

Mia notices my room request again and says goodbye to her

live stream crowd. Then, just like last time, the screen goes black before asking me for camera and microphone access. Both of which I decline.

"Hello again, Drake," she says with a crooked smile. The name throws me off for a moment, before I remember that drunk Garrett gave her the name of my ladies' man friend, Drake. Mia would love Drake. Of course, he would love her too, but probably only once or twice.

"Being shy again, I see."

I type out my response.

I'm just here to see you.

"That's sweet. But I liked seeing you last time."

Maybe later. Let's just talk today.

I watch her read my messages, a tight-lipped, curious expression on her face. I wonder what she's thinking right now. If the mystery of the man on the other end of the line is enough to keep her interested. Does she always give these men that dimpled grin and genuine warmth she's giving me now? Have I ever seen her look at me like this in real life?

"What would you like to talk about, Drake?"

Tell me about yourself. I like to hear you talk.

Her expression softens. "Okay…" She reclines on the bed, looking up into the camera as she cuddles against a pillow, and I lie on the couch, almost mirroring her position, as she tells me everything I already know about her. And yet, it's like I'm hearing it for the first time.

She talks about gymnastics, her failed attempts at cosmetology school, college, bartending, singing, and then again, her artistic skills. How many times did I tease her about her lack of direction and constant failures? Why did I have to pick on her so much about it?

I don't feel like picking on her now. Instead, I type out my response.

At least you tried.

Sometimes trying is the hardest part.

You don't want to get to an age and realize that you missed out on something because you never gave it a shot.

She laughs. "Well, tell my family that. They probably all think I'm one huge failure."

I'm sure they don't.

So how did you end up here, doing this?

She shrugs. "I guess I finally found something I'm good at."

Do you like it?

"Sometimes. I like meeting new people. I like the way they make me feel about myself. And…I like the money. So, I can't really complain."

Are you happy?

She reads the question and seems to deliberate for a moment, twisting her lips as she thinks about it. "Yeah. I'm happy."

I'm not convinced. What was that look for?

Her pensive expression breaks into a smile. "Nothing. I just… wish I could connect like this in person. For some reason, it's so much easier over the phone or in messages or even on camera. But the minute I try to feel something with anyone in real life, I put my guard up."

My thumbs hover over the keyboard for a moment. Even more than the video chat last night, this feels intimate. Mia is telling me shit she would never tell *me* if she knew I was the one on the line. There's no way. It's like I'm meeting this girl for the first time.

"What about you? I've talked enough about me."

What do you want to know?

"Hmm…what do you do for a living?"

Might as well stick with the lie. If I'm going to pretend to be Drake, then I'll be Drake. *God, this feels so fucking wrong.*

Construction.

"Oh, you work with your hands then," she replies with a flirty smile, and I hate myself for the grin that stretches across my face. "Do you have someone in your life? A spouse or significant other?"

Nope.

"Why not? A good-looking body like I saw last night, you should be out there with a real woman, not here with me."

I guess I'm like you. I can't connect to real people.

Her expression morphs into a pout but not a fake one. She looks genuinely sympathetic.

"When was the last time you had a girlfriend?"

A long time, I reply.

She wouldn't believe me if I told her how long. But I'm strangely comfortable in this chat and feel the urge to tell her more. Or everything. Maybe it's the anonymity, but I want to spill secrets to her that my own best friend doesn't know. And I almost do, but then I realize that this is Mia, and if she ever finds out who is on the other end of these calls, she'll know everything about me, and I've worked too hard and too long to keep them hidden. Especially from her.

But there are a few things I can give her.

This probably won't come as a surprise to you, but I prefer to watch.

Seeing her read my messages is enough to drive me wild, the way her expression changes as she reacts to each one. It's more enjoyable than I expected it to be. Mostly because this is Mia and I am still drunk on the idea that she can be so open and sweet.

"Well, you did more than watch last night," she responds with a laugh. It's more natural than the one I've seen on her live streams. More the real Mia.

Yes, I did. You caught me at a weak moment.

She laughs again. "It wasn't that hard to convince you, Drake." The tone of the conversation grows quiet and a little serious as her eyes drift downward, away from the camera. "Do you usually watch more than you partake?"

Yes.

"Would you rather watch me...or touch me?"

Fuck. This took a turn. A good turn, but not where I was

expecting it to go. Or maybe I was. Maybe this is what I've been trying to get out of her this entire time. More of her. More vulnerable, naked, splayed out like a meal my eyes can devour. I'm sure as fuck not turning back now.

I'd fucking love to touch you.

When her hooded eyes lift to the screen, she reads my message and bites her bottom lip. "Okay, then. Touch me," she replies, and my brows furrow. As she reclines on the bed, adjusting the phone so it's hovering over her—the same way I wish I were—she gently glides her fingers over the front of her body. She's still in that bikini top and those jean shorts, and my mouth is watering with the reminder that she's just upstairs. And any moment now, I'm going to have that view I so desperately wanted.

"Pretend my hands are yours. And tell me what to do with them," she says in a low, sultry whisper. "Touch me, Drake."

Fuck me. Fuck me for using my *goddamn* friend's name when all I really want is to hear her say mine.

In fact, fuck all of this. If I'm going to tell her what to do, it's going to be my fucking voice. I quickly hit the microphone button and do my best to lower my tone and keep it at a gravelly mumble.

"Slide off your bikini top. One side at a time."

She smiles at the camera, her cheeks turning pink at the sound of my voice. "Oh, hello there."

"Do it," I mutter.

Her fingers gently pull the right triangle of fabric down, revealing her soft pink nipple, the bud already taut and ready.

"Pinch your nipple. Just until it hurts. I want to hear you whimper."

She licks her lips, her chest growing heavy as she does. Sliding her fingers over one breast at a time, she twirls the sensitive bud in between her finger and thumb, and I watch her face for the moment the pain kicks in. A high-pitched moan slips through her lips, so I know she's reached that point.

"Keep one hand there. Let the other slide down slowly."

My cock is leaking in my shorts as I watch her touch herself, moving at a deliciously slow pace as she drags her fingers over her belly. And when she reaches her shorts, I tell her to unbutton them. The other hand is still working on her breast, squeezing and pulling enough to keep her at the precipice of pain and anticipation.

I don't want to touch myself this time. I just want to watch her. Focus on *her* pleasure. Her movements. Imagine that it is my hands on her flesh, without the distraction of my cock between us.

"Show me how wet you are," I whisper, and I pray my voice is masked enough, but since she's still touching herself and not running down the stairs to confront me, I'm going to assume it's enough.

My eyes don't leave the screen as she slips her eager hands into her shorts, and I watch her face as she makes contact with her pussy. Her mouth falls open and her eyes shut halfway. Then, she slowly pulls the hand out of her shorts, showing me the moisture coating her finger, and I let out a guttural moan.

It slips out. A little too loud and sounding a little too much like me. But she's so distracted that she doesn't even notice.

"Taste yourself," I tell her, not entirely sure if that's crossing a line or if she even will, but I'm pleasantly surprised as she moves her middle finger to her lips. Opening her sweet mouth, she presses the digit against her tongue, savoring the taste of her own arousal. Suddenly, I don't know if I'm going to succeed at keeping my own dick out of this. It's currently straining so hard it hurts, and it's fucking begging for attention.

Later.

For now, she's my focus. Only her.

"Does that taste good, kitten?" I ask, the sexy pet name just rolling off my tongue.

She whimpers, sucking on her finger as she nods.

"Are you wet for me?"

"Yes," she moans.

Just as I'm about to give her more directions, an alert pops up on my screen, informing me that our hour is almost up and I'll have to agree to another $450 dollars to continue. Fuck.

Well, maybe this is a good thing. Keep her waiting, wanting. Draw it out.

"I have to go," I whisper. "But I want you to make yourself come after the call. Imagine it's my fingers in your sweet cunt, okay?"

"Yes," she replies obediently.

"Will you send me a picture of your wet pussy after you come?"

Without hesitation, she replies, "Yes."

"That's my good kitten."

With that, she smiles, her cheeks flushed with arousal.

"You like it when I call you that?" I ask.

Lips parted and eyes on the screen, she nods. "Yes."

"See you tomorrow?"

"Okay," she whispers, biting her lip again. Then the screen goes black, and I can't get my hand around my cock fast enough. The entire time I stroke myself, I do it knowing that two floors up, she's fucking herself too. And when I come all over my chest, I imagine that we're coming at the same time.

Rule #7: If you want something, you have to be willing to give something in return.

Mia

I WAKE UP SOMETIME IN THE MIDDLE OF THE NIGHT, STILL IN THE clothes I wore all day. I must have drifted off after that unexpectedly hot chat with Drake. And then I did what he told me to do after our chat. How could I not? He had me wound up and hot as hell.

So once our call ended, I made myself come by replaying the sound of his dirty words in my head, and it did not take long at all. Then, I took a picture of myself, like he asked, and I sent it.

After coming down from that high, I started to wonder if I was getting a little too attached to this mystery guy. I would normally never masturbate after a call because the guy told me to. After I get off work, I'm *off work*. Meaning I put it all away and don't think about it until I flip that camera on again. But after just two chats with Drake, I can't shake the feeling that he's different.

It's probably just the anonymous thing. And the fact that I've seen his abs and his dick, and both were impressive.

But even without the sex stuff, I feel comfortable enough to actually open up to him. To show him the real me. Not the fake, camgirl me that is always *on*, giving my patrons just enough to keep them interested without letting them in too deep.

Which is ridiculous.

He's probably just another pervy guy on the app who wants to see some tits and ass, and he's willing to pay for it. There's no way he cares about the real me, no matter how much he pretends to. None of them do.

I pick up my phone and check the time. Two thirty-five.

I toss and turn for a while, replaying the private chat with Drake. Moments from my day with Garrett keep slipping through as well. Something seems off with him. That call out of the blue yesterday and then him showing up and going on a walk with me. Is this really about my dad? Or has he just started being nice to me because he wants to? He hasn't been as cruel or as mocking as he usually is.

And that whole talk about sex on our walk was way out of character. To Garrett, I am and have always been his annoying little sister. No amount of makeup or cleavage is ever going to change that. I'm dreaming if I let myself believe it could be any different.

Even if he were attracted to me, Garrett does not take relationships seriously enough to actually be in one long-term. He is destined to be a cocky bachelor for the rest of his life, and I don't think that's something he'd ever mourn.

When sleep eludes me for another thirty minutes, I give up and climb out of bed. The house is silent, but I like the silence sometimes. Life often feels so loud that I enjoy sitting in the stillness for a while, alone with my thoughts, all of which are currently consumed by the sound of some sexy stranger's voice, echoing on repeat in my head.

I pad silently down the stairs, but it's dark and quiet. When I hear the laugh track of an old sitcom playing in the basement, I keep going down the steps. The TV is playing in the living room, and I see Garrett on the couch, his face illuminated by the glow of the television.

"Hey." His voice carries faintly across the dim room.

He looks barely awake, with tousled hair and dark circles under his eyes. It's strange to see him so grim looking. Garrett is usually bright and cheerful.

"Can't sleep?" I ask, hovering by the staircase. I don't want to come any closer without an invitation.

Then, to my surprise, he lifts his blanket, inviting me to come sit next to him. I hesitate, not quite sure how to react, since the Garrett I know would tell me to go to bed or ignore me.

"Not really," he replies. I take his invitation and sit on the cushion next to him, so there's a good foot of space between us. He lays the blanket over me so I'm wrapped in warmth.

"What are you watching?"

"*Golden Girls*," he replies with a laugh. "It's the only thing on at three in the morning."

"I love this show."

He lifts his arm and drapes it across the back of the couch. "Me too."

We watch together for a while, laughing in unison at Blanche's sex jokes and Dorothy's one-liners. When the next commercial break comes on, I glance up at Garrett and notice a blankness in his expression I've never seen before.

"Everything okay?" I ask. I can't quite explain what's off about him, but it's almost like there are so many thoughts swirling in there that he's not really existing to the outside world.

And the last thing I would ever expect is for him to open up to me.

Which he doesn't. "Yeah, I'm fine. You okay?"

He lifts his arm away from me, as if he's worried that almost touching me is a problem.

"I'm fine," I reply.

"So what's new with you?" he asks, making small talk. "Any new...ventures?"

I turn toward him. Garrett has always teased me about my failed attempts at life, and I remember how encouraging Drake was, how he said trying was better than regretting the missed opportunity later.

"Why would I tell you? So you can make fun of me for failing at something again?"

He looks affected, a shocked expression on his face as he turns toward me. "Why would I make fun of you?"

"Because that's what you do. You know, it's better to at least try at something than regret not trying later on," I say, but I don't miss the way he rolls his eyes and looks away.

"Wise words."

"Well, it's true."

"Mia, I'm not making fun of you. I just asked what you've been up to. I'm proud of you for trying different things."

"No, you're not," I say, turning toward the TV. For some reason, I feel my lower lip tremble and my eyes sting with tears. Why do I even care? It shouldn't matter to me what Garrett thinks about me.

Except that it does.

"For the record," I continue, "I really like my job now, and I'm making enough to finally move out of our parents' basement."

"Oh yeah? Doing what?" There's a harshness in his tone that stops me from answering. He's such a cocky asshole sometimes. The last thing I would ever do is actually open up to him about what I do. He would only judge me more.

"Never mind," I mutter, throwing the blanket off of me and moving to stand. But his hand is on my arm, pulling me back down. I glare at him, mouth hanging open in surprise. "Let me go."

"No. You're being a brat. Just answer the question."

"I'm not telling you anything," I argue, trying to get up again. This time his arms wrap around my middle and drag me down onto his lap.

"Why not? What do you have to hide, Mia? Because I don't believe your lies about being in *data entry*."

He's mocking me and it has my blood boiling. So I take a swing at him, trying to slap him across the face, but he's too fast, catching my wrist in his hand. I'm struggling against his hold until we're wrestling, but he's so much stronger than me that, within minutes, he has me facedown on the couch with all of his body weight resting on my back.

"You're such an asshole!" I yell into the cushion.

"Why does everything have to be a fight with you?" he argues, a hint of mocking humor in his tone. "You're so goddamn feisty."

"Me? You're the one lying on me like you want to fuck me!"

He laughs in my ear, a low, gravelly chuckle. "Trust me, brat, if I wanted to fuck you, I would."

I struggle against him some more. "Well then, I guess it's a good thing you can't stand me, so I don't have to worry about it."

I swear I must be imagining things because I feel his hips grind against my backside, and there's definitely something *stiff* in his pants as he does it. Heat courses up my spine in a flurry of arousal and confusion. Why on earth is Garrett getting hard?

Does wrestling with his stepsister really get him aroused?

"On second thought…a little hate sex might be fun." His breath is against my ear and I gasp at his words. Heat floods my belly at the thought. Is he being serious?

I've given up all my fight against his hold now. Instead, I find myself pressing my hips back against him. Almost as if I'm searching for the growing erection in his pants.

"Garrett," I murmur, and the energy between us quickly changes from playful to…something else.

"Do you want me to get off you? Just say the word, Mia."

But I don't say a word. I lift my head from the couch, feeling his breath against my cheek, turning my face just enough that his mouth ends up only an inch away from mine. His hands, which were previously holding my wrists in a fierce, painful grip, move to my fingers, so our hands are clasped.

Then he grinds again. And I let out a loud moan, pushing my hips back again.

This is crossing a line. We shouldn't be doing this, but I still don't really know what *this* is and there's no denying how much we both want it, so I don't say a word.

His lips brush my neck and jaw, then move up to my earlobe

before he whispers, "What is this new job you're not telling me about, Mia?"

"I can't tell you," I reply, moving my head in search of his lips.

"Do you want me to touch you?" he asks as one hand drifts down from my arm, over my body, and squeezes between my belly and the couch. My bottoms grow wet as his fingers graze the sensitive flesh below my belly button. I'm assaulted by a tingling arousal from his touch.

I can barely reply. It's too strange to vocalize, but God yes, I do want him to touch me. So bad.

So I give him a weak whimper and "mm-hmm."

"Then tell me. Don't keep secrets from me."

"No," I mumble as I squirm under his body, desperate to get his fingers where I want them.

This is *insane*. Just a couple hours ago, I was video chatting with Drake and now I'm halfway to having sex with my stepbrother. What is happening?

Then, without warning, his body is off the couch and the weight of him on top of me is gone. I sit up in a rush and gape at him. "What?"

He laughs and then shrugs. "If you want something, you have to be able to give something."

Anger burns through me so hot that I grab the throw pillow and chuck it angrily at his face. "You jerk!"

Jumping off the couch, I storm away toward the stairs. I was putty in the palm of his hand, and he had me moaning and salivating for him like a cat in heat. It's humiliating.

"You're such an asshole."

"If you change your mind, I'll be down here waiting," he calls after me, but I'm already halfway up the stairs. My body is still buzzing with exhilaration, but I won't be going back down to him. He's never getting me like that again.

Rule #8: An ass is an ass— whether you're being one or admiring one.

Garrett

My run was hard this morning. Harder than usual.

Getting out of bed. Putting on my shoes. Walking out the door. Hard, hard, hard.

But I did it. I shoved away the gross lurking gloom that sometimes rears its ugly head, and I went for a run despite feeling like shit. And it didn't matter that it was nearly an eleven-minute mile or that I wanted to stop seven times. I made it clear around the nine-mile loop, and that's something.

The events of last night—or was it this morning?—keep replaying in my mind. During my entire run, my mind was on an endless shame-regret-disgust loop. Did I go too far? This is new territory with Mia, but teasing her is all I really know. I don't want to scare her, though, and I sure as fuck don't want to hurt her. I shouldn't have forced her down like that, but in my defense, I really thought it was just playful wrestling. How was I to know my dick was going to get so excited?

One thing is for sure…that physical attraction I wanted to investigate is definitely alive and well.

I shove the shame and disgust thoughts away for a moment to remember how soft her body felt in my hands, how quickly I got aroused with her against me, how good she smelled, and just how *badly* I wanted to let my cock slip inside her and make her mine. Truly mine.

Whoa. Where the fuck did that come from?

When was the last time I had that thought or urge? Longer than I'd care to admit.

I resigned myself to being broken long ago. The drive to fuck was gone, and I became easily content to stay on the sidelines and just watch. Sex has been a spectator sport for so long. So why now? And why the fuck *her*?

Maybe Emerson and Charlie are getting inside my head. The way they look at each other, touch each other, constantly lean on each other as if they actually fucking complete each other. It's just screwing with my sanity. Making me want something I've always sworn I didn't. And that's still true. The idea of dating has absolutely no appeal to me.

So why does the idea of doing that with my own fucking stepsister not sound half-bad? What sort of twisted psychosis shit is that? I'd rather go back to feeling the shame and regret honestly.

My head has been so fucked this week.

There's motion off to the right as I turn the last corner back to the house and see a bikini-clad Mia doing yoga on a stand-up paddleboard in the middle of the lake with my mother. They're both trying to maintain serious, calm expressions, but each of them break out in giggles at the slightest wobble in their form.

I feel better seeing Mia smile. I didn't see her this morning, and I was honestly afraid she would be sulking all day or allowing my shitty behavior to ruin her relaxing summer. But she looks good out there. Which means I should definitely get the fuck out of here before they see me and I ruin their time together.

"Garrett!" my mother calls, and I grimace. "Get over here!"

Reluctantly, I jog down to the bank and wave at my mom. Then, I brave a glance in Mia's direction, and our eyes meet for a moment. She doesn't look as angry as I expect her to; instead, she looks nervous as she glances back down.

Yep, I definitely made shit weird when I dry humped her into the couch last night. I'm an idiot.

"How was your run?" Mom asks.

"It was good."

"It's nice to see you running again."

I instantly clench up. Squinting my eyes, I look away. Why are mothers so open about everything? Why does she have to bring up the dark shit like it's nothing? I clear my throat and nod.

"Yeah," I reply with nothing else to contribute. I do notice Mia's attention suddenly back on me with a little more curiosity than before.

"Well…my replacement is here," my mom adds with a wink.

"What?" Mia replies, looking at her.

I notice the way Mia adjusts her bottoms and wraps her hands around her middle when she sees me watching. As if she's trying to hide something about herself.

"Come on, Garrett. Your turn," my mother calls, paddling herself to the dock. I help her climb out, and she wobbles a little more once her feet are on solid-ish ground.

"I just ran nine miles. Do I really need to do paddleboard yoga now?" I ask, and I spot some reluctance on Mia's face. My mom has no idea that forcing us together right now is incredibly awkward, but I guess it's a good thing she doesn't know.

"It's okay. I'll get out." Mia cuts in with a look of disappointment hidden under that forced smile.

Mom's not having any of that. "Don't you dare. You just got out here. Plus, Garrett needs to stretch after that run."

I hesitantly slip off my sneakers and tear off my sweaty shirt. It might be nice to actually have some alone time with Mia. My mom hands me her paddle and I lower myself onto the empty board.

Mia's watching me with a tight-lipped expression as my board cants to one side then the other, and I know for certain that, at some point, I'm going into the water.

"Are you sure about this?" she asks, holding back the urge to laugh.

"No," I reply.

Mia giggles as I take forever finding my balance. The tension between us fades into the background for the time being. And we focus solely on how I must have the world's worst balance and can't seem to stay upright on a *stand-up* paddleboard.

"Why don't you just sit down? It's easier to start that way."

I laugh, looking at her with a blush on my cheeks as I drop to my ass on the board. Holding the paddle across my body, I row toward the middle of the lake with her. She's kneeling, her spine straight and her shoulders back. In the late afternoon light, she looks so beautiful it's actually breathtaking.

"You have to find your balance," she says as I wobble again, nearly falling off.

I'm still on my butt—how is that even possible? "Yeah...I don't have a lot of balance."

"Deep breath. Just relax. You're trying too hard."

"Ha. Said no one ever."

"Garrett, I'm serious. Just take a deep breath and relax."

When I glance over at her, she's the picture of serenity. I love the way her cheeks look with a little sunburn under her eyes and no makeup.

All right, all right. Deep breath.

I do as she says, and on the long exhale, it feels as if I'm releasing air that I've been holding on to for too long. It feels...nice.

"Better," she says softly, her gentle voice carrying across the calm waters. I can't for the life of me understand why she's being so nice to me, especially after last night.

"Better," I say, repeating her. It's quiet for a while as we paddle without speaking.

Finally, she looks over at me as she says, "Aren't you going to apologize to me?"

"Apologize for what?" I reply, although I know. And while I'm aware I should apologize, knowing and gathering the balls to actually do it are two different things.

"For being an asshole. For *attacking* me," she says as she curls a lock of wispy hair behind her ear.

"You didn't seem to mind..." I reply with a teasing grin.

"Yeah, exactly. You totally played me. And if I hadn't stood my ground, you would have taken advantage of me."

"Is it still considered being taken advantage of if you were so eager for it your pussy was practically searching for my dick?"

"Oh my God," she screams. Using her paddle, she splashes me with a wave of water. "We are *not* having this conversation. My pussy was not *searching for* your dick. I don't even want your dick."

"*Oh, Garrett,*" I say in a taunting, high-pitched tone, mimicking how she sounded last night.

Even as she turns her face away from me, I catch the way she's biting her bottom lip, trying to hide her smile. "I hate you."

"That might be true, but I didn't do anything to you last night that you weren't thirsty for."

"Because you caught me at a weak moment," she replies.

"Oh yeah?" I ask, paddling closer to her. "Been a while for you?"

"You could say that," she mumbles under her breath.

"Well, I promise you, it's been longer for me." I'm not sure why I'm giving that away, but knowing that Mia seems to be struggling romantically has me feeling some sort of way. Like somewhat pleased...that I'm not the only one. Or that no one is able to satisfy her. Either way, it's good to know.

"So you were thirsty for it too," she says, looking back at me. "I *felt* it."

I can't help the grin that pulls across my cheeks as I stare at her. I love how unabashed Mia is when it comes to sex, and I guess that comes from being a camgirl. Or maybe it's why she's such a good one, because even with her stepbrother, she's not going to shy away from talking about how my cock got hard for her.

"I am only a man," I reply.

"Well, keep it in your pants," she snaps. "Because you and I are *never* going there."

"Whatever you say. But I'm going to get you to tell me about this secret new job of yours, one way or another."

She shakes her head, as if exasperated by me, and chooses not to argue with me on this topic. Instead, she changes the subject. Chewing on her lip, she asks, "What did your mom mean? About seeing you run again. When did you stop?"

This isn't the topic I want to switch to, but I can't exactly avoid it now. "Nothing. I just...didn't run for a whole year."

"When was that?"

"I don't know. Maybe nine or ten years ago."

When I look back at her, she's staring at me with a pensive expression on her face, and I swear it sometimes feels like Mia can see right through me. Like I can't even keep a single thought away from her, and while that might seem romantic or sweet, to me, it's terrifying. If she saw inside my mind, I'm afraid of how she would react.

"Are you ready to stand up?" she asks, trying to lighten the mood.

"Not really."

She giggles. "Don't be a little bitch. Now, get on your knees."

"Hey, that's my line," I reply, and she glares at me.

"Garrett! Be serious for a second!" She tries to keep a stern expression, but it quickly morphs into a laugh.

Mia has such a full laugh—full of what, I don't know. Full of life or something. It's infectious. The kind of laugh that makes everyone around her join in. It's literally impossible to keep the grin off my face. And other than the one night a week I meet up with my friends at the bar, I can't remember the last time I really laughed—or smiled.

"Okay, okay," I say, moving awkwardly to my knees. My board

wobbles, of course, but I manage to stay on as I position myself into a kneeling pose next to Mia.

"Not terrible."

"Thanks. Now what?"

"Now, plant your hands, tuck your toes, and push up." Suddenly, Mia's ass is in the air, and I can't seem to look away. Her brightly painted fingernails are planted against her board and her toes mirror the action. Her thick, muscled legs stretch all the way up from her toes to her plump ass in that yellow bikini.

Does she have any idea what she's doing to me?

Mia has always had the perfect body. The only time she didn't was when she started to look too thin back in high school. Or maybe it's the fact that she's always seemed comfortable in her own body, exuding confidence as if she doesn't care about the slight swell of her belly or the soft pillows of skin poking out from the sides of her bikini bottoms. Whenever she sits down, her hips create this little crease on the sides that would drive a man wild.

"Stop staring at my ass and do it," she barks.

Fuck, she caught me gawking at her body like a horny teenager. Around Mia, that's exactly what I feel like. I'm thirty-six, not fifteen.

And she's only…twenty-three.

Fuck, Mia is *twenty-three*. Why does that thought feel like I'm being hit by a semi? Like I'm suddenly realizing that the little girl is gone, replaced by a mature woman. It's not like I didn't know she was twenty-three. But I remember being her age. I still *felt* like a kid, and I certainly acted like one. I was fresh out of college, drinking and partying *way* too much, and acting so reckless it's a miracle I'm still alive.

But Mia is not like that at all. She's ten times more mature than I was at her age, and it's not some excuse I can use to justify suddenly lusting after her and grinding her into the couch just to feel the friction on my dick.

"Garrett…" she groans, grabbing my attention again.

"Yes, yes. Sorry. Toes under. Hands planted. Hips up." As I shove my backside into the air, I'm surprised to find that I actually don't fall into the water. Letting my head hang, I keep my eyes on her as I feel my calves stretch. Her long blond hair waves in the slight breeze, the ends wet against the board, and she turns her head toward me, a bright smile on her face.

"Holy shit. You did it!"

"Now what?"

"Now, walk your feet and hands together until you can slowly roll up to standing."

"Ha," I reply. "You're joking, right?"

Miraculously, I watch her do it, and she makes it look easy. She steps forward until her feet are planted just behind her hands. Damn, she's flexible. And her ass somehow still looks perfect from this angle. I mean…an ass is an ass. Even upside down, I can admire it.

As she slowly rolls upward, I watch beads of sweat cascade down her spine. I'd like to trace my fingers along the trail they just left.

Focus, Garrett.

I mimic her actions, taking a much smaller step forward, since my tight calves would never let me bend in half the way hers let her. As I start to roll upward, her touch on my arm startles me. Steadying me, she runs her hand from my shoulder, over my biceps, to my hand.

"You got it!" She squeals as I stand all the way up on my board, tightly holding her hand in my grip like an anchor.

"Oh, this isn't so bad," I reply, but I don't let go of her hand.

"You might actually be good at yoga."

Her grip slips from my hand before I can say anything, but our gazes catch. There's a long, tense moment when it feels like everything between us has changed, and I don't know if it's just me or if she feels it too.

"I'm sorry," she mumbles softly. "But I can't help myself."

"What?" I manage to say before the hand that was just holding mine shoves against my shoulder, and I go careening into the water. Just as I break the surface, I hear that full, delicious laugh of hers. And it sounds so good to my ears, I couldn't possibly be mad.

Even I can admit, I deserved that.

Rule #9: An open door is an open invitation.

Mia

"YOU TWO SHOULD MEET US DOWN AT MIKE'S TAVERN LATER," MY stepmom says, ruffling my wet hair. I wince as her hand drifts over my sunburned scalp. "Mia, you need to put on more sunblock and wear a hat."

How can I explain to Laura that I was too distracted by her son being both dickheaded and charming at the same time, making me want to fuck him and murder him? In that order.

There was really no time for proper skin care.

"Um…sure," I reply, grabbing a piece of watermelon from the chopping block. I glance over at Garrett, who's scrolling through his phone. When he looks up at me, there's a sense of hesitation on his face. Maybe getting Garrett a little buzzed at the bar will help loosen him up and make him forget about my *secret job* and give in to this growing sexual tension between us.

"Okay, your dad and I are going out to eat and then to Mike's," Laura says as she kisses my cheek. "Have Garrett bring you up later. They have karaoke tonight!"

On the other side of the kitchen, he groans. Meanwhile, my eyes light up.

"Oh, I'm so there."

"Count me out," he mutters.

"Don't knock it till you've tried it, Garrett," I say, teasing with a laugh.

After our parents leave, Garrett and I are alone, and it's awkwardly tense again. There's a strange sense of flirtatious anticipation between us now, as if we've accidentally discovered something we were never meant to find and now there's no going back. And I sort of want to see this through.

Of course, I can't let *him* know that.

The good news is that we've recovered from the fight last night, but things are still so strange between us. After I pushed him into the lake, he tipped my paddleboard, and soon, we were swimming and dunking each other like little kids, howling with laughter the entire time.

When we're like this, I can't quite tell if Garrett and I are friends, siblings, less, or more. It's all so confusing. I just wish I could figure out for one minute what is going on inside his head. I wish I had the slightest clue as to how he feels about me. Am I still just the annoying little sister, or does he truly see me as a woman? If last night is any indication, it's definitely more the latter.

Even though it's never felt this way before.

"I'm going to go shower," I announce as I waltz out of the kitchen. I can feel his eyes on me as I head for the stairs. Just before disappearing around the corner, I glance back and our eyes meet. I don't hold his stare for long, but it's amazing how much is conveyed in one single gaze. The question is…what exactly did I just convey by looking back at him? Did I basically just invite him to come watch me? Shower with me? Screw me?

I can't stop thinking about it as I get ready for my shower, a slight tremble in my bones. Once I reach the upstairs bathroom, I start to pull the door shut behind me, but for some reason, I decide at the last minute to leave it cracked. Why? Logistically speaking, because our parents aren't home and Garrett has no reason to be up here.

Why did I *really* leave it open? Because I want to believe he'll find himself on the other side of it.

Which is insane because there's no way Garrett would ever watch me in the shower. So why would I even think that? Maybe because I want him to?

When I strip off my clothes, I think about Drake and what he told me over our chat, about him being a voyeur, about *watching*. The thought alone sends butterflies to my belly. How could something so seemingly impersonal feel so intimate? The idea of those mysterious eyes on me…as if existing just for his gaze alone makes me feel sexier and more desired than anything else.

So maybe that's why I leave the door open, inserting Garrett for Drake in my fantasy. I imagine he's peering through the crack, watching me get naked. And when I climb in the shower, with its glass doors and clear view, I can almost feel his gaze on me. As the glass fogs up from the hot water, I don't know if he's there, but honestly, it wouldn't bother me if he was; in fact, I wish he were.

Which might be the only reason I pull the detachable showerhead from the wall, turning down the heat of the water as I press the intense spray between my legs. I recline against the wall, shutting my eyes, and I picture Garrett—or is it Drake?—standing on the other side of the cracked door, watching me as I make myself come with such force my spine arches, and I let out a muffled cry.

After my shower, I turn off the water and reach for my towel hanging on the hook. Wrapping it around my body, I step out onto the mat.

The rapping noise against the door makes me jump, and my heart somersaults in my chest. It slowly pushes open as Garrett says, "Knock knock."

What is he doing here? Is this…about that eye contact earlier? Is he here to…have sex with me?

No. No, no, no, no.

I'm standing there dripping on the bath mat with my mouth hanging open as Garrett enters the room, my mind a foggy mess. He prowls toward me until he's only standing an inch away. I barely reach his shoulders, so I have to stare up into his eyes.

"Wha…" I mumble idiotically.

He leans so close I stop breathing, and I can't believe this is happening. I mean, I did leave the door open, subconsciously inviting him in, didn't I? I basically sent him a *come fuck me* stare as I left the kitchen, and combined with the open door, it was all the sign he needed. I wasn't subtle about it, not really. So I shouldn't be surprised that my stepbrother is pressing his body against me while I'm in nothing but a towel, leaning closer and closer until our mouths are about to touch.

My trembling fingers lose their grip of the towel, and it falls to my feet, leaving me naked in front of Garrett. The arousal and cool breeze have my nipples tight and brushing delicately against his shirt. A crooked smile lifts one side of his mouth, but his eyes stay focused on mine.

Then, just when I think he's about to kiss me, he starts to pull away. Confusion wracks my brain as my brow furrows. He doesn't stop moving until he's stepping backward, and I look down and notice the bottle of bodywash in his hands.

"Sorry," he says with a wicked grin. "We're out of soap in the downstairs bathroom."

My mouth falls open again, but before he turns and leaves the bathroom, he lets his eyes rake over my still naked body. Then, a victorious expression colors his features as he turns to leave. Meanwhile, I'm standing here dumbfounded that I let him get to me.

Again.

———

Mike's Tavern is just down the hill from the house. It's dark by the time Garrett and I start to make our way there. Every time a car passes us, he puts himself between me and the road, holding me to the side like I'm a toddler at risk of darting in front of a moving car. I laugh a little each time it happens, but inside, I love it.

Our parents are at a table in the back, and they spot us immediately. They wave us over, and as usual, they are not alone. When my gaze catches on a new face at the table, I pause. Not because I don't know who he is but because he's young, good-looking, and my stepmother has her arm on the back of the chair. I can tell before I even approach the group that she is trying to set me up with a handsome boy my own age.

My stepmom is a social butterfly, which is great for my dad, who tends to be a bit of a loner. It's nice seeing them with friends and enjoying a full life. Even if he's always looking more tired than he used to—a sign that the cancer is still taking its toll.

"Mia, come sit over here!" Laura calls. "I have someone I want you to meet."

The guy smiles and awkwardly waves at me. Garrett's scrutinizing attention is on me and this new stranger I'm being ushered toward.

"Hi," I stammer. Laura scoots over a seat, leaving the one between them for me.

There's only one other empty seat at the table down near my dad, putting Garrett and me as far away from each other as possible. Probably a good thing, but I'm still left feeling strangely disappointed.

Once I sit down, I glance up at him, and his eyes are laser focused on me, his jaw clenched, and his shoulders tight. If I didn't know any better, I'd say he looks a little jealous.

"Mia, this is Reese. He's Marcia and Todd's son. He just graduated from Yale!"

"Wow…congratulations," I say, forcing a smile in his direction. Reese is handsome, with lush black hair and bright golden-brown eyes.

"Reese, this is my beautiful daughter, Mia," Laura says as she touches a lock of my silvery blond hair.

But then a voice booms across the table. "She's not your daughter."

Everyone goes silent and all eyes drift over to Garrett. And like everyone else at the table, I'm staring at him wide-eyed as he cowers in shame as if he just realized what came out of his mouth.

"Of course she is," Laura responds, putting an arm around me.

The table resumes its casual conversation, and while Reese and Laura chatter back and forth about school and his parents' lake resort business down the road, I keep glancing over at the man sulking at the other end of the table. What the hell was that all about? All of a sudden, he has mommy issues and he's jealous that his mother sees me as one of her own? It's never been a problem before.

In fact, I like it when Laura calls me her daughter. I don't remember my own mother, but from what I've heard, she was lovely. It doesn't change the fact that she doesn't exist in my memory, though. Instead, it was Laura chaperoning my field trips and buying my first maxi pads and taking me prom dress shopping. She never had a daughter and I never had a mother... so who cares if she calls me her own?

The only other reason I can think of that he would freak out like that is if his mother calling me her daughter makes it too weird for him, considering what has transpired between us in the last twenty-four hours. There's a sexual energy there, where there wasn't one before, and it'd be a lot easier for both of us to process if our parents didn't treat us like blood-related siblings.

The waitress brings over our drinks, and Garrett's attention rarely leaves me as Reese and I chat. For some unknown reason, guilt gnaws away at me, especially when he makes me laugh or touches my arm. Reese is a software engineer with dreams of working at Google. He tells surprisingly good jokes, but other than that, there's no chemistry between us. Regardless of how good-looking he is, I'm not dying to see him naked.

After our second round of drinks, the waitress brings over the karaoke menu of songs and some slips of paper to fill out. I snatch it up excitedly.

"Oh no. Here she goes," my dad announces when he sees me browsing the song list.

"You like karaoke?" Reese asks, sounding a little uneasy.

"I fucking love karaoke," I reply without looking up.

"That's cool. So you can sing?"

I laugh. "I can't carry a tune in a bucket."

When I glance up at him, he looks uncomfortable. "What?" I ask. "It's karaoke. You're supposed to sound bad!"

"You're not...embarrassed?"

I laugh again. If only he knew about my secret job.

When I look toward Garrett, this time he's not radiating jealousy. He's sort of smirking at me. Then he shakes his head and takes a deep breath. He's probably gearing up to give me shit about my singing, but I don't care. I *love* karaoke, and even he can't ruin this for me.

Meanwhile, I jot down four songs on the tiny piece of paper and hand it to the waitress.

"And two shots of Fireball, please," I call out to her before she gets too far away.

"Oh, no thank you," Reese says, and I turn to him with an arched brow. "I don't drink Fireball."

Another laugh slips through. "Those are both for me."

Rule #10: It's better to be a stepsister-loving pervert than an insensitive, Ivy League douchebag.

Garrett

Mia sounds terrible. She's currently shaking her ass through an off-key version of "Dancing Queen," and it's the worst thing I've ever heard, but the crowd has suddenly come to life. Everyone is clapping and dancing and singing along. And she looks as if she doesn't have a care in the world.

In her cute jean shorts and flowery tank top, she's beaming as her screechy voice carries across the room. She looks truly free, hopping up and down with the microphone, and I can't tear my eyes away. Not from her smile or from the way her hips shake with each bounce.

When I glance over at *fucking Reese*, the Ivy League square at the other end of the table, he's wearing an uncomfortable grimace as he scrolls through his phone. I want to take the damn thing and throw it into the water pitcher on the table. This guy isn't Mia's type at all. He looks dull as fuck, and she'd be bored to tears with someone like him.

I don't get jealous. That's not what this is. I just don't like this guy, and regardless of what's gone down this week, Mia is still family to me, and I'm her protective older brother. I don't like the idea of some guy getting a free ticket to her panties just because he graduated from Yale and his parents own a lake resort.

When Mia comes bouncing back to the table, we all applaud her, and she gives a little bow with her red cheeks and messy hair. There's not a scrap of embarrassment on her face. Must be nice to have fun and not give a shit what anyone thinks. I wish I had a shred of what Mia has.

"Bravo, sweetheart!" Paul says as he stands up to hug her.

"Thanks, Dad."

She sits down, still next to *fucking Reese*, and we have another round of drinks before the parents—ours and Reese's—all decide to call it a night. I can tell with one look at Mia that she's not ready to throw in the towel just yet. She still has three more songs to sing.

So we tell them goodbye, but when everyone rises and walks to the door, I stay put. If *fucking Reese* is staying, then so am I.

When my mother gets to the door, she calls me over. "Why don't you come with us?" she asks, looping her arm through mine, and I clench my jaw.

"I'm not leaving Mia here alone."

"She's not alone," Mom replies, actively pulling me to the door. "She's with Reese."

"Do you even know that guy? You're just going to leave your *daughter* with a complete stranger?"

She balks. "First of all, Mia is an adult. Second of all, I'm not leaving her alone. She's in a bar, where everyone has known her since she was in third grade. And lastly...why are you so protective of her all of a sudden? I mean, I'm glad you're finally getting along, and I think it's sweet you've taken this big-brother role so seriously, but maybe you need to ease up a bit."

I pull my arm away from her. "Maybe you need to take your *mother* role a little more seriously. I'm not leaving her."

With that, I walk away, taking my guilt with me. I didn't

mean to snap at my mother or blame her for being a bad one, but she'd never really understand why I couldn't leave Mia here. There are still a shit-ton of unanswered questions where my stepsister and I are concerned, and I'm at the point where I either see it through and do something about all of this new tension or just leave town completely and try to let it go.

I think we all know which route I'm going to choose.

When I sit back at the table, Mia is laughing at something Reese said, and it grates on my nerves.

"What's so funny?" I mutter, doing a pretty shitty job of appearing unaffected by their sudden friendliness.

"Oh, nothing. He was just telling me about how he had to use his fake ID in college."

"So how old are you then?"

"Twenty-three in August," he confidently replies. My eyes trail over to Mia, but she's too busy worrying her lip and stirring her straw around in her drink to look up at me.

Is this the kind of guy Mia goes for? A smart guy, close to her age, who's probably not a moody asshole who owns a sex club and has watched her masturbate not once, but *twice*, without her knowing it.

Yeah, I did sneak upstairs and peek in on her taking a shower, but somewhere in my sick, demented mind, I figured that if she left it open a crack, then she was actually inviting me to do so. And after that *fuck me* stare she shot me before heading upstairs, who could blame me?

Maybe I should just leave them alone. I won't leave the bar entirely; I still need to make sure she makes it home safely, but I should probably just find a lonely corner of the bar where I'm not a pesky third wheel.

Right as I'm about to force myself away from them, the announcer calls her name for another round of karaoke. She beams as she jumps up from her seat and the patrons seated around the bar actually cheer when they see her jog onto the stage.

When the music starts, I immediately recognize the song. "Criminal" by Fiona Apple. Not exactly the same tempo as Abba.

I feel my spine stiffen as I watch her clutch the microphone stand with both hands and hug it close to her body. Oh, fuck. I can already tell by the way she's swaying to the beat that this is going to be difficult to watch. Not because it's cringey or because her singing is just as bad as it was before, but because my eyes won't be the only ones devouring my too-sexy-for-her-own-good stepsister.

I don't look away for even a second as she sings—still badly—while swaying her hips and practically grinding against the microphone stand. The crowd is eating it up, whooping and whistling, and it only encourages her to do it more.

"Is she always like this?" Reese asks from behind me. When I turn toward him, he's smiling up at the stage, and it's like ice to my bloodstream.

"Always," I reply grimly.

He laughs. "She's quite a girl. I bet there's never a dull moment."

I'm watching her as she crawls onto the nearest table with the microphone in her hand, dancing on her knees and making the crowd go crazy. A couple of older ladies jokingly throw dollar bills at her, and she's laughing her way through the song.

Her singing might be god-awful, but her stage presence is perfection. Those stage lights love her, and she has a natural ability to control a crowd like nothing I've ever seen. So a career in music might not be right for her, but Mia belongs onstage.

"Never…" I reply, but when I glance back at Reese, he's staring down at his phone again.

Fuck this guy. Turning back toward Mia, I watch her finish the song. And when the crowd cheers for her, I cup my hands over my mouth and whoop the loudest. She glances up at me and her eyes twinkle with excitement as our gazes meet.

It's at this moment that I decide to stop going back and forth with what my body wants. It clearly wants to fuck her. And I guess if that's what my body wants—and clearly what hers wants too—far be it from me to argue with that kind of persuasion. This new chemistry between us is just physical anyway, so we might as well get it out of our systems. She said she's been in a dry spell too, so it's likely just pent-up sexual aggression and a healthy dose of resentment that's been building for years, but whatever it is, I bet it will make for some out-of-this-world sex.

When she comes back to the table, I stand up to greet her. That douchebag, Reese, isn't paying attention anyway. So I grab Mia by the waist and pull her toward me. Her eyes widen as I do.

"That was incredible," I mumble quietly.

"Thank you," she replies with uncertainty. She must be confused as to why I'm not making fun of her poor singing skills and holding her a little too closely in public.

So I lean down and whisper in her ear, "Leave with me right now."

Her eyes widen even more at my dark invitation, searching my eyes as if she's trying to confirm what I'm implying. "For what?"

"You know what," I reply in a deep whisper.

"Can't you see I'm on a date?"

"No, you're not. I brought you here."

"Well, I like *him*," she whispers, and I stare at her in confusion.

Ouch. "No, you don't. You think that guy could possibly give you what I can?"

She flinches and tries to pull away, but I don't let her get far. "I already told you, we're not having this conversation. You've teased me enough. I'm done."

"Mia, stop fucking around," I mutter, feeling suddenly impatient.

"I think I like seeing you so jealous," she replies with a wicked grin.

This time, she successfully pulls away, moving back to the table to sit next to Reese.

"We need shots," I mutter as I flag down the waitress, ordering a pitcher of beer and a round of Fireballs, which Reese actually takes this time.

The rest of the night feels like a blur. She sings a couple more songs. I'm her loudest and most obnoxious supporter while *fucking Reese* continues to pay minimal attention, only giving her his time when she's back at the table. At one point, I turn around to find him with his arm around her, whispering something in her ear that has her smiling.

Suddenly I know what a territorial dog feels like when someone encroaches on their property, touching what is theirs. I have to bite back the urge to snarl as I glare at them. But what right do I have to say anything? Mia is not mine; I have no intention of making her or anyone mine. So why should I steal her chance at happiness for my own stubborn pride?

"I have to go to the bathroom," I mumble, although neither of them hear me. I resign myself to leaving while I'm at the urinal, ready to put away my selfishness, regardless of how drunk I am and how badly I want to stay.

As I come out of the bathroom, I hear Reese's voice down the hallway that leads to the back door.

"I'm telling you, it's her!" he exclaims into his phone. I press myself against the wall, so he doesn't see me as I listen in.

"No, I haven't asked her if she's a fucking camgirl, but look at those pictures I sent you. It's definitely WickedKitten."

Goose bumps erupt along my arms and neck.

"Dude," he laughs. "Of course I'm going to fuck her. She's been trying to touch my dick all night. As soon as I get her away from her creepy fucking brother, I'll take her back to my place. I bet she lets me film it, and I'll send it to you."

Fuck this guy. My blood turns to scalding in a heartbeat as I march toward him with a sneer pulling on my lips.

"Give me this," I bark. I grab his phone out of his hand without warning.

"Dude, what the fuck?"

I toss it on the floor as I slam him against the wall. "Listen to me, you little shit. I don't care what the fuck you saw or what you think about Mia. If you try to lay a hand on her, I promise I'll break it off, understand?"

He shoves against me, but I'm stronger and more determined, so I lock him against the wall with my forearm pressed to his throat.

"It's so obvious you want to fuck your sister, you pervert!" he manages to squeak out, although I've got him pinned so tight he can barely breathe.

"Yeah, well, I'd rather be a pervert than a douchebag."

"Garrett!" a familiar female voice screams from the entrance to the hallway. "Let him go!"

On instinct, I pull away, staring at her and wondering just how much of that she heard. Reese sputters and coughs, trying to suck in air as she reaches for his phone.

But Mia gets to it before him, and as she picks it up, she asks, "Are you okay?" Then she glances down at the screen to see her own picture, which we both see clear as day. It's bright as fuck, and she's naked, sprawled out on the mattress of her bed. I watch Mia's face go stark white and her eyes widen like saucers.

I snatch the phone out of her hand and shove it toward Reese. "Delete it. Now," I bellow.

Mia stands frozen between us as Reese composes himself, not moving with the phone in his hand.

"Now!" My voice thunders through the dim hallway. Finally, he starts punching buttons on his phone, and I watch the photo disappear.

"It was you, wasn't it?" Reese asks her. "You're some porn star, right?"

"I'm not a porn star," she replies.

"Yeah, well, whatever. You get naked for money."

"That's enough," I bark at him, but he ignores me. The way he's talking to her, flashing her picture around, sharing it with his friends, I know it's humiliating to her, and it's making me want to pummel his face with my fist.

Then he reaches out for her, and I see red.

"Let's get out of here," he says. "I already know what your hourly rate is, sweetheart. I can pay it."

My fist flies on its own accord, connecting with his jaw in a resounding crack. Time stops moving for a moment as Mia and I stare at him. Then, at the same time, we look at each other, the energy of the moment sobering us instantly.

Reese is whining about the pain when I grab Mia's hand and drag her out of the bar in a rush. Before she and I are out the door, she shoots back one quick "fuck you" to Reese.

Rule #11: A truth for a truth.

Garrett

"Mia, wait up," I shout, but she's speed-walking home. After we bolted from the bar, Mia has avoided even looking at me. She took off in a sprint up the long, dark road that leads back to the house, and all I can think about are the people leaving the bar after too many drinks and not seeing the short, furious woman walking too close to the road.

It's not until we're standing in front of the house that I finally catch up to her. She's rushing for the door, but I'm not ready to let her go just yet. I grab her arm to stop her, but she quickly pulls away. "Leave me alone, Garrett!"

"Me? What the hell did I do?"

She spins on me with angry tears in her eyes. "Aren't you going to give me shit about the naked photos? Or the fact that I almost fell for an asshole who just wanted to use me for bragging rights? Or about the fact that I'm a camgirl?"

She draws out the last one, making it clear that that was her secret all along. I see the shame in her eyes, and I don't even have the guts to tell her that I already knew she was a camgirl because that would require me telling her *how* I know that.

"I'm not going to give you shit about that, Mia. Is that really what you think about me? That all I do is tease you?"

Her face changes to shock. "That *is* all you do!" she shouts. "Well, it used to be, but you're acting so weird this week. It's like I don't even know you."

"So I changed. People aren't allowed to change?"

"And what is all of this talk about leaving with you and you giving me what he can't? You know…Reese was right. You do want to fuck me, but I just can't understand *why*. This…whatever this is…was never here before."

I'm so busy staring at her mouth while she yells at me, all fired up and looking cute as fuck. And just hearing her talk about how I want to fuck her has me unhinged. I'm a little drunk. She's a lot drunk.

In the back of my mind, I know it's wrong, but it doesn't stop me as I quickly close the distance between us, shoving her against the side of the house as I lower my mouth within inches of hers. "I wish I fucking knew why, but I can't stop thinking about you. Don't get me wrong—you still drive me insane. You're bratty as fuck, and I don't know if I want to strangle you or shut you up with my cock in your mouth, but seeing that photo of you tonight put me over the edge, Mia. I don't care that you're my stepsister, and I don't give a fuck that you're a camgirl."

Our mouths crash together with wild energy. She tastes like berries and cinnamon, and I take her pouty bottom lip between my teeth, tugging just enough to make her whimper. She meets my mania with her own, latching on to the back of my neck and pulling me closer as our tongues tangle and our bodies grind. We are frantic, devouring each other, hands and lips fighting for as much contact as possible. I kiss her neck, her earlobe, her chest as her hands fumble for my belt buckle.

God, she tastes so fucking good. There's something familiar about kissing her and also like I'm learning a whole new side of her just through this kiss. It has me wanting to learn *everything* about her. With my mouth.

I stop the movement of her hands at my belt when I reach down and grab her by the back of her legs, pulling up until she wraps them around me. She moans as she feels my hard length grind against her. Then I carry her around to the back of the house, toward the door that leads to the basement. Our mouths don't break contact for one second.

Once I get the door open, we stumble inside, and I take her straight into the bedroom. Leaving the lights off, I drop her onto the mattress.

"I fucking need you, Mia. You have no idea."

"I need you too," she cries, reaching for me. I tear off my shirt before climbing over her and resume kissing her neck.

My mind is swirling with thoughts as I savor the taste and feel of her, an overload of sensation, and behind all of that is a chorus of excitement. Thank fuck this is finally happening. Finally for me, and finally for us.

"Garrett," she gasps, and I stop to look down at her. "A truth for a truth?"

My brain is struggling to grasp her words. I just want to keep touching her and kissing her. "What? Yeah, sure."

Then, I'm back on her, pulling up her shirt and peeling her bra aside, so I can latch my lips around her nipple. My cock is straining against the zipper of my pants, and her hands are still there, lingering around my belt, and I'm fucking *begging* her to touch it.

"Okay, tell me the truth," she says with a gasp, as I squeeze the pink bud of her right breast between my fingers. "Were you watching me today? In the shower?"

"Yes," I reply without hesitation.

And her response is a breathy moan as if she gets off on the idea of me watching her.

"Do you like that, baby? You want me watching you while you make yourself come?"

She bites her lip as she replies, "Uh-huh."

"Good, because I like watching you, Mia. I like watching you play with this pretty pussy."

I slide my hand down her body until I reach the bottom of her tiny shorts, and I ease two fingers between the denim and the fabric of her wet panties.

She cries out again. "Garrett, touch me, please."

It's too easy to drag her panties and shorts to the side to access the wet lips of her cunt. And I love the way her soft, hairless skin feels against my hand. When I find her clit, I muffle her cries with my mouth, kissing her hard as I circle the sensitive nub. Her hips grind against my hand, lifting from the bed.

Her hands fall away from my belt, but I don't care at the moment. As badly as I need this, I can wait. I want to explore every inch of her before she touches my cock.

God, without even entering her, I can feel how tight she is. I can't help myself as I dip my middle finger in, and holy fuck, it's almost too tight to get one finger in.

She whimpers, still grinding her hips upward toward my hand. "That feels so good."

"You're so fucking tight, Mia." I growl into the skin of her neck.

Her response is a delicious laugh that I feel through the kiss against her throat. "Well, that's what I was trying to tell you. That's my truth."

"What is? That you're tight?" I reply with a laugh.

"That I'm a virgin, you idiot."

I try to laugh again, but it doesn't come out. Instead, I freeze and stare down at her, trying to gauge if she's kidding or not. My middle finger is still buried knuckle deep inside her.

"Wait, are you serious?"

Her smile falters. "Yeah, it's not a big deal. I want to have sex. I just wanted you to know."

Slowly, I pull my hand out of her shorts and hover over her body, so we're no longer touching. My mind is so focused on this new information, trying to make sense of it.

"Are you really going to freak out about this?" she asks, sounding impatient and annoyed.

A groan slips through as I roll away from her. "Fuck, Mia. How…"

"Why does it even matter? Who cares if it's my first or my fiftieth? You seriously don't want me now?"

"I just need a moment to think, okay?"

But being the stubborn little brat that she is, she doesn't listen. She slides her hands around my waist and eats up the space between us, gazing up into my eyes as she whispers, "Didn't that feel so good, though? Why do we have to stop?"

I squeeze my eyes closed. "First, because you're drunk. And I can't do that."

"But we were just about to—"

"Mia, you can't lose your virginity to your thirty-six-year-old stepbrother. You just…can't."

"Why?"

"Because you don't even like me. You're only turned on because I'm flirting with you and touching you to make you feel good, but you'll regret it later. I promise."

"Why don't you worry about yourself and leave the virginity decision to me?"

"Okay, but the fact remains that we're still drunk," I say, slightly relieved to have a valid excuse. It's not that I don't want to fuck Mia because she's a virgin. In fact, I love the idea of being the only man to touch her. The only one to feel her body from the inside. To fill her up and know the sounds she makes as I pound into her.

But this new information adds a whole layer of complexity to this already confusing situation. I'm not ready to really digest all of this yet.

"Come on," I mumble, pulling back the comforter, so we can both climb under it. "We both need to sleep off the alcohol. And we'll talk about this tomorrow." She pouts, but I see the sleepiness in her eyes.

And I was right. As soon as her head hits the pillow, she starts to drift off. I grab my shirt off the floor and slip it back on before exchanging my jeans for sweats and climbing back into bed next to her.

I watch her sleep for a while, trying to understand how someone like her could have gotten so far without having sex even once. And how on earth she could want to break that streak with someone like me.

Rule #12: Virtual mystery men over self-absorbed stepbrothers every day.

Mia

THE FIRST THING I REGISTER WHEN I WAKE UP IS GARRETT'S familiar scent. I'm surrounded by warmth, and I open my eyes to find my face pressed firmly against his chest. He's wearing a T-shirt, but it's riding up enough that my hand is draped over his bare stomach.

He's still asleep, his head tilted to the side as he breathes quietly. So I admire him for a moment, the sharp lines of his cheekbones and jaw, and the perfect slope of his nose. The fullness of those lips that I now know are *amazing* to kiss. Especially with the scratchy texture of his five o'clock shadow.

How long have I dreamt about kissing Garrett? Since I was old enough to even know what a kiss was. And now that he's finally treating me like he might actually be attracted to me, I'm terrified that it's all one elaborate joke. Any moment, he's going to pull the rug out from under me, and I'm going to feel like a fool. I'm not normally so apprehensive to let my guard down, but with Garrett…the stakes are just too high.

Resting my head back on his chest, I run my fingers softly

over the tuft of hair running down his tight stomach. He shivers and fidgets in his sleep.

I know I really shouldn't, but I can't help myself. So I trail my fingers upward, sliding under his shirt and along the ridges of his abs to touch his pecs.

He moans and squirms again. I'm getting too bold, but then again...he's admitted to peeping on me in the shower, so he owes me. Getting a little too daring, I move my hand down, past the hemline of his pajama pants and over the swollen ridge of his cock. My fingers only lightly brush the hard surface before he wakes up.

With a loud moan, he grabs my hand in his and pulls it away from his pants. I panic for a minute, afraid I've been caught, but when I glance up at his face, he's staring down at me with wild lust in his eyes.

"We're not drunk anymore," I say in a sultry tone, and for a moment, he lets my hand rest against his morning wood, grinding his hips upward into my palm. Then, before it can go any further, he yanks my wrist away and drops it.

"But you *still* are a virgin," he replies, and I sink into the mattress with disappointment.

Then he runs his hands through his hair with a stretch. It takes him a few minutes to wake up before he turns toward me. "Jesus, Mia. How on earth could you get to *twenty-three* without having sex?"

"Have you met men?" I reply with a laugh. I lie on my side, my head resting on my hand as I stare at him. "Honestly, it just always felt like whoever I was with only wanted to be with me for one thing. I wanted to have sex, but I wanted to connect with that person too, you know? I wanted to feel so comfortable with them that I could tell them what I want and not feel like I was just being used as something to stick their dick into."

He grimaces. "Not every guy is like that," he says, turning toward me.

"I know that…" I say, letting my voice trail off. I never felt that way about Garrett. If only I could tell him about all the naughty fantasies I had about him as a teenager. Sneaking into his bed at night and climbing under the covers so we could touch each other in secret. "That's why last night would have been perfect."

"Why?" he asks. "Because you were drunk?"

"Because I trust you, you idiot."

When he turns his head toward me again, there's a strange sense of sincerity in his expression, something real that I don't normally see when I look at Garrett. Nothing between us is ever serious, but telling him that I trust him seems to have triggered a genuine response. Like he might actually be taking me seriously.

Then he quickly rolls out of bed. The stiffness in his pants is gone along with all the fire between us. "Mia, I'm not the one you want, I promise. Not for your first time. You want a guy who's going to give you more than a one-night stand, who's not fucked in the head, and who's not your goddamn stepbrother."

I can't believe what I'm hearing. For the past two days, Garrett has been driving me crazy, teasing me and making me want him, but now that I've opened up and admitted that I'm a virgin, I'm practically repulsive to him. Was he just messing with me again? Teasing me to the point of having me begging him for sex?

I'm an idiot.

"Oh my God," I say, jumping out of bed and staring at him with a smug expression. I quickly grab my phone off the floor, where it must have fallen in our frantic make-out session last night, and I shove it into my back pocket.

"What?" he asks.

"I just realized what this is." He's staring at me, waiting to hear what I'm about to say. "This was all a joke to you. Some elaborate prank. Just to get me wet and begging for you, only so you could turn me down."

"It wasn't a joke," he replies, looking offended. "I'm trying to protect you, Mia."

"Do you have any idea how *humiliating* it is to be turned down by your own stepbrother because you're a virgin? Let alone turned down at all!"

"Mia—"

"No!" I snap, putting my hand up toward him. "You didn't want me with other guys like Reese, but then *you* don't want me because I *haven't* been with other men. It makes no sense, but the only thing that does make sense is you torturing me, and I'm officially done letting you."

I storm out of his room and rush up the stairs, praying that our parents aren't on the second floor waiting for me. Luckily, the house is empty as I continue up to my room, slamming the door behind me as I crash on top of my bed and scream into my pillow.

I hate him. Why are my emotions such a joke to him? I want to cry and yell and just vent about all of the angry things I'm feeling, but I can't talk to any of my friends back home about this. It's too embarrassing to admit that I was turned down by my own stepbrother. Plus, none of them are all that great at listening. They're great friends to have fun with, but I don't have anyone to really talk to, to share things with and confide in.

Unless...

I fish my phone out of my back pocket and notice my battery is at two percent. After I plug it in, I stare down at the FlirtyGirl app. I've never done this before, reached out to a client like this, but something about Drake tells me that he wouldn't mind. I believe he really would listen. And maybe it's just attention I want, but I have a good feeling Drake is more genuine than the rest.

I swipe open the app and find his username. He's offline. But I could send him a message. If he has his notifications on, he'll receive it. It's a long shot, but I'm desperate—and hungover, maybe even still a little drunk, which might explain why I'm actually doing this.

Hey.

I hit Send and then immediately start to panic. That message looks way too creepy, so I quickly back it up with, **Any chance you're online?**

If he sees this, he's totally going to think I'm just fishing for another paid hour of video sex. Shit.

No charge. Just want someone to talk to.

"Ugh," I moan as I let my face fall into the pillow. "I'm pathetic."

But then my phone buzzes in my hand.

I'm here. Talk to me.

I stare at his words in shock. Then I quickly reply, **You probably think I'm crazy. I just need someone to talk to.**

You're not crazy. Talk to me, kitten. Tell me anything. I'm listening.

He's not real. This can't possibly be a real human man. None of them have ever responded to me like this. Not without some hint at wanting to see my tits in the process. Just to be safe, I keep our chat in the messages instead of going into a video chat. I look like hot garbage anyway.

Are you ready for a ridiculous confession? I ask.

Yes, he replies.

I think I'm in love with my stepbrother.

The line is silent for a while, and I start to panic that he *does* think I'm crazy. Why did I lead with that? And to a client? What's really strange is that I feel comfortable enough to talk so openly about my private life with a client. I wish I knew why, but I honestly have no idea.

It's taking him too long to reply. There are no typing bubbles on the screen. Just silence.

I told you I'm crazy.

Does he know how you feel? he says, ignoring my "crazy" remark.

I laugh as I read his question. No. Garrett thinks I hate him, and although I think *hate* is a strong word, he definitely has no idea how I really feel. I call him cocky and obnoxious, and he calls me annoying and bratty, and even if he is flirting with me now, he'd much rather keep our relationship as stepsiblings with benefits than try to make it anything else.

I could never tell him. He would laugh in my face if I ever told him that.

I highly doubt that, he responds.

Do you think he has feelings for you?

I laugh again. No. I thought maybe he wanted to sleep with me, and we almost did last night but then...

Then what?

Then he turned me down. It was humiliating.

I'm sorry.

It's not your fault, I reply. It was stupid of me to be so vulnerable. For years, I thought he hated me. He always saw me as the annoying little sister, so I could never be honest about my feelings. I figured that if he saw me as a pest, then that's what I would be.

Wow.

Letting out a sigh, I stare at my own messages, letting this sink in. I can't believe I'm telling him all of this, but then again, he's just a guy on the internet. It feels good to finally get it all out, though.

I'm sorry for unloading all of this on you. I guess I just needed to talk to a guy who really sees me. I can't believe after only two chats, I feel this comfortable with you. This is crazy.

He types for a while, the little bubbles bouncing on the screen as he puts together his next message, and I wait not so patiently. Finally, his message pops up.

I do see you, kitten. And your stepbrother is an idiot. He clearly doesn't see the real you, and that's a shame. Sounds to me like he doesn't deserve you. But you can talk to me anytime. And I won't ask for anything in return. I never want you to think I only like you for one thing.

My jaw literally drops. How does he seem to know all the right things to say?

You're making me forget him completely right now.

Good, he replies.

I still feel like a jerk for unloading all of this personal stuff on you. I'm really sorry, I say.

Stop apologizing! he replies. Look, I'll tell you something personal about me to make you feel better, okay?

I bite my lip, waiting to hear something, *anything*, personal about Drake. It feels like a window into a world I'm not supposed to see into. And I have my suspicions about what he's about to admit. Like him admitting to fucking a teacher back in high school or having a threesome once or something mildly embarrassing. I do not expect the message that pops up next.

I haven't had sex in almost ten years.

My eyes nearly pop out of my head. *Ten years?* I've seen his body on camera, and yeah, it was a little dark, but it was definitely in shape and absolutely nothing to keep hidden from women for a decade.

Wow, I respond.

You're speechless, aren't you?

A little bit, I reply. **Wait...are you a priest?**

LOL. No. I'm not a priest.

Then...how?

The typing bubbles bounce on the screen for a moment as I wait for his response.

I don't know. I just found sex to be so unfulfilling. There was never a real connection, no spark. So after a while, I just stopped trying. And time got away from me.

It feels like he's pulling these words directly from my own brain. Feelings I've felt before. And, obviously, I can't relate to the sex part, but I know the lack of connection part very well, as if the sincerity in people is gone and nothing feels real anymore.

I know exactly what you mean. It's like...no one really sees you.

Exactly.

So wait... I say. **You clearly do other things, right?**

Ha ha, like masturbate? Yes, I still do that.

You've seen me do that, remember?

Oh yeah.

Duh, I reply. **I almost forgot about that.**

How could you forget about that? It was one of the hottest nights of my life.

Can I tell you another secret? he asks.

Of course.

That was my first time on an app like this.

You mean I'm your first? I respond with a smile.

First and only. You popped my cherry, he says, and I'm smiling from ear to ear as I type my reply.

Good. I like being the only girl for you.

An hour and a half goes by while we chat, and the subject never comes back to Garrett and the way he humiliated me this week. Instead, we talk about life in general. Our favorite things and our jobs. He tells me stories about work and his friends.

Garrett never comes upstairs to bother me during my chat with Drake. I'm sure he's already moved on with his life. And that's fine. Drake makes me feel better about myself anyway.

Rule #13: If she gives you the cold shoulder, remember, even ice melts.

Garrett

She's avoiding me. I mean, why wouldn't she? I humiliated her, turned her down, made her feel like shit for being a virgin, and then the kicker—suddenly I find out she's been in love with me her whole life, and I've been treating her like shit.

After that long conversation with her on the app as *Drake*, I know I should get some rest. Maybe go for a run. Fuck, at this point, I should probably get in my car and drive back to Briar Point before I do something I'll regret, but I have to see her.

Being Drake means that I can be the open-book, open-arms listener that she needs, but it also gives me a place to unload some secrets of my own. Like the ten years thing. A secret not even my best friend knows.

In the last three days, my whole fucking world has been flipped on its head. My stepsister is a camgirl. Suddenly, I'm attracted as fuck to her. And to top it all off, she's in love with me.

I *should* do everything in my power to make her hate me—to *really* hate me. Help her get over me by being even more of an asshole to her. Show her I'm not worthy of her time or attention.

But I can't help but love the idea that Mia actually cares about me. When was the last time I ever let a woman get that close to me? Over ten years ago, I know that.

Not that I'm actually considering something real with my stepsister. That's not who I am.

It's the afternoon by the time I finally get showered and dressed and head upstairs. The house is quiet, so I assume my parents are out doing whatever they do with their friends. I certainly hope they didn't sneak into my room before they left to find Mia sleeping in my arms.

When I reach the main floor, I find Mia sitting alone in the dining room, listening to music with her earbuds while sketching in her journal. A smile tugs at my lips as I remember the god-awful sketch of her cat she showed to her viewers on her live stream. The devil herself, Betty, glares at me from the windowsill, as if she's warding me off from getting close to her owner.

As I enter the kitchen, Mia glances up at me and then back down at her book. There's something cold and stubborn in her expression. She's mad at me, and she has no idea she's just spent her morning pouring out her heart to me over chat. I should feel bad about that, but I don't.

Yikes. I'm an asshole, aren't I?

"You're not still mad at me, are you?" I ask, leaning against the kitchen counter and staring at her. She's in a white crop top and a long floral skirt. When she doesn't respond, I walk over and snatch one of her earbuds out of her ears.

"Hey!" she barks.

"Don't give me the cold shoulder. It's juvenile."

"You're juvenile," she replies angrily.

"Will you just talk to me?"

"No," she replies, and I honestly wonder if this is the same girl who just confessed to being in love with me. Clearly, she can't stand me.

"Will you let me apologize?"

"No." She stands up and pushes past me toward the kitchen. I don't stop her or grab her, no matter how much I want to. I watch in silence as she takes a glass from the cabinet and fills it with ice. Then, she takes a can of soda out of the fridge, and just before opening it, she turns to find me watching her.

"You're mad at me because I won't take advantage of you, you realize that, right?"

"No," she replies, finally looking into my eyes, "I'm mad at you because you're toying with my emotions. I don't understand what's going on with you, Garrett, but I don't want to play these games. Thank you for looking out for me last night with Reese, but I think it's best if you and I just go back to the way we were before."

She leans against the counter and opens the can of soda in her hand.

I realize as I watch her that I don't want to go back to the way things were. Not at all, and I still don't quite know what that means, but it's the only thing keeping me in my place, staring at her with heavy emotion swirling around inside me.

"What do you do for those men on the app?" I ask, and her eyes dart up to my face with the abrupt subject change, one she's clearly not comfortable talking about.

"It's none of your business," she bites back.

"Do you touch yourself for them? Let them watch you with toys?"

"You admitted to watching me in the shower yesterday. You have no room to talk!"

I take a step toward her, and her wild eyes shoot up to my face.

"No wonder you liked that. You're an exhibitionist, Mia."

"I am not," she argues. I watch the delicate movement of her throat as she swallows with each step I take toward her until I'm about a foot away.

"Yes, you are."

"Then you're a voyeur!" she snaps.

"Sounds like we could have a lot of fun together," I reply with a mischievous smirk.

"No. We are not doing this again, Garrett."

"Well, I don't know what else to do with all of this new chemistry between us, Mia, but I think I'm starting to understand." I eat up every inch of space between us, pressing one of my legs between hers as I crowd her so much, she has to lean back on the counter. "I don't want your virginity. I just want to play with you a little."

A whimper escapes her lips as she trembles against me. "Like how?"

My smile grows as I lean my mouth down toward her neck. Instead of kissing it, I blow softly against her flesh, watching the way it shivers in response. "Show me what you show them."

It takes her a moment to work up a response, and I know I don't play fair, using her body against her, making it difficult to argue when everything between us feels so good. "Why should I? What's in it for me?"

"You like to be watched, Mia. It makes you hot, doesn't it?"

"I'm still mad at you," she says, but it's the gentle nudge of her face against my cheek that tells me she's not as angry as she wants to be.

"So let's get this over with. No sex but a little fun, and then at the end of the week, we'll go back to the way things were. We'll get it out of our systems. You're like an itch I need to scratch, Mia, and I can tell you feel the same way."

She whimpers again. "Fine," she hums, and I smile with pride. Then I glance down to see the ice in the glass she's holding, and I get an idea.

"Take a piece of ice out of your glass," I say in a low command.

She hesitates before slowly moving her hand toward the glass. After reaching in and pulling out a piece, she waits for further instruction. I pull away to watch her as I say, "Touch yourself with it. Start with your chest."

After a deep, nervous inhale, she places the ice against her body and shivers on contact. Then, with her eyes on me, she moves the cold piece slowly across her chest. I pull the top of her deep V-neck shirt to the side, and she follows the movement, bringing it over the flesh of her breast. Goose bumps erupt in the wake of the cold.

Next, I peel back one side of her bra, exposing the round, pink bud of her nipple. My dick twitches in my pants at the sight. I'm fighting the urge to touch her, reminding my cock that I watch—not touch.

Mia drags the ice cube over her nipple with a small gasp, and I watch as it quickly contracts, hardening at the tip.

"Tell me how that feels," I say in a low murmur.

"It's…intense," she whispers.

"Let's make it even more intense, shall we?"

Gazing into her ocean-blue eyes, I lift the fabric of her skirt. Then, I guide her hand with the ice downward, and I watch with eagerness as it drifts over her tan belly and down to her inner thighs.

She gasps loudly, arching her back as she struggles to breathe. Her body is trembling with the intensity of the ice against her sensitive flesh, and it's so fucking beautiful to watch. I'm about to snap.

My aching cock is resting against her hip, and I grind subtly against her, seeking the friction it craves. Everything about Mia turns me on. How did I never see this before? The fullness of her lips and the freckles scattered across her skin like stars. The way her body fits perfectly against mine.

I want to touch her. I *need* it.

Hooking my thumbs under the elastic of her panties, I pull them down to her knees and nudge her hand, covered in water from the melting ice, to her center. She tries to fight me, but eventually, her fingers find her clit, which I can tell because she lets out a shriek and clutches onto my arm as her body seizes.

It's fucking beautiful to watch, but I'm struggling to keep my hands to myself. It's been too goddamn long.

"Is your pussy hot, Mia?" I whisper in her ear. "It's melting that ice fast, isn't it?"

She nods. I move my hand over hers, feeling the water drip through her fingers as she swirls the ice cube over the warm folds of her cunt.

Sliding my fingers through hers, I tease her delicate skin, remembering the tightness around my single digit last night when I slipped inside her. I'm losing it.

"Does it make you hot knowing we could be caught?"

She hums her reply.

"Someone could walk in at any moment and find you touching yourself."

She purrs against me, fidgeting her hips back and forth, fighting against the cold to find her pleasure. The intensity of the ice is making the heat of her fingers feel that much better.

And I can't get enough of the look on her face as she chases her climax, but when she lets out a cry, shoving her hips against my hand, the last string holding me together snaps. I can't take it anymore and suddenly watching isn't enough.

I grab an ice cube from her glass and pop it into my mouth. Her eyes widen as she watches me drop to my knees in frantic need. I'm not careful or delicate about it as I pull her body toward my mouth, attacking her cunt with my mouth.

She lets out a scream, digging her wet hand in my hair as she grinds against me. The ice on my tongue has her going wild, and right now, there's nothing better than her perfect scent and the sounds she's making. Her panties slide all the way to the floor, and I can't get enough of her. I can't believe my mouth is on Mia. This is insane, but she tastes, smells, and feels so fucking good.

"Garrett!" she cries out.

Nudging her backward, I guide her to the counter, and with one quick lift, I have her sitting on the surface, legs splayed open to me like a meal. And I bury my mouth against her. The ice is quickly melting, which is exactly what I want. By the time it's gone, I want to have nothing but her coming on my tongue.

"God, you taste so good, kitten," I mumble against her sex. As soon as the pet name leaves my lips, I tense up. Fuck, why did I let that out? Is my shameless secret exposed already?

Luckily for me, she's so distracted by the sensations of hot and cold on her body that she didn't even hear me. Instead, she's panting and gasping for breath, and I think she's close.

Her legs wrap around my head as her body starts to tremble. I suck eagerly on her clit as she rides out her orgasm, letting out squeaks and whimpers of pleasure.

When her climax ends, the ice is melted and there's water dripping down her legs. I kiss my way up her body. As I reach her face, I kiss her lips softly, but she doesn't kiss me back. She can still be mad at me if she wants. As long as I can watch her do that again.

"We shouldn't have done that," she whispers as if she's just realized she let her stepbrother lick her clit until she came.

"Mia, I love the way you look when you come. It's so good I think I could get addicted to it."

As she gazes up into my eyes, I know she's thinking what I'm thinking: if we're doing this to get it out of our systems, we're fucked—because this feels too good to quit.

Rule #14: Never judge a book by its cover.

Mia

I'M RACKED WITH GUILT AS I COME DOWN FROM ONE HELL OF AN orgasm. I'm not quite sure why I feel so guilty, though. Maybe because I spent the morning chatting with Drake or because I'm supposed to be mad at Garrett but can't seem to say no to him. Either way, I don't feel good about what we just did.

Even though it was *so* good.

He's staring at me with a smug grin, and I want to punch it off his face. Or kiss it. It's really a toss-up at this point.

Suddenly, the front door opens without warning, and Garrett and I scramble, pulling apart in a rush as I quickly snatch up my underwear before either of our parents notice. Garrett grabs a kitchen towel to clean up the mess of melted ice on the floor, and I do everything I can to hide the blush on my face as my *dad* enters the kitchen.

"Hey, guys," he says as he sets down a bag of groceries on the counter.

"Hey, Dad," I mumble with a forced smile. As he leans in to plant a kiss on my cheek, I die inside of utter humiliation and shame. If only he knew what we were just up to. Laura follows behind him with a slightly buzzed look about her and fresh sunburn, which means they've been on the boat today and must have stopped at the market on the way back.

"What are you two up to?" she asks, and I refuse to look in Garrett's direction as he answers.

"Oh, not much. Just picking on each other a little bit."

"Go easy on her," my dad chimes in, and I resist the urge to climb the stairs and hoist myself off the third-floor balcony.

"Why is there water on the floor?" Laura asks, glancing down at the puddle Garrett must have missed.

"Oops," he replies. "Mia dropped some ice." And as he drops down to clean it up, I glance in his direction, just in time to see him wink up at me with a sly grin.

God, I hate him.

"How was your day?" I ask our parents, changing the subject.

"Good, but we had to come in early. Looks like a storm's rolling in," my dad answers.

"What time did you come in, missy?" Laura asks, interrupting my dad. "You weren't in your room this morning…" The look she's giving me is half-giddy curiosity and half-stern parental concern. I know what she's thinking, though—that I went home with Reese—which I obviously did not.

"I don't want to hear anything," my dad announces before quickly leaving the kitchen, and Laura laughs in giggly drunkenness. Apparently, my dad doesn't want to risk hearing about me going home with a guy from the bar.

But to my surprise, Garrett replies, "Oh, she stole my bed. We both stumbled in around two, and there was no way she was making it up those stairs." I give him a quick, terse glare.

"And where did you sleep?" Laura asks.

"On the couch in the basement." He lies so easily it surprises me.

"Well, that was nice of you," she says, ruffling his hair. "Such a good big brother."

I choke on the air I'm breathing as those words come out of her mouth, and she looks at me with a quizzical expression as I resume coughing for no reason.

As Garrett laughs, I quickly flip him a middle finger.

Twenty minutes later, the rain starts to fall, filling the house with relaxing white noise, and my dad and Garrett both fall asleep in the two recliners in the living room, watching some baseball movie I've never heard of, leaving me and my stepmother alone.

"It's really coming down out there," she says. "Want some tea?"

"Yes, please," I respond, sitting on one of the stools around the island. I watch her for a moment, trying to imagine how she would react if she found out what Garrett and I were doing before she came home. How he had his face buried between my legs, licking my pussy like an expert, and if they had walked in five minutes sooner, they would have had a front-row seat to one of the best orgasms of my life. I've only had two other mouths down there, and neither of them were very good at it, so I had to fake my climax. Not this time. Garrett didn't give me much of a choice; he had me coming so effortlessly, I wonder if he spends his free time licking clits. Of course, he works at a nightclub, so I'm sure he has plenty of experience.

And while I'm certain she wouldn't want to know about all that, I'd like to believe Laura would be the most accepting of our relationship—not that Garrett would ever let it get that far. According to him, we're just *playing*, but I'm still not quite sure why. Is he just horny for some action or does he suddenly find me irresistible? Either way, I'm not going to jinx it and will just play along. At least for now.

"So…" she says after she puts the kettle on and turns to face me, giving me a knowing look. I tense in my seat. That look on her face has all the makings of a mom who knows everything.

"So…?" I feel myself shrinking. *God, please don't ask me about Garrett. I can't do this now.*

"What did you think about Reese?"

"Oh. Reese." I force a smile. I really don't want her knowing about what a jerk he turned out to be. It'd be almost impossible to bring it up without outing myself as a camgirl in the process, and I sure as hell hope he doesn't go blabbing to his parents either. "He was super nice. And very good-looking."

"Right? When Marcia introduced us to him last week, I thought…this boy needs to meet my Mia."

This fake smile is getting harder to hold.

"Your brother wasn't too overbearing, was he? I tried to get him to leave with us, to give you two some alone time, but he is so damn stubborn sometimes. He's protective of you, and I think that's really sweet, but you're all grown-up now. Garrett might have a hard time accepting that."

I'd say Garrett is accepting that just fine, but I can't say that out loud either. Instead, I hold up this incredibly stiff smile and nod.

"Garrett and I are getting along pretty good this week," I say, which sounds innocent enough. I mean, that's the truth.

"You are. Don't think I haven't noticed," she replies with a raised brow.

Fuck, what is that supposed to mean?

"I know he's hard on you sometimes, but that's just how Garrett is. It's not an excuse, but I'm just telling you that sometimes teasing and making jokes is how he shows affection."

My heart warms in my chest. Given how much Garrett has teased me in the past fifteen years, he must be madly in love with me.

The kettle whistles loudly, saving me from having to respond to that statement.

When she turns back, filling our mugs with water, I see a contemplative look behind her eyes. "I'm glad he came," she says quietly.

"Me too, for once."

"It's good to see him smiling so much. I worry about him sometimes."

I pause, my eyes lifting to her face. "Worry about him how?"

Her jaw clenches as she stirs honey into her tea. "Garrett... has always had...high highs and low lows."

As I reach for my mug, I let those words sink in, trying to fit them into the picture of the man I know. Does Garrett have low lows? I don't think I've ever seen them.

"Can I ask you a question?" I say carefully. Before I continue, I turn, glancing around the corner to the living room, and see him sleeping soundly on the recliner.

"Yeah, honey. Of course."

Then, I broach this one cautiously. Why am I so nervous to ask this? "What did you mean yesterday when you said it was nice to see Garrett running again?"

Her eyes stay fixed on my face for a moment before she lets out a long sigh. Pulling her tea bag out, she squeezes it around the spoon before tossing it in the trash. Then she brings the cup to her lips and blows against the steaming liquid. I wait patiently for her answer.

"I'm trying to decide how much I'm allowed to tell you."

I swallow the lump in my chest. I knew there was more I didn't understand, and I'm dying to know, but I'm also terrified. I'm not sure why. Knowing something so private and personal about Garrett feels like an invasion of his privacy.

Finally, she puts the cup down and takes a seat on the stool across from me. "When Garrett was younger, he used to get in these...moods. Dark moods and benders. Almost as if someone flipped a switch and the bright, happy light inside him just went out, and then he would disappear for days, doing God knows what. I worried about him so much. But then he started running, and when he went to college, things seemed to get better.

"Then about ten years ago, he started a new job, and things were going well. He seemed to be thriving. And then suddenly... the light switch flipped off again."

"What happened?" I'm leaning over the counter, whispering so he doesn't hear.

"It was your thirteenth birthday. He didn't answer my calls all week and then showed up at the house a complete mess. We got in a little fight, and then he stormed off."

The lifeless expression in her eyes is harrowing. As if she's reliving a nightmare. I'm hanging on her every word, feeling my heart crack and wanting to immediately run into the living room and curl into his arms to hold him.

"What happened?" I whisper.

"Your dad and I went to his apartment." Tears brim in her eyes. And I wait for her to finish, but suddenly, she shakes her head and blinks away the tears. "I don't want to tell you this part, Mia. It's not…not how I want you to think of Garrett. He wouldn't want me to."

My chest is heaving and I'm left with my mouth hanging open. "But he was okay…" I say, as if knowing he survived whatever it was is enough.

"He wasn't okay. But he is now."

Tears sting my eyes, and suddenly, my chest feels so heavy it's impossible to pull in a breath. I don't know what she means exactly by *wasn't okay*, but it's pretty clear that we almost lost him. And I had no idea.

"Why don't I remember this?"

"You were only thirteen. You went to your friend's for the weekend, so you had no idea, and I didn't want to worry you."

"But he's my—"

"Exactly," she says, interrupting me. "As much hell as Garrett has given you over the years, he has always looked out for you. He wanted you to see him as the funny and sometimes annoying big brother and protect you from the dark stuff. I shouldn't have told you this much, but you're an adult now."

I close my mouth and lean back, unable to see this version of Garrett behind the one I know. And my heart suddenly feels blindsided. How have I spent the last decade hating him so much when he's only been trying to protect me?

Garrett is still asleep after we finish our tea. I decide to go up to my room alone and catch up on some unanswered messages on the app. I sent out a blanket statement to my regular patrons that I'd be on vacation for a few days, but quite a few have still reached out.

Gregg sent me a hundred dollars to spend on a new bathing suit that he wants to see a picture of me in. I feel wrong even reading the message, and I leave the gift as pending because I don't know if I can accept it now. Between Drake and Garrett, I just need a minute to think without work interfering.

I decide to close the app for now and save it for a later time, when I can really focus on it.

Instead, I think about what happened in the kitchen and what the hell is going on between Garrett and me. Just the memory of his lips against my skin and the frantic need in the way he dropped to his knees sends butterflies straight to my core. There is electricity between us. It's palpable and real, and I feel my heart getting attached to the idea that Garrett is, in some way, mine.

I wish it wouldn't get attached. He's never going to commit. He keeps his feelings guarded, making it impossible to form any kind of serious connection, but I can't deny that the idea that he would open up his heart to me is a feeling I could get drunk on.

Trying to get out of my head, I consider reading or watching something on my phone, but as I curl up on my bed, pulling my throw blanket over me, I open my photo app instead.

Scrolling through the albums by years, I go back quite a few, until they're ones from middle school. I didn't see Garrett much those years, and now that guilt eats away at me for not realizing there was so much going on with him. I may have only been a kid, but now that I know he was struggling, it hurts to think he did that alone.

I find some photos of us together at Christmas. I was twelve, and he was twenty-five. The photo is a selfie of us in the car, and I remember that he was taking me to the movies when we were supposed to be Christmas shopping. I look ridiculous with my big shiny braces and acne-riddled complexion, but he looks almost the same. There are minor changes in his face, a few less lines, lighter and brighter skin, but for the most part, it's just him.

Then I scroll a few more, and I search the photos for any sign of what Laura was talking about. Was he struggling at this time? Because, in these moments, we're laughing, making stupid faces, stuffing our faces with popcorn and wearing 3D glasses in the movie theater. He looks happy.

I'm not stupid. I know being happy in one photo doesn't show what's lurking underneath, but even if the photo didn't capture it, why couldn't I?

And if I didn't catch it then, does that mean I might not be catching it now?

Rule #15: Be careful who you play with.

Garrett

THUNDER CRACKS, RATTLING THE WINDOWS ON THE HOUSE, AND MY eyes fly open. I pick up my phone off the nightstand to check the time. It's three in the morning. So much for getting a full eight hours.

I've tried the sleep aids and the supplements and the white noise machine, but nothing seems to work. I'm lucky if I get in four hours at a time.

That nap on the recliner today didn't help much either. When I woke up, Mia was in her bedroom, and she didn't come out. I couldn't go for a run in the rain, and being in the house was making me stir-crazy. The last few hours have felt long and torturous.

Suddenly, there's a figure standing in my doorway, and I freeze. Her long blond hair is hanging down over her shoulders, her figure silhouetted in the darkness.

She pauses there for a moment before crawling into my bed.

"Hey," she whispers so delicately I barely hear it. With her head on the pillow next to me, we stare at each other in the darkness, the only light coming from the moon through the window.

"Hey," I reply. "Storm wake you?"

She nods.

Something is up. I can feel it. It's in the way she's staring at me, her eyes searching mine as if she's looking for something. And even though we had our fun in the kitchen, I assumed she was still mad at me from this morning. But she's lying next to me peacefully. We're not bickering or jabbing each other with insults, so this is not like us at all.

"Can I sleep here again?"

"Of course," I reply.

We lie together for a while in comfortable silence, and I honestly can't remember the last time I was around someone without talking for so long. I always assumed the laid-back comfort I felt around Mia was because of our sibling relationship, but looking back on the last few years, I'm starting to see things differently. Even if we were always giving each other hell, it was just easier to be around her.

She moves to her back, staring up at the ceiling as she breaks the silence.

"Remember when you came to my high school graduation and booed when they called my name?"

My cheeks heat up as I turn toward her, and I expect a scowl, where there's a smile.

"Yeah…" I reply.

"Or remember when you gave my prom date condoms right in front of Mom and Dad?"

Great. So she wants to relive all of the times I was a shithead to her.

"Or when you wrapped a box of tampons in an iPhone box and gave it to me for Christmas?"

"This is a fun trip down memory lane," I say sarcastically.

"You've been tormenting me for years." Her eyes are fixed on the ceiling, a warm expression on her face, and not at all what I'd expect. Mia has hated me for years for being such a bully to her, but suddenly, it's like she's seeing it all differently.

"You must really hate me," I reply, lying on my back, one arm folded under my head. As she turns toward me, her crystal-blue eyes catch the moonlight and sparkle with more warmth than I've ever seen. Something in my chest swells at the sight—at being the one those beautiful eyes focus on. It makes me feel like the only man in the world who matters to her.

Then, she crawls into my arms, resting her head against my chest in the same way she was this morning, her long blond strands like silk against my skin. The coconut scent of her shampoo wafts up to my nose, and something stirs inside me. Not quite lust, but not quite love either.

It has me thinking about Emerson and Charlie. Is that what he feels when he's with her? If so, I can understand why he's so attached. I can understand now why he loves without shame or regret. Because having Mia in my arms like this fills every crack and crevice inside me. There are no shadows or anxiety or fears. It's just peaceful, quiet comfort.

"I don't hate you, Garrett," she whispers against my chest.

"Good. I don't hate you either."

Her arms wrap around my chest as her breathing starts to slow and she lets out a deep yawn. It's so domestic and tradi-tional, something I've always rejected the idea of, but now that I have her here, cuddling with me while the rain pours outside... it's not so bad.

"I had fun today," she murmurs in a sleepy slur.

"You mean the ice cube in the kitchen, I assume."

"Yes, idiot."

This time, I'm the one yawning, and the warmth of her body and the drone of rain against the windows are pulling me under.

"Good. I did too."

Her hand drifts downward, over the front of my pants, and I jolt, grabbing her hand before she can do any more. As enticing as playing again is, I don't want to lose the sleep that's just within my reach.

"Tomorrow," I mutter against her head. "We'll play some more tomorrow."

"Okay," she replies with another yawn.

With my lips against her head, I mumble, "I have something fun in store for you."

"If this is what you had in mind for me today, I'm not impressed," she whines as she pauses on the side of the trail, bending over to rest her hands on her knees and gasping for air.

I laugh as I pat her back. "Stop your bitching. It's not that bad."

There's a hiking trail within walking distance of the house with a moderate incline and some breathtaking views. But what we're really walking up here for…is the privacy.

We used to take this hike a lot when we first started coming to the lake house, and my perverted mind has been holding on to this fantasy of possibilities in these secluded woods for years. Now I'm ready to live them out. With the last person I'd ever expect to.

What still confuses me is the idea that if I ran into Mia at a bar or even at the club, would I see her the same way I see her now? Would she just be another beautiful woman I'd fail to connect with? Is our connection the result of years and years of platonic chemistry and a deep, familiar relationship?

I want to believe that I'd be attracted to Mia no matter what circumstance or universe we'd meet in and that this isn't some creepy stepsister obsession I've developed. Or maybe I'm only this comfortable with her because I'm a coward, too afraid to even try building a relationship with a stranger.

That thought still nags at me. What if I'm unable to connect with anyone for the rest of my life? I was so content with being alone, but with each passing day, that idea grows more and more depressing.

"What are you thinking about?" she asks, knocking me with her elbow.

"Nothing," I lie.

"You're not…regretting—"

"Regretting what?" I ask her. "Getting frisky with my stepsister? I'm not. Are you?"

"Not as much as I probably should," she replies with a grin. "We're both adults. Not blood related. I mean…do you think our parents would even be that angry?"

My expression changes into one of shock. "Yes, I do. Your dad might actually try to drown me in the lake. People see us as siblings, and I'm thirteen years older than you, Mia. I've known you since you were a child." I grimace. "That's not going to go over well."

"I'm not going to let him drown you," she says. "As long as you make this hike worth it, because I gotta tell you…this is not the sexy surprise I had in mind."

She shoves me in the chest, and I get the strange suspicion, based on the way she touches me, that she'd rather wrap her arms around my waist instead. The cuddling in my bed last night was different. It didn't count. And when we woke up this morning, we went right back to being us again. No touching or intimate whispering. Back to being more…enemies with benefits, I guess you could say.

"Well, then tell me, camgirl," I say, teasing as I crowd her, moving us toward the edge of the trail, "have you ever touched yourself in public?"

Her eyes light up, staring at me in shock. Then, her surprised expression morphs into a mischievous smile. "No…"

I crowd against her some more, and she steps backward again, until we are in the woods together. Turning behind her to see the crowded grove of trees that hide us, realization dawns on her face.

"Here?"

"Yes, here," I reply. Leaning down until my mouth is next to her ear, I mutter, "I want to watch you come with strangers just a few feet away. You'll have to be quiet, though. Can't let them hear you."

Her smile grows, but as I push her farther back into the woods, she tenses before looking up at me to say, "No."

I pause. "What do you mean, no?"

It's not the response I expected. Mia is an exhibitionist, and I want to be the one to take her to the limit of her comfort, pushing her to her max to see just how much she can take. And a nearly desolate hiking trail in the middle of nowhere is hardly a challenge. *Don't back out on me now, Mia.*

To my surprise, she doesn't argue. Instead, she takes my pants by the front and pulls me along, deeper into the expanse of trees, just far enough that we can still see the trail but have a touch of privacy.

"What are you doing?" I ask.

"I don't want to touch myself anymore. How about you watch me…touch you?"

My heart nearly pounds its way out of my chest as I gaze down at her, her lips pinched between her teeth as she starts unbuttoning my pants.

"What?" I stutter. "No."

The giggle that escapes her lips is equal parts sweet and devious. "What do you mean, no?" she replies, mocking me. The way her fingers are fumbling with my zipper is making it hard to breathe as her fingers graze the inside of my briefs.

"Mia," I say, almost about to let it slip that it's been a very, very long time since my dick was touched by another person and that I'm not mentally prepared for it to be getting any attention today. But I'm too far gone now. Just the mention of her touching me has me over the edge and desperate for it.

I don't think my dick could get any harder, but Mia quickly proves me wrong when she reaches in and wraps her warm hand around my aching length.

I groan as loudly as she does. *Holy shit that feels good.* I forgot how amazing someone else's soft, warm touch could be.

With a giggle, she says, "You have to be quiet. Don't want people hearing you." No chance of that—I couldn't keep it down if I tried.

I almost wish she knew just how long it's been since I had a woman touching my cock, so she could know just how special this is. But she has no idea. For all she knows, this is just another hand job to me. But it's *so* not.

She strokes me slowly, her grip tight enough to tease me, but not too tight to have me blowing too early. This wasn't what I had planned today. I thought I'd bring her out here and watch her stroke her clit in broad daylight on a trail during tourist season.

But when she lowers to her knees in front of me, I realize…I picked the wrong girl to toy with. Mia is not meek or shy or afraid to fight back. I should have known this. I might have made it sound like I could play with her, but this girl plays back.

While my mind is going a mile a minute, she suddenly gazes up at me and licks a wet circle around the bulging red head of my cock. My jaw falls open and my brain shuts off completely. Not a single thought registers as she takes me into her mouth.

Jesus fucking Christ.

"Oh fuck, Mia," I whisper. My fingers dig into her white hair at the scalp, messing up her ponytail as she lets me slide my way in toward the back of her throat.

She moans around my solid length, taking it as far back as she can go.

She's incredible. Fucking amazing. And even if I had been getting blow jobs in the past decade, this would still be the best one. Her mouth is so impossibly warm and wet and her movements aren't rushed or too eager. She's slow and delicate and perfect, feels like heaven around my dick.

With her hands gripping my hips tightly, she bobs her mouth up and down, moaning and slurping her way through my reckoning. She's ruining me at this very moment, unraveling me piece by piece, until I barely remember my own goddamn name. How the fuck did I let this happen?

"Goddamn, baby. Look at you," I mumble, staring down at her.

Her big blue eyes gaze up at me, tears pooling in them as she swallows me down.

"My cock is down your throat, Mia. It looks so fucking good from this angle. I can't stop watching you."

I feel my balls tighten with the threat of release, and I immediately stop her movement.

"Wait, wait," I bark, pulling out. Closing my eyes, I take in deep breaths as I force myself not to come all over her. As the feeling finally subsides, I open my eyes and gaze down at her. She's waiting with her lips parted. "Open your mouth, tongue out," I say in a commanding whisper.

She does as I say, and I gently rest my swollen dick against her tongue.

"I want you to just hold my cock on your tongue. Don't move, hear me? Just let me look at you."

She obeys beautifully, not even wrapping her lips around me or fidgeting in the slightest. She knows I'm already at risk of losing it, so she stays as still as a statue, so I can just savor the feel of her soft, wet tongue against my cock and the amazing view in front of me.

We both flinch at the sudden sound of voices from far away. We wait, her mouth still frozen as a couple walks up the trail behind me.

I gaze down at Mia and put one finger to my lips as I ease my cock farther into her mouth.

The people are dangerously close now—and so am I.

"Look at me," I whisper, and she gazes up again, tears welling in her eyes. With my hand on the back of her head, I force myself farther down her throat until I see her flinch with the need to gag, so I ease myself back.

It's the proximity of the people on the trail and knowing that we could be caught at any moment with her mouth holding my cock that is so filthy and hot. I know she can feel it too.

"Close your lips around me," I whisper, and she does. "Now, suck."

The intensity of her mouth practically swallowing my shaft brings me to the edge. The suction is exquisite, warm and wet, and I'm cursing myself for depriving myself of this for ten years. With a hand on the back of her head, I fuck her mouth.

"I'm gonna come in your mouth, Mia." I groan a little too loudly. A couple quick strokes later and my orgasm slams into me. I unload against her tongue. The sight is fucking surreal: her beautiful blue eyes on me as I cover her mouth with my cum. The pleasure hits in waves, lasting longer than I think I've ever lasted, shooting from the base of my spine and reaching every inch of my body in intense euphoria.

Once my cock is spent, I pull away and watch her. She's staring up at me with wide eyes, tongue out, and I can tell she's a little nervous.

"You can spit it out," I say with a laugh.

With a look of relief, she leans over and expels my cum into the grass and leaves on the ground. I can't keep in my howl of laughter as she gags and spits. When she's done, she wipes her mouth with the back of her hand, and I can't keep my hands off of her.

Dragging her to a standing position, I kiss her hard. I don't care about the salty taste on her tongue. I just need her in my mouth.

"Sorry," she mutters into my kiss.

"Don't be sorry. That was so fucking hot."

"Really? I wanted to swallow it, but I just couldn't do it."

I laugh again. "I'm so proud of you."

She giggles as I kiss her again. "Thank you."

As we make our way back down, I keep replaying that last moment over and over in my head. Why did I say those things to her or kiss her the way I did? Maybe it was post-orgasm delirium or something because that does not sound like something I'd say at all. It sounds too much like something a man in a relationship would say.

Rule #16: Truly possessing another person is a privilege.

Mia

THE STORM CLOUDS START ROLLING IN ON OUR WAY DOWN THE trail, and we're both getting soaked on the last ten minutes of the hike. Garrett offers me practically every piece of clothing on his body, but I laugh at him as we run back to the lake house.

"This is the only time you'll catch me running," I joke as we jog back. He looks down at me and gives me that disarmingly bright smile that makes my heart skip a beat and my insides turn to goo.

When we reach the deck, running under cover, we stand there catching our breaths—me more than him. He barely even looks winded while I'm gasping for air, and probably looking like a wet, sunburnt potato. I can't tell if our parents are back yet, since they park in the garage, but Garrett doesn't seem to care because he latches an arm around my waist and drags me toward him.

"What are you doing?" I gasp, looking around to see if anyone is nearby.

"You're cute when you're all wet."

I try to shove him away, wanting to fix my hair. "Am not! Stop it!"

He laughs, nuzzling his face in my neck and running his warm tongue along my jawline, picking up the wet drops of rain from my skin. Warmth pools in my panties at the soft friction of his tongue.

"What are you doing to me?" I whisper as I melt in his arms.

"Not nearly as much as I'd like to."

"Someone could see us."

"I think that's the point," he replies jokingly. His hands run all over my body like he can't get enough of the contact between us. Like his hands could literally devour me.

What was in that blow job?

Garrett seems unraveled, acting different than before. Yesterday it was all...let's play with each other and have some voyeur/exhibitionist fun, but now he's treating me like more than someone to play with.

And as hot as the idea of being seen is, I really can't let my dad see me out here getting groped by my much older stepbrother.

With that thought, I pull away. Peeling Garrett off my body is almost painful, but I manage to slide away from him. "I'm going to take a shower..."

"Can I come?" he asks with a devious grin.

I groan, really wanting to say yes. "We have to be careful, Garrett."

"Is that a yes?"

It shouldn't be. I should say no right now. But God...the thought of him naked in that tiny shower with me, rivulets of water running down those abs and through his chest hair...yes, please.

"Maybe we should check to see if our parents are home first," I reply, backing up until I hit the front door. He reaches around me, finding the door handle and turning it open with only inches between us.

"Hey, Mom?" he yells once it's open. When he's answered only by the silence he must have expected, he takes my lips in a hungry, bruising kiss. I yelp into his mouth as he lifts me into his arms as if I weigh nothing...which I do *not*.

My legs wrap around his waist, and our lips don't part as he stumbles up the stairs, my body clutching to him for dear life. I'm shocked and painfully aroused by the time he reaches the top floor, and we crash into the bathroom together, slamming the door behind us.

Then we're tearing our clothes off in a rush. My mind is reeling. Is this it? Is he finally about to do what I've wanted him to do for almost five years? The thing he denied me a couple days ago? I'm ready. I'm so fucking ready—but in the shower? Is that even a good place to do it? God, I have so much to learn.

I'm suddenly struck speechless by the sight of him, standing naked in front of me. And there I am, naked in front of him. And we're both sort of hypnotized by this all of a sudden.

"I can't believe this is happening," he mumbles quietly as he reaches into the shower and flips the handle on.

"I was thinking the same thing," I reply. And then our bodies are pressed together, and he's kissing me as he drags me into the shower. The water is too hot at first, but he turns it down. His hands roam down from my face to my neck and then to my breasts, which he squeezes and pinches and then kisses, filling me with warm sparks of excitement and what feels like...pride. My body turns him on.

Then his touch drifts lower until he's lightly massaging my clit and making my legs almost useless. I'm a warm pile of pleasure as he slides his finger between my folds. My arms clutch his neck for support while he touches me.

"Mia," he whispers against my mouth.

"Yes?"

"Put your hands on me."

Oh. I was so distracted by him touching *me* that I forgot to touch him. So I eagerly wrap my hand around his cock, and he jolts from the pressure. Slick with the water from the shower, I stroke him, squeezing the head.

He pulls away from our kiss and looks down at my hand, his mouth hanging open as he watches with a lust-filled expression.

"Slower," he mutters.

So I ease up my pace, squeezing the head slightly on every upstroke. He bites his lip while his eyes stare intently on the motion of my hand.

"Attagirl," he whispers, and I let out a sweet moan of pleasure. He's still touching me, but just the sound of his voice in that sultry tone turns me on.

"Are we still playing?" I whisper into his kiss.

"Yes. Why? Not having fun?"

"I am..." I reply in a breathless murmur when he curls his finger inside me, finding a spot completely new to me.

When his finger leaves my heat, I open my eyes and stare at him in confusion. Then, I watch him reach for the showerhead—the same one I used on myself the other day. And I already know where this is going when he takes my hand and places the showerhead there.

"Show me how you use this, baby."

My breath hitches. Goose bumps erupt all over my body, even in the heat of the shower, with the spray still pelting my skin.

I've never felt more sexual or more alive in my entire life. I do this almost every day. I let men watch me, but when it's Garrett's eyes on me, it's different. It's like they were always there, always meant to stay there. So natural that I feel stranger when he's not looking at me than when he is. He's not another person in the room...he's more of an extension of *me*.

So with our eyes locked, I move the warm spray down my body until the heat pummels my most sensitive spot. My stomach contracts and my spine curls as the breath forces itself out of my body.

Leaning against the shower wall, I stare back at him, bringing myself closer to climax. His hand is wrapped around his cock, and he's stroking it the same way I just was. But our eyes don't leave each other's. I can see him jacking himself in the periphery of my vision, but it's the look in his eyes I want. I want his most vulnerable, private expressions. I want to see into his soul.

I'm so lost in the intensity of our eye contact that I'm practically sideswiped by the sudden onslaught of my orgasm knocking the wind right out of me. My muscles tighten and I cry out, grabbing onto Garrett for support as I'm knocked down over and over by the sensation.

When I open my eyes, I watch the white jets of his cum disappear into the spray of water. He grabs me and crashes our bodies together, kissing me hard. The showerhead is hanging in my hand as I latch on to him, needing his touch, his kiss, his nearness.

When we finally come up for air, I use the showerhead in my hand to clean us both off, and we laugh a bit. Then we wash ourselves up, gentle smiles on our faces, stealing kisses every moment we can. And it really has me wondering how bad this is going to hurt when the week ends.

———

So how did things go with your stepbrother? Did you talk to him?

I bite my lip, staring down at the screen. It feels almost wrong now to still be talking to Drake when there's clearly something going on with Garrett, but Garrett and I are just playing. He made that very clear. And tomorrow is the last day at the lake house, but there are still so many unanswered questions between us. What happens after this week?

Not exactly.

Uh-oh. What does that mean? he asks.

It means...I don't know. We're keeping things physical, I guess.

There's no response for a moment, and I start to worry that I shouldn't be telling him this stuff about my real life. This is way too real for a conversation with a client, but Drake isn't really one of my clients anymore. We've told each other really personal stuff that I don't normally share with other guys.

"Who are you talking to?" Garrett's voice makes me jolt as he leans over my shoulder, staring at my phone. I quickly pull it to my chest to hide the chat box with Drake because I don't know how Garrett would react to me talking to Drake the way I do.

Of course, I don't know what Garrett and I are, so I should probably figure that out first. After the hike, he seemed different. A little less like the jerk who toys with me and more like a man who…actually likes me. It threw me off.

I think it threw him off too. He's been weird ever since.

"None of your business!" I snap, swatting at him to get him out of my space. He's laughing as he heads to the fridge to pull a bottle of water off the top shelf.

"Is that your little camgirl app?"

I spin toward him. "You calling it a *little camgirl app* is super condescending and offensive. You know that, right?"

"Of course I do," he replies before taking a swig. "I just like ruffling your feathers." He sends me a wink. Then he pulls his own phone out of his pocket, and I turn around to get back to my conversation with Drake.

I'm sorry. I probably shouldn't tell you that. You don't want to hear about the stuff I do with him.

It's fine, he replies. I know he'll never make you feel the way I do.

I bite my lip again, trying to hide the smile on my face so Garrett doesn't start teasing me again.

Tell me, kitten. Did he make you come?

My cheeks redden, and I turn around to see Garrett focused on his phone, a blank expression on his face, so I quickly type out my reply.

Yes. Does that make you jealous?

No. I'm not jealous. I already told you. I know who you really belong to.

Tell me more. What did he use to make you come?

His mouth, I say.

God, I wish I could taste you myself. If I find myself between your beautiful legs, I'm never coming up for air.

Butterflies dance through my belly as I imagine him there. But the more I try to imagine Drake, my mind keeps picturing that moment with Garrett in the kitchen, his mouth against my sex, a mixture of warm and cold making me crazy as he brought me to climax.

What would I do if Drake walked through that door right now? Would I find myself moving toward him? Or toward Garrett? It feels impossible to choose, so I guess it's a good thing that will never happen.

I wish you could.

I want to be the woman who breaks that dry spell for you.

Oh, kitten. Trust me. I wish you could too.

My mouth twists into a knot. The next words I type out are daring and crazy, and I can't believe I'm saying this.

It can be arranged.

I know I should probably tell him at some point that I'm a virgin, but what if he reacts like Garrett did? What if he doesn't want me? Again, I start to feel bad about talking to another guy on the same day I've fucked around with Garrett, but Garrett will never commit to me, so why should I commit to him?

Drake's response is disappointing.

It's complicated.

I choose not to explore that further. If it is truly complicated, I don't think I want to know why. I've got my own layers of complications to deal with. Speaking of, I turn around and glance at Garrett, still standing there, drinking his water and scrolling through his phone. His eyes lift when he feels me watching and our gazes meet for a moment.

"Do you like it?" he asks suddenly, and I'm caught off guard. For some reason, I feel like he's caught me talking to Drake, but I know that's not the case.

Squinting at him, I ask, "Like what?"

"Your job," he replies, nodding toward my phone. "Doing whatever it is you do for the people online? Do you like it?"

It's strange talking to him like this. Garrett was always the last person I would open up to about my work, but after everything we've done with each other this week, I don't feel so strange about it now.

"Sometimes," I respond.

"And you'd never meet any of these men in real life, right?"

"Of course not," I reply without hesitation. How did he know we were just talking about this? "Also…why do you care? Are you jealous?"

"No. I just worry about you."

The response is so sincere it makes me pause. Then I think about the conversation I had with Laura yesterday, about how Garrett has always tried to protect me and how I never knew. I feel something warm in my chest at the idea that I've meant more to Garrett than I ever realized.

"No, I promise. I never meet up with clients. I protect myself."

"Good. And it's genuinely what you want to do, right? Not something you feel like you have to do?"

I swallow the lump building in my throat. A question I don't really know how to answer. The shame surrounding being a sex worker is probably the hardest part of my job. The way society makes me feel like I have to hide it or be ashamed of it, as if taking this job is any worse than taking one at the gas station or library. Work is work. To be able to say I don't dislike my job is more than most people can say.

"Does it bother you? Knowing what I do?" I ask.

He walks over, pocketing his phone before he plants his hands around me on the table, leaning in close, and my heart rate starts to pick up.

"Someday a man will come along who won't like what you do. He'll want you to himself because he thinks you're nothing more than a body he can control, and it will be because he's insecure. A real man knows that truly possessing someone is a privilege, and it's not their body you'll own. It's so much more. I want you to know the difference, Mia."

I can't breathe as I stare into his eyes, the space between us tense and electric, ready to blow at any moment. But when I expect him to lean in and place a kiss against my lips, he doesn't. Instead, he pulls away and starts to walk toward the stairs that lead to the basement.

"Which one are you?" I ask.

He pauses and turns back toward me. "I'm still working on it," he replies just before disappearing down the stairs.

Rule #17: When it's time to walk away, walk away.

Garrett

IT'S OUR LAST NIGHT IN THE LAKE HOUSE, SO I'M NOT SURPRISED when her soft footsteps creep down the stairs and into my room. We don't say a word as she crawls into bed, slipping between the sheets next to me.

Over the past few days, we've made one thing pretty clear: we don't fool around in bed. She's slept in my bed twice now, but we both seem to agree that it's too close to sex to play here. The temptation to slip her clothes off and slip into each other is too great.

I'm too old to play around with a twenty-three-year-old. I know that, but the mood between us this week has been the mood of a couple horny stepsiblings who can't help themselves. And if that's what I am, then, oh well. I'm not ashamed. I've gone so long without sex, I might as well be a virgin again, and fucking Mia as part of an experiment would be wrong. I came here to figure out if my sudden attraction to Mia is something physical or more than that, and even though those questions aren't answered, I do know that the physical aspect is too hot to ignore.

We don't say a word to each other as I gather her into my

arms and kiss her with urgency. I've barely been able to kiss her all evening, with our parents around, and I haven't had a single chance to touch her. I can't believe how much I've missed this, miss her already. It's only been a few days, but it already feels like I can't live without it.

And tomorrow, I have to start living without it for good.

Silently she slides against me. Lightning flashes, bathing the room in light for only a second before the thunder cracks again. She flinches in my arms, so I squeeze her tighter. Her face is resting on my chest.

But before too long, the ache to touch each other gets too powerful and we're kissing again. There's so much we're supposed to say at this point, like establishing boundaries and expectations. I'm not so good with words, but I do know how to do this. I want to express my feelings for her with our bodies. I literally watch people do it every day.

So I tell Mia how I feel with the movement of my mouth over hers, squeezing my eyes closed as I tug her bottom lip between my teeth and bite just enough that she cries out. She answers me by wrapping her arms and legs around me, holding me as close as possible.

I place my body over hers as my hips grind against her. She hums into my mouth and tightens the grip of her thighs. My cock hardens quickly between us, and I seek the friction of her body, grinding harder and harder to the rhythm that sets my body on fire.

"This is almost better than sex," I mumble into her mouth. "Wanting you this much."

"Garrett, please," she cries out, and I lie my body over hers, grinding harder and harder, watching the way her back arches and her breathing almost stops.

"God, you're so beautiful when you're about to come. I'm addicted to it, Mia."

Her nails are digging into my back as I use the hard length of my cock against her clit to take her to the edge.

"Faster," she pants into my kiss, and I answer her request by digging my cock even harder against her and moving my hips even faster. Then she does the rest. Grinding her hips against me, she uses my body to make herself come. Her muscles squeeze around me impossibly tight as she cries out, and I place my hand over her lips to keep her quiet.

"So fucking beautiful," I mutter, and she's barely come down from her orgasm before she's reaching into my boxers and wrapping her hand around me. Then, she strokes me fast, knowing that I'm so close already. Moments later, I'm pulling up the front of her long T-shirt and painting her chest white.

It's weird that at a moment like this, while she's covered in my cum, I'm actually proud of myself for *not* fucking her...as if this is better.

Man, do I need to get my priorities straightened out.

I did what I came to do. I wanted to see this through with Mia, to explore whatever it was I felt that night on the video chat. And I explored it. And her.

I'm supposed to have things figured out at this point. But somehow, there are even more questions swirling around my head. I've got her texting me on the app every moment that she doesn't have her hands busy with my cock or in the throes of another orgasm.

And the only thing I've figured out this week is that I'm royally fucked.

As I slam the trunk of my car with my duffel bag packed inside, I notice Mia standing near the driver's side. I glance around carefully to make sure we're alone before we say anything.

We couldn't be leaving this lake house any more unsure about what the fuck we're doing. There have been some intense moments of intimacy that, I'll be honest, felt a hell of a lot like a relationship. But her virginity is still intact, and I withheld from being the asshole to take that. Still, the physical stuff was amazing, so do we just call it a day and part ways?

Is that what I want?

Ignoring the fact, of course, that I'm still talking to her online as Drake at all times.

"Well," she says, crossing her arms, "I guess I'm glad you came."

"Nice choice of words." I laugh.

She bites her bottom lip and looks away, holding back her own laughter. "You know what I mean."

"Yeah. It was fun."

"It was fun," she says, looking up at me. Her skin is tanner than when I got here five days ago, and I find myself staring at the hints of sunburn on her nose and cheeks. Then, of course, I think about the tan lines under her clothes, and I have to force my mind to stay out of the gutter for one fucking second.

"Are you excited to get back to work?" she asks.

"Yeah, I think so. What about you? Are you excited to flash your tits for creeps on the internet?"

She rolls her eyes. "You're just jealous."

"Nah," I reply, stepping toward her. "I've seen your tits. That image is safely tucked away right up here." I tap the side of my head.

She smiles for a moment before getting serious. "So…this is it, right? We're still not going to do this back in Briar Point, are we?"

I'm searching her tone for any hint of what she wants. Does she want to keep doing this?

It doesn't matter. We are done. I'm calling it quits right now. I'll even stop texting her as Drake. I need to just go back to my regular life at Salacious, so everything can be normal again.

"This is it," I say, and I watch her eyes as a hint of disappointment flashes through them.

"Okay," she says with reluctance.

God, I want to touch her. Just one last time. Before we head back to the real world, to the way things were before this weird twilight zone affair started. I take a quick glance up at the house, and since I don't hear my mom or Paul talking, I know it means they're not near the doorway. So I grab Mia by the hand and lead her to the house, so we're out of view of the windows.

Then, I press her against the wall. "Since this is goodbye, I just need one more…"

With that, I slam my lips against hers, tasting her mouth like it's the last time I'll ever kiss her. Because it is.

Her mouth eagerly latches onto mine, our tongues twisting in delicious friction. She tastes so good; I savor the feel of her lips. It's a short kiss, but it's enough to satiate my appetite.

When we pull apart, she doesn't linger to look at me or ask any more questions. She just keeps her back to me as I climb into the car, only waving at me once as I disappear down the driveway.

It's not until I'm home that she texts me. On the app, of course. Technically, I guess she's texting Drake. At first, I ignore it, tossing it on the bed unanswered. It's time to cut all ties. If I could un-stepbrother myself from her, I would, but as far as I know, we're stuck sharing parents for the foreseeable future.

I'll just ghost her as Drake and that will be it. This whole weird stepsister phase is behind me now. I almost go for a run. I almost go to the club. I *almost* do a lot of things, but that one fucking unchecked message is haunting me and won't let me go.

Okay, I'll just say goodbye.

Picking up the phone, I click the message and see her beautiful face. There is no text. Just a picture she sent—a beautiful smiling selfie. No words. Nothing.

"Fuck," I mutter, staring at her photo. Why does she have to be so fucking confident and vulnerable and easy to talk to?

All right, change of plans. I'll just ease Drake out of Mia's life. We'll chat online for a bit—no more video chats because I can't risk her finding out the truth. And after a while, one of us will just end things online, and everything will be fine. God, what the fuck am I thinking?

As long as I don't see her in person and she never comes to the club, I have nothing to worry about.

With that, I type out my response and hit Send.

Hey, beautiful. Tell me about your day.

PART 2

The Club

Rule #18: Crazy ideas are sometimes the best ideas.

Garrett

"YOU LOOK REFRESHED," EMERSON ANNOUNCES AS I WALTZ INTO the boardroom on my first day back to Salacious after five days at the lake. He stands from his chair and greets me with a half hug, half pat on the back.

"Thanks. I feel refreshed," I reply.

"Good. The tan looks good on you." His eyes linger on my face for a moment with a mischievous expression painting his features.

I squint my eyes at him. "What's that look for?"

As we take our seats around the table, with a smile, he replies, "You know what it's for."

Ah, Mia. Of course. Why did I have to tell him everything? I hate the way he's looking at me right now. Like I'm one second away from being blissfully attached like he is.

Bad news, I'm not.

"For the record, I didn't fuck my sister," I say.

At that very moment, Hunter walks in, his dark, curly hair catching my attention and the sharp blue suit he always wears.

Right as he hears my announcement, regarding the non-sister-fucking, he laughs. "Well, that's good to hear."

"He means his stepsister," Emerson adds.

"Oh, that's only a little creepy then."

Emerson looks back at me. "What happened? Why didn't you?"

Why didn't I? Did he miss the part about her being my stepsister? How about her being thirteen years younger than me and someone I've known longer than is socially acceptable? "Well, let's see," I say. "Mostly because she's a *virgin*."

Emerson's eyebrows pinch inward in confusion. "Mia?"

Exactly the response I was expecting. No one would take one look at my gorgeous stepsister and think for a second that that girl was cut out for celibacy. She's adventurous, beautiful, and outwardly sexual in a way I didn't notice until this week.

"Yes."

"Isn't she like…twenty-three?" Emerson asks.

"And drop-dead gorgeous," Hunter adds.

"Yes and yes."

Emerson is still deep in thought, holding his chin in his hand as he stares at me. "But wait…what does that have to do with anything?"

"I'm thirty-six," I say with a fair amount of shock in my voice. How can he even ask that? "I have no business popping anyone's cherry at my age."

Hunter joins in the conversation, sitting across from me at the table with Emerson at the head. "I'm confused. Is something going on between you and Mia? When did this happen?"

Inwardly, I groan. I really don't need the whole company getting involved. I left the lake yesterday, and Mia and I had fun, but we're done. We spent the week doing exactly what I said we would—playing. No sex. A little fun. And no regrets. It was the first time my dick was touched by a woman in way too goddamn long. No strings, no complaints. And now, we can both return to our lives like nothing happened.

Except that we still talk almost hourly as Drake and Mia—instead of Garrett and Mia—and she keeps hinting at us meeting in person. That's a hole I've dug for myself that I don't want to face right now. Because I still can't quite get the taste of her lips out of my mouth, and when she finds out I'm Drake, and that I've been lying to her this whole time, I'm going to lose her twice.

"It's complicated," I grumble, rubbing my forehead with my fingers. "She's a camgirl and I happened to see her online and might have joined under a fake name and watched her a couple times. Next thing I know, we're doing everything but fucking."

"And you came clean about the fake profile?" Emerson asks with a hopeful expression on his face.

I give him a one-word response. "Ha."

He lets out a disappointed sigh, and it kills me. Emerson Grant is the last person you want to disappoint. "Garrett," he replies, my name sounding like a punishment.

"This is why we didn't have sex. I don't need to feel any more like a piece of shit for what I've done already. Taking her virginity would be the icing on the cake."

Emerson is sending me a stern look. "I don't like when you do that," he mutters.

"Do what?"

"Call yourself a piece of shit when you're clearly not."

Well, that was…unexpected. Am I supposed to apologize for that? Like Emerson Grant has ever known what it was like to feel like a piece of shit. Even when he was banging his son's ex, he probably didn't beat himself up feeling like the world's worst dad.

Okay, he kind of did, but that was a single incident. I highly doubt my perfect best friend knows what low self-esteem even feels like.

We need a change in subject. "How's the club?" I ask.

The way his face screws up into a pained expression has my heart dropping. "Well, numbers are steady. But the hall has been a little lackluster lately."

Fuck. "What? Why?"

"Last week, we had three rooms filled at once and only four spectators in the hall."

Fuck, fuck. Groaning again, I slide my face into my hands. I should have known I'd come back to a mountain of work. I never should have left.

"I think we need to start vetting who we let take the rooms," Emerson adds.

Immediately, my brain shifts into idea mode. We can fix this. It's not a lost cause. "I'll get back some of my regulars. We can get a group in there. They love that." My gaze slides over to Hunter, who looks personally affronted, as if I'm specifically asking him to partake in a gang bang.

"Why are you looking at me?"

"Talk to Drake," I say. "He'll do it. Room fee waived, of course."

Speak of the fucking devil himself, Drake walks into the room.

"Talk to Drake about what?" he asks with a sly smile on his handsome face.

"Jesus," Emerson groans. Drake isn't an owner of the club, but he is head of the construction crew responsible for building it, which means he has a free lifetime membership, which he uses to its full potential. And he tends to find himself at our meetings, more often than not, which is not something Emerson particularly likes. He doesn't *dislike* Drake exactly, but it's clear Drake's flippancy and nonchalance when it comes to the club and life in general have always irked Emerson. Not to mention, Drake doesn't hold back with his flirting, and if Emerson so much as catches him glancing in Charlotte's direction, he turns murderous.

And speak of the devil again, Emerson's girlfriend-slash-secretary, Charlotte, walks in with Maggie. They take the last two seats around the table while Drake stares at me, waiting to hear what I brought up his name for.

"Drake, if we could get you a room in V hall, do you think you could gather up a little group to put on a show?"

Now that gets everyone's attention. Chitchat suddenly comes

to an end as everyone watches him for his response. His eyes light up with excitement.

"Just girls or guys too?"

My eyes get a little wider. Well, that's not something I knew about Drake, but I guess you learn new things about people every day.

"Whatever you want," I reply.

"Cool. I'm down," he says casually, as if he didn't just accept an invitation to publicly fuck a group of people while in a workday business meeting.

When I glance in Hunter's direction, I notice his jaw has tightened and his nostrils flare. If I didn't know any better, I'd say he doesn't love this idea very much.

Too bad for him because I'm elated. This will be great for the voyeur hall. "See?" I say in triumph, looking at the boss man at the end of the table.

He looks less than impressed. "We need more than groups and regulars. We need professionals."

My brow furrows. "Like what, porn stars?" This is the first time he's ever brought up hiring professional performers for the club. It was never about the entertainment. It was always about the people and their experience.

"Yeah. Or...camgirls?"

And with that, my blood runs cold. "No," I bark, pointing a finger at him. "I know what you're thinking and I'm saying absolutely not."

Emerson is fucking relentless, though. "We could really use her perspective, Garrett. She could help us with the hall."

I force a long inhale, willing myself to calm down. "No. My stepsister thinks I run a nightclub. She's not stepping foot into Salacious. Ever."

He exhales. "Okay, I understand. But that's not all."

Oh great. "What?" I ask.

"VIP had a negative intake month," he says, and my heart falls again.

"Down fourteen, up twelve," Maggie adds. I feel all eyes in the room on me as I take in this information. This is my territory. Keeping people happy and keeping them coming—literally and figuratively. But obviously, I'm failing.

"Don't panic," Emerson replies, noticing my souring mood. "We just need new, enticing ideas to bring people in. They can have sex at home, but we need to give them a reason to do it here."

Hunter interjects. "I have the BDSM demonstrations scheduled for next quarter. A Shibari showcase and an impact-play workshop."

"Good," Emerson replies with a nod. "People want to try it. They just don't know how. What else?"

"We need an event. A big event," I say, knowing that that's the simplest answer. The auctions do well, but we need something fresh. Something different. Something so magnetic and sexy and tempting, prospective members can't say no to it. Something with a following or fan base we can utilize.

And I hate that my mind has settled on this idea because, technically, Emerson already brought it up. But he's right. If we bring in performers, it could be the boost the club needs. We're at the three-month mark, and it's a make-or-break period for new clubs. We can either establish a solid foundation or we can crumble under the pressure.

"What do you have in mind?" Emerson asks, like he can see my wheels turning.

"You're right," I mutter. "If we brought in camgirls and porn stars, they could advertise to their fans. Put on a live show. It would bring in a huge crowd."

"I like it," he replies.

"It would have to be invitation only. Cap attendance and offer them a free month of membership for attending the event with optional VIP upgrade."

When I glance up at him again, he looks pleased.

"We're going to need more than the hall, though. It can't

handle a crowd. Drake, could you set up a temporary structure in the main hall?"

"Like a theater?" he asks.

I sigh. Is this crazy? It feels crazy. Would they even do it? Perform up onstage, doing...what they do?

"Yeah, like a theater."

He nods, jotting down some notes on his paper as he and Hunter discuss some more ideas for the space. Pulling back from the conversation, I try to calm my nerves from knowing the club is suffering. My anxiety can't grab on to the idea that we're going under or I'll be a mess. Out of the corner of my eye, I catch Emerson watching Charlotte as she scribbles notes on her notepad.

"You getting all this?" he asks, placing his hand on her knee under the table.

She glances up and gazes into his eyes with a warm expression full of love. "Yes, sir."

"Good girl," he whispers, before pulling her close and pressing his lips against her forehead.

I glance away, noticing the new ache in my chest from watching them. Before I left for the lake, I thought Emerson was crazy for giving in to this relationship so willingly, for being vulnerable and opening up his heart to possible damage down the line, not to mention the overall stress of having another person to please and keep happy.

But then I think about how easy things were between me and Mia over the past week. How easily we laughed, and how even when we were tormenting each other, there was still something satisfying there.

Pulling out my phone, I quickly send her a message.

Hope you're having a beautiful day, kitten. I miss your smile.

This is insane and I'm going to pay for this later, I know that. But pretending to be someone else makes typing these things a little easier. Like I can convince myself that none of it is actually real. I can tell Mia how much she means to me as Drake. It's not like that's how I really feel. Right?

Rule #19: Don't cry for men who don't cry for you.

Mia

"I LOVE IT," I SAY WITH A SMILE, POSING IN FRONT OF THE CAMERA for Gregg as he proudly admires the shimmery, metallic-looking fabric of my dress. It's a dress for a stripper, literally. I'm not even being facetious. This literally came from a shop for pole dancers and performers, but he doesn't know the difference. To him, a skimpy dress on a woman is more natural than a suit on a rich man.

"It looks beautiful on you. I'm so glad you like it."

"I do. And it's good to see you smiling like that."

"Then, don't leave," he replies, and my fake smile falters.

"I wish I didn't have to, but I have class in fifteen minutes. We can have a real chat later maybe."

It's a lie. I don't have a class. In fact, I don't have anything, but I'm forced to make up lies to cover up the fact that I can't seem to do this anymore. Whether it's for Drake or Garrett, I don't really know. I just know that until I figure out who I'm with—if I'm even with either of them—I can't get naked for men on the internet. That's something I should discuss with them first.

If only I could bring it up with them.

He made it very clear yesterday before we left that things between us were done. It was just physical anyway. Playing, as he called it. Even if he is avoiding the truth that sometimes it felt like more than playing.

It was fun, but it was also...something real. There was a connection there. Real chemistry that I have never felt with a man before. And I know he felt it too. But Garrett is afraid of commitment, and he seems to have it in his head that he's not cut out for relationships. He gave up on us before there was an *us*.

And it's hard to make Drake a realistic priority in my life when I've never even seen his face before, and he's clearly hiding something from me. If he didn't have a secret, then why wouldn't he video chat with me? Show me photos of himself? How come he can express these deeply personal secrets but he can't let me see him? It doesn't change the fact that I feel a connection with him that I don't feel with Garrett. As if they both give me something different, and if they could just morph into one person, they'd be perfect.

"I'm proud of you for going back to school, sweetheart," Gregg replies, distracting me from my complicated thoughts.

"Thanks, baby. I'm really excited about it."

Lies, lies, lies.

"Send me more pictures when you have some free time. I miss you."

I smile at him, leaning close to the camera. "I miss you too."

Then, we hang up. I flop onto the couch in the basement of my parents' house, and I let the feeling of guilt wash over me as I accept Gregg's payment for the hour-long chat—plus tip. I didn't even show him my tits. I can't keep doing this.

I either need to stop worrying about Garrett and Drake and get back to work, or I need to quit entirely.

Both sound awful.

Before closing the app, I get a text from Drake.

Hope you're having a beautiful day, kitten. I miss your smile.

I smile down at the phone as I type out my reply.
Want to video chat?
I'm at work.
Hang on. Let me close the door.

I laugh as I wait for him to respond. Then without warning, I get an incoming video call request. I quickly hit Accept as I lay on the couch, putting my phone in the holder on the coffee table.

"Hi, baby," I greet him as the other line picks up.

He has his camera turned off but his microphone on, which is fine by me since it's the sound of his voice I want to hear anyway.

"Are you in your office?" I ask.

"Mm-hmm," he replies, his voice a deep, gravelly tone.

"I wish I were there with you," I say, feeling a little emotionally raw at the moment.

"Tell me what you would do if you were here," he whispers into the speaker, and my spine lights up, sending a thrill through my entire body.

My smile broadens as I stretch on the couch, letting my dress ruck up my legs until my thong is visible. Then I let my imagination wander as I think about all the things we could do if we were together.

"I want you to bend me over your desk and hold me there while you do whatever you want to me. Touch me, kiss me, bite me, fuck me. Until I can't take it anymore. I want to fuck until we are so spent and tired that we can't even stand. I want more than just one hour, Drake. I want a thousand of them. And I want all of them with you."

He growls into the speaker. "Oh, kitten."

"Are you hard for me, Drake?"

"Yes, kitten."

There's something in his tone that strikes me as familiar, and I pause. Something that reminds me of…

No. My mind is playing tricks on me. Garrett would never do this. It would take way too much vulnerability. Not just the video chatting but the deep conversations and talking about emotions. He would never. Sometimes, I wish he would.

Just in time to distract me from my thoughts, I hear him unzip his slacks and then he mutters, "Use a toy, kitten."

It's like he read my mind, and I quickly reach into the drawer of the coffee table and retrieve a small rose petal–shaped vibrator. Its hum is nearly silent as I turn it on, and he growls again when he sees it.

It's a good thing I'm the only one home because the moment the sucking sensation of the vibrator hits my clit, I cry out. It's a delicious buzz that sends a thrill all the way down to my toes.

"This won't take long, Drake. I hope you're ready," I say in a breathless pant while I squirm on the couch.

He grunts and groans to the sounds of his fist stroking his cock, and I let the sounds fill my imagination, and my climax washes me away. Judging by the sounds he's making, he's coming too.

His heavy breaths and some music in the background are all I can hear as I recline on the couch and wait for my heartbeat to slow down.

"Drake, I don't know how long I can do this," I say, the words slipping through before I can stop them. I have no filter moments after I orgasm apparently.

"Do what?" he asks.

"This. Whatever this is. I like you. Maybe…more. But I'm so afraid you're going to break my heart. At some point, you have to let me into your life."

"I know…" he mumbles, his tone despondent. And the sadness in his voice doesn't make me feel any better. In fact it sounds…hopeless. As if there's nothing he can do about it, and I'm doomed to feel like this forever. Or at least until it ends. Whatever he has going on in his life, I will never be a priority.

"I'm in love with two men who don't want me," I whisper, and I really have no idea where the fuck that came from. Tears well in my eyes as I quickly sit up and fix my dress. I can't believe I just said that. I'm humiliated, and the other end of the line is silent for too long.

"Kitten…" he whispers.

"I have to go. I'm sorry. I just think… I'm under a lot of stress. I need to think."

"Please, don't—" he says, but I click the red End Call button before he can beg me to stay or feed me lies. What the fuck have I gotten myself into?

I need to get out of here or do something because the more I sit here and think about how sad I am to possibly lose Drake or Garrett, the more I know I'll cry, and I'm not going to do that. I'm not shedding tears for men that don't shed tears for me.

Glancing down at the clock, I see it's almost nine. I feel like a bomb about to explode, and I need to vent out these frustrations. There's only one person I can think of at the moment who I want to see, and I may not know where to find him, but I know I can figure it out.

Rule #20: If you go snooping around sex clubs, chances are you'll walk in on an orgy.

Mia

THIS IS CRAZY. I'M STANDING OUTSIDE A NIGHTCLUB IN DOWNTOWN Briar Point, in a dress literally made for a stripper, ready to face my emotionally hindered, ignorant, dumbass stepbrother, basically to beg him for sex. Why? I have no idea. Mostly because I feel like a ticking time bomb, and I'm tired of waiting and playing by his rules and putting my own wants and desires behind his.

It's time to put these men to the test, and Garrett is up first.

I'm ready to give him an ultimatum: sex or nothing at all.

No. A relationship *with* sex or nothing at all.

Oh God. He's going to say nothing at all. Of course he is. He's already made it clear that he's not interested in baggage in the form of a girlfriend, especially an annoying, younger stepsister.

Fuck it. Worth a shot anyway. If I finally take this leap with Garrett, then maybe I can finally leave Drake behind.

When the driver dropped me off at the door of the club, I didn't quite expect this. It's so quiet. I thought there would be bass thumping through the walls and drunk girls stumbling out the door with Axe body–sprayed men.

Instead, it's a discreet black door on an old brick building with the black metal logo hanging above the door: *SPC*.

The ominous nightclub only goes by initials online when I did a quick search of the phone number Laura gave me—which she said he reluctantly gave her after she hounded him for it in case of an emergency. It's making me wonder what kind of club Garrett really owns. Is it a strip club and he didn't tell me? I mean…it would sort of make sense. He's been so aloof about the details, but I guess I assumed all this time that it was just another dance club.

Oh well. I can walk into a strip club (looking like a stripper). Smart, Mia.

There's a bouncer at the door, but he's not the beefy, tatted kind you usually see at clubs. He's in a black suit, looking a little too fancy to be a bouncer. Still, he opens the door for me, and I take a heavy breath before walking inside.

Here goes nothing.

After stepping through the door, I'm in a dimly lit lobby. Everything in here is black. Black curtains, black carpet, black counter, behind which stands a woman in a sleek, black pantsuit.

"Hi. Welcome to Salacious. Are you a member?" she says, greeting me. I catch the way her eyes skate over my body, probably judging me by my call-girl getup. I can already tell that this establishment is way too nice for a dress like this; it's made for strip clubs they put up by airports, not members-only clubs like this. I came to the right place, right?

"Um…actually, I know one of the owners," I stammer, sounding ridiculous.

She nods with her lips pressed together. I'm no dummy. The look on her face screams *sure, you do*.

Too bad for her I'm not some doe-eyed virgin, too scared to walk into a strip club or battle some hostess drunk on her own power. I straighten my shoulders, clear my throat, and look her square in the eye.

"Garrett Porter is my brother, and I'd like to see him. Right. Now."

Her eyes widen as she stares back at me. Then her bottom lip falls, as if she's about to argue, when someone appears through a dark curtain I didn't even realize was a doorway.

I've only met Hunter a couple of times. Garrett brought him and his then-girlfriend-now-wife, Isabel, over for Thanksgiving once when they had just moved into their new house and didn't have a table to even eat at. The other times were mostly short moments, and I know Thanksgiving, in particular, was at least four years ago, so I was only nineteen.

I don't expect him to recognize me at all, but when he glances up from the tablet in his hands, in midsentence with the girl behind the counter, I watch his eyes nearly pop out of his head.

"Mia?" he gasps.

"Hi, Hunter," I reply with a smile. Hunter is so good-looking in a rugged, manly sort of way. He has a head full of curly, black hair that he keeps trimmed short and buzzed on the sides, letting a few stray curls fall over his tan forehead. He has dark eyes and full lips, making him a walking wet dream. Isabel is a very lucky woman.

He pulls me into a warm hug, and I practically sneer at the hostess. When he pulls away, he holds my shoulders and stares at me as if I've just come back from the dead or something.

Then his eyes drift down and over my dress.

"Wow…you've really grown up," he says with a hint of uncomfortable reluctance. "When I saw you, I assumed you weren't even old enough to be in here. How old are you now?"

"Twenty-three," I answer.

"Wow," he replies. "Are you here to see Garrett? He must have called you after our meeting today."

"Umm…yeah," I lie, because I'm not sure I'll get past that black curtain if I don't make it seem like I'm one hundred percent wanted here. If Garrett were okay with me being in his club, he wouldn't have kept it a secret. Because it's definitely not a dance club, although I'm still not entirely sure what lies beyond that curtain.

"Awesome. Come on, I'll take you to the office."

"Thanks," I reply, sending the girl a big fake smile before Hunter guides me through the black curtain.

The main room we walk into is huge, with tall, warehouse-high ceilings and a second-floor balcony around the perimeter. There's a giant bar off to the left and a stage with a DJ booth in the middle. The music is more sultry than the kind of club music people would dance to; in fact, there are no people dancing at all.

There are, however, two giant cages on either side of the stage with topless women moving to the music. But it's not like any strip club I imagined, where men would sit around them, stuffing bills into their G-strings.

There are tables scattered around the room with people filling most of the seats, some couples and other small groups. Hunter leads me through the main room so fast, I barely get a chance to take it all in, but it's certainly not at all what I expected. It's like some super discreet, exclusive strip club…but where are the strippers?

There are a lot of doors along the two floors, so maybe they're in there?

Suddenly, Hunter is ushering me through a staff-only door that leads to a hallway that runs the length of the main room. We walk together down the long corridor, making small talk as we go.

"I'm glad he called you," he says. "He was against it at first, but I know you can bring something awesome to the club."

I'm striding next to him, trying to absorb what he's saying, but I can't seem to keep up. *Called me for what? What would Hunter think Garrett would need me for?*

I don't want to let him see my confusion, so I answer noncommittally. "Yep. Me too."

"You know how he stresses," Hunter says. "Maybe you can help keep him calm about the whole thing."

"Sure," I say. Because I do know how stressed Garrett can get. And whatever it is, I do want to help him, and I don't want to blow my cover before I can. So I quickly change the subject. "How's Isabel?"

"She's good. Owns her own yoga studio now."

"Nice. Good for her. Tell her hi for me."

"I will," he responds as we reach a door at the intersection of two hallways. It opens to a huge office space that looks like all the owners share. Next to this door is one labeled *Security*, but it's closed. There are various other doors down here, which look like supply closets and electrical equipment rooms. I don't peep around too much, but I do scan the empty office for Garrett, who doesn't seem to be around.

"Well, he was in here," Hunter says as he pokes his head around the corner. "Why don't you sit tight in here, and I'll go hunt him down."

"Sounds good," I reply sweetly as he leaves me sitting in a foreign office in a strange club with a whole lot of uncertainty.

But I'm really not the kind of girl who sits around and waits.

So as soon as Hunter disappears down the long hallway, I poke my head out of the office. Some of the doors are labeled, but some are not. And I can tell by the sound of the music that some of these doors will lead back into the main room.

I am too damn curious to sit here and wait for him. And I have a feeling when Garrett does find me, he will quickly usher me out without any answers. Fuck that.

Quietly, I turn the knob on the first black door. It opens to a dark hallway—much darker than the main room. Quieter too. Taking a peek inside, I see people standing in random places, staring at something I can't quite make out. And it's giving me museum vibes, but it feels too intimate, so I quickly back out and escape to the staff hallway.

Wandering farther down the hall, I find a door that leads to a brightly lit and silent stairwell. I quickly close myself in. It's only one flight, and when I reach the second floor, I find another ominous door. It's unmarked, but I hear music playing on the other side, so I ease it open and step into a dark foyer that leads to yet another door, probably meant to filter out the light from the stairwell.

I almost turn back before going through the second door, because it's slightly quieter up here, but then I hear something—a high-pitched yelp that sounds distant and a hell of a lot like someone is fucking on the other side of this door. Maybe that would be a good sign to leave, but I can't help myself. I'm too fucking curious to walk away now, so I carefully peel the door all the way open and slide the black curtain aside to sneak in.

I'm standing speechless on the perimeter of a room in the midst of...an orgy. I don't really know how else to put it, but my eyes don't even need to focus for me to see what's happening here.

It's a lounge with a cushioned sofa lining the wall and a recessed sitting area in the middle with more seats, each of which sits a woman getting absolutely railed. The music is loud enough to mask the sounds of sex, but it's still there.

My mind is scrambling. This is what Garrett does? This is his club?

Is this what people do in exclusive strip clubs? I haven't seen one fucking stripper, though.

Two minutes ago, I was reminiscing with an old friend who's been to my parents' house on Thanksgiving, and now I'm standing in the middle of a fuck fest. Nothing makes any sense right now.

Movement catches my eye and I notice a woman walking through the room, seemingly unbothered by the display around her. She has long, sable hair and full, pouty lips. She's probably one of the most beautiful women I've ever seen, and she carries herself like a modern-day Cleopatra.

I can't take my eyes off of her as she passes by a round sofa, stopping to say something to a man in the middle of receiving a blow job from *two* women. Then without warning, her eyes are on me.

She's walking toward me, and I start to panic. I need to get out of here, but she's reeling me in.

"Oh, baby girl, you look lost," she says sweetly as she touches my arm. On instinct, I flinch.

Pulling her hand back, she smiles. "I didn't mean to scare you, but I noticed you were staring, and people don't generally stare up in the VIP room."

"VIP room?" I reply in a breathy gasp.

"Yeah. Are you lost? It's a little calmer downstairs if you'd rather go there."

"This isn't a strip club, is it?" I ask, and the woman replies with a low chuckle.

"Wow, you are lost. How did you even get up here?"

"I'm one of the owner's sister." I have to keep my eyes on the thick lines of makeup over her eyes or else I'll get too distracted by the movement and the moaning behind her.

"Owner's sister?" she echoes, and there's a definite furrow in her brow as if she's thinking something through. Finally, realization dawns on her face. "Holy shit. You're Mia."

Confused, I nod.

"I've heard about you. I was actually looking forward to meeting you. But let's get out of here. It's not really the place for… conversation," she says, glancing back at the action around her.

With that, she takes my hand, and I let her lead me across the room and through a curtained doorway, leaving the sounds of sex behind us.

Rule #21: If Madame Kink offers you a tour, you take it.

Mia

Once we pass through the curtain, we're in a slightly brighter room. I spot a bar and some tables. More couches... minus people fucking on them.

The sexy woman in black leads me to a high-top table and gestures to the bartender for two waters as I sit down, reeling from the room we just walked out of.

"You've heard about me?" I ask, figuring that was a good place to start. Since I have no idea who this woman is or what this place is or even why the hell Hunter said Garrett would have called me to help out.

"Yeah, well, not from Garrett, naturally," she says as she takes the seat across from me. "He never tells anyone anything. I get all of my info from Charlie."

"And who are you?" I feel like an idiot, and my eyes keep dancing around the room, watching for Garrett to show up. We're still upstairs, and judging by the red rope dividing this bar from the stairs that lead to the main room, I assume we're still in the VIP area.

"I'm Eden," she says, putting a hand out for me to shake. Her nails are long and painted a glistening gold. Everything about her is immaculate. "I'm a good friend of the owners, but I guess you could just call me a regular."

"And Charlie?"

She giggles. "Wow, he really didn't tell you anything, did he?"

I clench my jaw and press my shoulders back as I shake my head. If he were standing in front of me, I'd punch him right now. Sure, I probably shouldn't have gone snooping around, but in my defense, I didn't think I was on the set of a porno.

"Charlie is Emerson's girl. She said you were mentioned in today's staff meeting. Which is why Garrett called you. To talk about the event."

"What event?"

"The Voyeur Night. He wants to bring in camgirls and actors. I think it's fucking brilliant. I used to do a little cam work back in the day." She says it with pride as the bartender drops two ice waters in front of us. "Thanks, Geo," she says sweetly.

"You did?"

"Yeah, it wasn't really for me, though. I thought I'd like to be watched, but I think I prefer the physical connection more."

"Yeah..." I mumble, taking a sip of cold water. I never thought I'd prefer the physical too, but Garrett's opened my eyes a lot this week.

"So...Garrett obviously didn't prepare you very well. Did you even know you were in a sex club?"

"A sex club?"

She laughs. "I didn't think so."

"Wait." With my elbows on the table, I lower my face to my hands and let all of this process before I ask another question. Sex club. Voyeur night. Performers? "You think he wants me to *perform*?"

No. No. No. Garrett didn't actually call me. It's just a coincidence that I stumbled into the club after this meeting, where I was apparently brought up, but still...this isn't right.

"Well," Eden says, placing a hand on my arm. "I think he wants your input. At least that's what Charlie said they were trying to convince him. Not to actually put you in the show, but according to her, he didn't want you involved at all. I think he's a little protective of you."

"What exactly would the performers do?"

Eden doesn't answer, but her eyes get a little wider, and I'm no idiot. I'm not naive or new to any of this. I'm a fucking sex worker myself, but I still can't believe what I'm hearing.

My Garrett owns a sex club and he wants to put on a voyeur event? None of this makes any sense.

"Oh my God," I mutter as I cover my face. "That asshole."

"Geo, I think we're gonna need something stronger," Eden says. Moments later, there's a clear shot sitting in front of me, and I don't even ask what it is before I'm tossing it down my throat. It burns its way down, and I cough up fire before guzzling my water.

"So let me get this straight," she says. "He called you and told you to come up here, but didn't tell you anything else?"

"He didn't call me," I mumble into my hands.

"Oh." Her mouth stays in an O shape before she throws back her own shot. Then she places the shot glass on the table and looks at me with a confused expression. "So why are you here?"

"Did you see what I'm wearing?" I ask. "I'll give you one guess."

One shot and I'm Little Miss Loose Lips.

The O shape of her mouth is back and a little bigger this time. "I was told you're his sister..."

"Stepsister," I reply. I don't even know this girl, and I'm just letting everything out. What the hell is wrong with me? I walked in here thirty minutes ago ready to ask my stepbrother to take my virginity, and suddenly, I don't know what the hell I want. Do I still want that? I feel like he lied to me. What else do I not know about Garrett?

First, it was the incident ten years ago Laura told me about, and now this? Am I kidding myself to believe that anything with

him is real? He keeps so much close to his chest, so why on earth
would I put my own heart at risk and trust him?

"Well...this is interesting."

"I'm sorry. I appreciate you filling me in and saving me from
that room," I say, gesturing back to the gang bang behind the
curtain. "I should go before I just make things weirder."

"Oh, come on," she says casually. "You're already here. Want
a tour?"

I open my mouth to decline, mostly because I still feel like I
shouldn't be here. Then I realize...why shouldn't I? She's right; I
made it through the door. Until Garrett finds me, I'm free to do
whatever I want. And something tells me this woman might be
the best person to get a tour from.

"Can I get another shot first?" I ask.

She smiles. "Just so you know, there's a two-drink limit, but I
get it. We all need liquid courage sometimes."

After throwing back another round of the smoothest vodka
I've ever had, I follow Eden around the second-floor balcony.

"These are the VIP rooms," she says. "They're mostly just a
little nicer than the ones downstairs. A few more *amenities*."

"Okay, this may sound like a stupid question, but what's in
the rooms? Are they just like hotel rooms?"

"Some of them are," she replies. "But the themed ones are
my favorite."

"Themed?"

With a giggle, she leads me toward the elevator at the end of
the hall. "Come on. I'll show you."

"They'll let us in?" I ask as the door closes us into the elevator.

"Oh, I'll do you one better."

I don't know what that means, but I clutch my dress tightly
to keep from letting my fingers fidget in front of me.

The elevator opens to the main room again, but I notice what
looks like a storefront on the right, so I pause in front of it.

"Oh, that's the shop. If you need anything like toys or lingerie or whatever, but the rooms all come equipped with condoms and lube. And some toys."

This is insane. I still can't wrap my head around this being what Garrett does for a living. Why wouldn't he tell me? Did he really think I couldn't handle knowing about his sex club? Sure, I can understand him keeping this secret before, when I was younger, but after the week we've had? We've done everything but screw, and he just happened to omit the fact that he's a sex club owner? It doesn't make sense.

Eden leads me across the main floor, and now there are people dancing in the middle, which does make it appear more like a dance club. I notice things now that I know this isn't just a strip club, like couples sitting awfully close together around the tables and more ominous doors along the walls.

And it occurs to me that there are people behind those doors. And I know what they're doing. But nothing about this place feels raunchy or exploitative. It's not like a strip club, catering to one demographic. I haven't done anything or seen what's behind those doors, but I already feel how liberating it is. How women can walk around alone without feeling watched or like prey.

There's another bar down here, but we don't stop as we pass it toward another black curtain in the corner. There's a bouncer standing near a red rope, and he simply nods at Eden as she approaches.

"She's with me," she tells him, and he nods his head again.

"Renting a room?"

"Nope, just watching tonight."

"You got it. Have fun." He lifts the red rope and pulls the black curtain aside.

Eden takes my hand and smiles as she says, "Ready?"

Ready for what?

It takes me a moment to realize this is the same room I peeked my head in moments ago, before I found the stairs and wandered my dumb ass into the VIP sex room. It's a museum-looking hallway with people randomly staring at the walls like they are dissecting a piece of art. But as we move into the room, and I see what's behind the windows, I realize the art is literally...more people fucking.

Still, my mind doesn't quite register what I'm seeing when I reach the dimly lit window on the right and a woman with a curly brown halo of hair is literally riding a man on a bed.

Blood nearly drains out of my body as I stare at the sight before me. The man is tied to the four corners of the bed, face up, with a blindfold over his eyes and a ball gag in his mouth. In one hand, he is holding something white clutched in his fingers. He can literally not move or speak as this woman rides the ever-loving shit out of him, and I'm not hallucinating; they are literally fucking. It's not some weird strip club show or BDSM presentation.

I can see where he is entering her, the throbbing red skin of his dick where she's bouncing herself on him. Her breasts are being held up by a red corset, but with all of her movement, she's knocked them free of their restraints.

Subtly, I turn my head and stare at the other people watching. There is a man sitting on the bench with another smaller man sitting on his lap. They're both watching with rapt attention as if this is a movie in a theater. And there are definitely people touching each other, movements I didn't catch before, but so obvious now as my eyes adjust.

As one woman turns toward me, I quickly glance away, feeling like I've just broken some unspoken rule about eye contact in the porn room.

"Isn't it amazing?" Eden whispers, leaning in from behind me. Goose bumps erupt along my neck from the feel of her breath against my skin.

"Garrett did this?" I ask.

"Yep. This is his creation. It's everyone's favorite."

I glance down the hall, and she takes my hand again, leading us down to the darker windows. There's no one renting these rooms, but I can see through the darkness that there are different setups: an office, a throne room, and a BDSM room with whips and floggers lining the wall.

"I can't believe he did this."

"Turns out everyone has a little voyeur in them," she whispers as we pause in front of a room two women just entered.

And he calls me an exhibitionist. Just watching the women get started in the room, my body tingles with excitement. Not with the idea of watching them, but with the idea of being on the other side of that glass. Knowing that others are watching. Completely exposed.

"You're thinking about being in there, aren't you?" she whispers next to me.

Turning toward her, I nod.

"Well, find that man of yours and get him to take you. I would if I could." With a wink, she smiles at me and runs her hand up my arm. If she only knew I haven't even had sex with a man, let alone a woman. If it wasn't for Garrett, I might have let her.

Would he even go into that room with me?

I don't have to wait long for that answer. Glancing toward the staff entrance on the other end of the hall, I'm staring into his angry blue eyes.

Rule #22: Fuck.

Garrett

Fuck. Fuck. Fuck.

Why is Mia standing in the voyeur hall with Eden *fucking* St. Claire?

This can't be happening. I remember what happened six months ago when Emerson nearly lost his girlfriend to Madame Kink herself. Not that Mia is my girlfriend…but she's still mine.

My mind goes entirely blank as I storm across the hallway toward her with one echoing thought: *Get her the hell out of here. Now.*

Somewhere in the mess of my thoughts, I remind myself to do it as discreetly as possible. As I grab her arm, she lets me tow her out in a quick shuffle toward the curtain that leads to the staff hallway, but the moment we're through it, where there is absolutely *no* public sex taking place, she yanks her arm out of my grasp.

"Let me go," she snaps, rushing down the hall and away from me.

"What the fuck are you doing here?" I whisper as I chase after her. She ignores me as she stomps away, but when I see her heading toward the wrong door, the one that would lead her back to the voyeur hallway, I grab her by the waist and haul her back.

I press her against the wall to stop her from evading me again. "Answer me, Mia. What the hell are you doing in my club?"

"Your club? You mean your *sex* club? How could you never tell me this?"

"Because I never expected you to come here," I argue.

"Let me go," she argues back, pushing away from me, but I can't let her leave yet. I'm still blindsided by her even being here, and I need to just talk to her. I don't want her to leave angry like this.

And then I fully take in what she's wearing. It's a skin-tight, short-as-fuck minidress made of shimmery metallic fabric that accentuates every curve of her body.

"What…are you wearing?"

"Oh, you want to control my clothes too?"

I corner her until her back is against the wall and my knee is pressed between her legs. "When you come into *my* club, you better believe I'm going to control you. Your tits are hanging out, Mia."

"Yeah, *my* tits," she replies, jutting her chin up toward me, and the sinister side of me loses control. I love when she pushes back, challenges me, stands up, and picks a fight. So I tug her hair, angling her face upward as I lean in for a harsh kiss. My hand wraps around her lower back as I drag her body against me. She only fights for a second, her fists pounding against my chest right before she melts into my arms.

Shoving her against the wall, I lift her dress up just a couple of inches, so I can pull one of her legs around me. God I missed having her in my arms, feeling her soft skin in my hands, and molding her chest to mine. She must have missed me too because she's stopped fighting and she's moaning into my mouth now, pulling me closer.

"You don't fight fair," she whispers against my mouth.

I reply with my fingers, running them up the inside of her thigh until I reach the moist fabric of her panties. "Are you wet from watching those people fucking?"

She tenses before pulling away from the kiss. "No, no, no. I'm mad at you."

The more she tries to get away, the more I fight to hold her. It feels liberating here, away from the lake house and our parents and the reminders that we shouldn't be doing this.

She finally fights her way out of my hold. "Garrett, I'm serious. I'm mad at you."

"Why?" I ask.

"Because you lied to me. And because you led me on at the lake house. Played with me and made me..."

"Made you what?" I ask with a teasing smile.

"Made me like you, dammit!"

God, she's cute when she's angry. Even as she slaps me hard across my face.

"I get that complaint a lot," I reply smugly.

She shoves me against my chest again with a frustrated grunt.

"All right, then if you want to leave, leave."

She juts her chin up at me obstinately. "No, I don't want to leave. I want to..."

"Want to what? What the fuck did you come here for in the first place?"

As her mouth opens to reply, she pauses. "Forget it." She shoves against me again, moving toward the door. I stop her by moving my body in front of hers.

"Come on now, what was it?"

"You know what it was," she mutters without looking me in the eyes.

"I think I do, but say it, just so I know we're on the same page."

"I want you to fuck me, Garrett!" she yells, and I do my best to keep the smile off my face, but I'm only a man after all, and that was both adorable and sexy as fuck at the same time.

She shoves me again. "I can't believe you knew what I wanted and then made me say it anyway."

"And what about what we said yesterday? That we're done playing. Remember?"

"You know what?" she says, lifting her chin. "You're right. I'm in a sex club after all. I'm sure I can find someone else to do it for me. I bet Eden could."

With that, she spins on her heels and walks toward the door again. I know she's full of shit, and arguing is just what we do, but I refuse to let her play that game with me.

"Like hell you are," I bellow, hoisting her short frame up by the waist and tossing her over my shoulder. She puts up a little fight, but it's unconvincing. If she wants down, she'll fight her way down. Mia can be mad at me all she wants, but she's not getting away from me. And she knows it.

"Where are you taking me?" She squeals as I carry her down the long hallway.

"You're done being a brat, Mia," I tell her as we reach the door that leads to the rooms along the other side of the building.

And I realize as we reach the first door on the left that Mia has left me with no choice. This is what she wants, and all the reasons we shouldn't do this have been overshadowed by the image of her in the voyeur hall with Eden.

I set her down inside the room, and she looks around before gazing up at me. Of course, I didn't bring her to just any room. I brought her to the one with large mirrors on every wall and even on the ceiling.

"This is what you want, isn't it? If you want to back out, here's your chance."

She takes one look at me and then she jumps into my arms, wrapping her arms around my neck and latching on to my lips with her own.

I bury my hands into her hair at the nape of her neck and kiss her with wild energy and frantic need. Pulling her bottom lip between my teeth, I pinch the tender flesh just to hear her yelp into my mouth. And just as I expected, she bites me back like I wanted her to, nipping my lip between her teeth so hard it hurts. We are a frenzy of gnashing teeth and tangled tongues, my hands in her hair and hers gripping the jacket of my suit in her fists.

As I shove her against the wall, I grind my aching cock against her, already leaking at the tip just at the thought of being inside her. The moment Hunter told me she was in the club, my dick started throbbing. By the time I reached her, it was painfully hard.

She hums into my mouth as I yank up the bottom of her dress, feeling the lacy panties underneath. I let out a growl when she eagerly spreads her legs for me. My hands hook under her thighs, and she clings easily to my body as I grind against her again. I want to tear my cock out and fuck her right here and now, against the wall, but I refrain. As badly as I need this, I can't hurt her.

Her eagerness is obvious as she fumbles with the buttons of my shirt. She shoves my jacket off my shoulders, then starts on the buttons while I'm sliding her dress straps down to find her waiting tits. It's not long before I have one in my mouth, so soft and beautiful between my teeth.

Fuck, I need her. There is no stopping us now.

My patience runs out quickly, and I can't take another second of foreplay. I quickly carry her to the bed and drop her onto the soft mattress, staring down at her as I slip each button through the holes of my shirt and shrug it off in a rush. She's pulling her dress over her head and unclasping her bra as I'm removing my pants, and before I know it, we're both naked and I'm climbing over her body with my swollen dick between us.

My head is spinning when her lush thighs embrace me around my waist. And as her warm hand wraps around my cock, the room around us disappears.

I'm rutting against her, my shaft seeking out the comfort of her body like it knows that's where it belongs. Those beautiful, thick thighs are tight around my waist, and I'm resting comfortably in the warmth of her legs.

My mouth doesn't leave her body, not for a second. It can't. Because if I stop, I'll realize what a bad idea this is. I'll remember that this moment is fleeting, and even if she's letting me touch her now, when we're both done here, she'll leave and go back to hating me again.

So I shut off my brain and slide my hands down, over her full breasts and soft stomach to the sweet aching center between her legs. When I dip my finger between her folds, I find her dripping, and it makes me moan so low and loud against her neck that I'm practically growling.

"You're so wet for me." God, I want to use her pet name at this moment, but I can't give myself away. Because from here on out, there is no Drake. After tonight, she'll forget all about him.

"Then, fuck me, Garrett. I'm ready." Pulling my face to hers, she stares at me with a serious, pleading expression.

"I'll get a condom."

"I have an IUD," she whispers against my lips. "I want to feel you. Please."

My body is on fire, goose bumps erupting all over every inch of my skin, more turned on by that one little plea than I've ever been in my life. She has me so wrapped up in her at the moment that I'd do literally anything for her.

Mia has always been mine. Even if it wasn't always like this, it was always meant to come to this. I know that's true, so I slide the head of my cock just a few inches into her wet heat, watching her face as I do.

She flinches when I reach resistance, and her gaze focuses on the mirrored ceiling behind me. I freeze, the head of my cock just barely pressed inside her.

"Mia," I say, bringing her attention to my face. "Eyes on me."

Those beautiful blue eyes I've known for almost half my life gaze into my soul with only trust as I thrust my cock in, piercing her tightness and sliding until I'm all the way inside.

She squeals, but she never takes her eyes off of mine. I stare at her with my mouth hanging open, amazed at how right this feels and how beautiful she is and how much I want to stay here forever.

Sweet Jesus, I've missed this. I've been so focused on this being her first time that I barely register how long it's been for me. And how even ten years ago, with some nameless woman I don't remember, it never felt like this.

Everything about this with Mia is better. The warmth of her body, the feel of her legs holding me close, the bond burning brightly between us as we gaze into each other's eyes, connected by more than just our bodies.

"Fuck, you feel so good," I whisper. I wish she knew how big this moment is for me. How long I've waited to feel this. I don't move, remaining buried inside her and savoring the sensation without seeking friction, although the craving to move is getting intense.

Her fingers reach down to the place where our bodies are fused, running over the base of my cock to where it disappears between her folds. I watch her face as she explores, shifting her hips to accommodate me, and with each small movement of her body, I fight the urge to thrust.

"Does it hurt?" I ask.

"Burns a little, but not bad."

Leaning down, I kiss her pretty pink lips, softer than before. Not out of need but out of want. Because I love the taste of her lips, and I want to pretend for a moment that I'm not so fucked up in the head and could be the guy for her. She finally pulls away from the kiss and latches her hands around my neck.

"Garrett," she murmurs, staring up at me with lust in her hooded gaze, "fuck me now."

"You want it hard?"

Biting her lip, she nods.

Losing control, I grab the headboard in one hand, bracing myself with the other, and I slam into her, watching her face. She cries out in a breathy exhalation of pleasure, mouth open and head back, and I pound inside her again.

Her moans are sweet and loud, her nails digging into my neck and shoulder. I have to force myself not to come too soon because everything is perfect. Her voice, her face, the way her tits move with my thrusts, and the tight welcoming heat of her body.

"More," she pleads. Our bodies move in perfect unison, and the look on her face and the pacing of her breaths tell me she's getting close.

I'm not ready to be done with her yet, though. I don't think I'll ever be done. At this point, I'll never want to pull out of her.

Shifting back to my knees, I pull her legs up to my shoulders and continue my thrusts, watching the way her expression changes with this new position.

"Right there, right there, right there," she chants in a low whisper.

Our eyes meet while I'm buried deep inside her, and it's so fucking surreal how right this feels. I've never felt this close to a woman I was fucking, let alone looked in their damn eyes like this.

"Please don't stop," she whispers. Reaching down, I strum the sensitive nub of her clit. She hums and squirms, and I know she's getting close.

"Come with me, baby."

"Oh God, I'm gonna come," she shrieks in a breathy cry. And I fuck her hard and fast, losing sense of everything else in the room but her and me and the feeling of her tight heat around my cock.

It's the sound of her orgasm that finally does me in. She screams, throaty and guttural, as her back arches, her nails biting the sheets in her fists and the muscles of her legs tensing over my shoulders. I stare down at the place where we are connected as I come, spilling into her over and over and over and, just like that, ending the longest ten years of celibacy with the last person in the world I should be with.

But she said she was saving herself for me, and maybe I was saving myself for her too. Not literally, of course. Three weeks ago, I wouldn't have dreamed of doing this with Mia, but I was resigned to never feeling like this with a woman again, and all along, I had no idea I could feel it with her.

As we both come down, I release her legs from my shoulders and collapse onto the bed next to her. I'm waiting for her to climb out of the bed, put her clothes on, and leave me again. What I don't expect is her turning her head toward me and saying, "How long before we can do it again?"

Rule #23: If you're mad, stay mad. The sex is better that way.

Mia

WHY THE HELL DID I WAIT SO LONG TO DO THIS? WHAT ON EARTH was I so hung up on? We're clearly both making up for lost time, since we're on our third round in the mirror room. I have no idea what time it is, but if we walk out of this club in the daylight, I wouldn't be surprised.

His hand finds my chin and lifts it up, so I'm faced with our reflection in the mirror, him pounding into me from behind. He doesn't like when I look away or close my eyes. The connection between us is stronger when our gazes are locked. And that makes everything feel better.

"You look so good taking my cock," he says with a groan, gripping my hips tightly in his fingers. "I could watch this all day."

"Don't stop!" I scream, reaching down to touch myself. With just a few circular strums of my clit and his relentless pounding, I come undone. He's not far behind, slamming in once, twice, three more times before he groans loudly and fills me for the third time tonight.

My hands are aching from my tight hold on the headboard,

and I start to sag before Garrett wraps his fingers around my throat and hauls me backward, so I'm pressed against his chest.

"I can't stop thinking about you leaking my cum all night," he mumbles darkly against my ear as we gaze into the mirror together.

A wicked smile spreads across my face as he runs his tongue along my cheek, just another way for Garrett to mark me as his. And I hate my stupid heart for getting attached.

I shove away from him and feel him slide out of me. "I'm still mad at you."

He laughs as he reclines on the bed, folding his hands behind his head. "That's fine. You can stay mad at me. I think the sex is better this way."

"I think you're right, so it's a good thing I hate you." As I try to climb off the bed for the first time in hours, my knees wobble and I almost go down to the floor. I quickly grab onto the headboard to steady myself, and without fail, that first drop of warm moisture makes its way down my thigh.

Okay, that's not the most pleasant thing. But I still don't regret not using a condom. I trust Garrett is clean, and I really am on birth control. I had an IUD implanted last year, *just in case*. Glad all that discomfort didn't go to waste.

Grabbing a few tissues from the table, I quickly clean myself up. Then, because I'm nosey, I start poking around the room. The bedside table comes equipped with cleaning wipes, lube, condoms, and bottles of water, one of which I eagerly grab and gulp down. There's a cabinet against the wall, and when I open it, my eyes go wide. Inside are straps, ropes, and chains of every shape and size.

"They're for these," he says, and I turn around to watch him flip open the top of the footboard to reveal steel rings on either side.

"Oh," I reply. "How...clever."

"There are a lot of *clever* things in the club." He gives me a quick, Garrett-esque wink, and I quickly turn away so he doesn't see me blushing. I'm still mad at him for fuck's sake.

"So are you going to tell me about this *event* everyone seems to think you called me about?"

His brow furrows. "They told you about that?"

My shoulders sag as I glare at him. "Apparently, you were talking about me at your staff meeting. So what did you say?"

"That you're a camgirl. Is that still a secret?" he teases me.

"I can't believe this whole time you were keeping this secret and I felt so embarrassed about you finding out about my job."

Thinking about my job has me thinking about Drake, but I shove the thought of him away. I don't need to think about him right now. I'll have to tell him about this, and I'm not sure how that's going to go. He knows we're not exclusive, but still...he could be upset to learn I've slept with Garrett.

"So are you going to ask me to perform too?" I ask, although I know the answer.

"Oh, fuck no," he replies, and I feel the smile creeping across my face.

"It's not like I'm your girlfriend."

He climbs off the bed, his naked body on full display, and I blush at the sight of him like this.

"No, but you are still my stepsister." He's standing inches away from me, gazing down with those dark blue eyes. Something about him calling me that has my stomach doing flips, and I'm not proud of that. I probably shouldn't like the idea of being his stepsister and fuck buddy at the same time, but I do like it. I guess I just like the idea of meaning *more* to him than just another girl.

"I'm going home," I mumble, searching the floor for my dress.

"Did you drive?"

"Took an Uber," I reply.

"Let me drive you home."

"You don't have—"

He glares at me. "No one should have to take an Uber after losing their virginity."

I can't help but laugh as I slide my panties up my legs. Bending down to get my shoes, my knees almost give out, and I glance up at him. "Yeah, maybe you should."

"Text my mom that you're staying at my place. Come home with me. It's closer anyway."

"No, I'm going home," I argue, albeit weakly.

"I'll make you breakfast," he says with a sly grin. "Just after I've had mine."

My knees wobble again. *Motherfucker.*

After we're dressed, we leave the mirrored room and head straight down the hallway. We stop at the end of the hall, and he touches my arm.

"Wait here. I'm going to tell Emerson I'm leaving and make sure we get a cleaning crew in the room before it's opened again."

"Okay," I reply before letting out a heavy yawn. And as I watch him disappear, I curse myself again. I'm letting myself get attached to the idea of Garrett being serious about me, but I know better, and I know in his head, he's still not going to get serious. It's still just *playing.*

As I'm texting Laura that I'm crashing at Garrett's place in the city after drinking with some friends, I feel a tall man approaching.

"Ready?" I ask, but when I glance up, I realize it's not Garrett. It's an even taller man with long blond hair pulled into a ponytail. "Oh, sorry. Thought you were someone else."

He laughs. "Have a good night, gorgeous."

I find myself blushing as he passes by, and when I see Garrett coming down the hallway toward me, there's a worried expression on his face.

"Everything okay?"

He glances at the blond man disappearing through the door before nodding. "Yeah. Let's go."

Lying in bed that night, I can't sleep. Garrett's restless next to me, tossing and turning too. The entire sex-club experience is playing on repeat in my head, and for a moment, I feel like I stepped into an alternate reality.

Every time I close my eyes, I see everything. The woman in the voyeur hall riding that man like a mechanical bull, but not in a gross, orgy-porn-scene way either. It wasn't meant for anyone else's enjoyment but their own, and there I stood...watching them. I mean...other people were watching them too. Including two men grinding against each other as they watched.

But nothing about it felt...wrong. Well, okay, it felt a little wrong but in a...good way?

I flip over again, trying to gather my thoughts into something that makes sense in my head.

"Are you awake?" I whisper.

"I thought you were mad at me," he mumbles.

"I am, but I have questions."

With a groan, he turns onto his back and drapes an arm over his eyes. "Ask away."

"All right, so obviously...people have sex there."

"Naturally."

"And up in the VIP area, they just do it out in the open?"

"Only in the VIP room, yes," he replies like it's the most normal thing.

"So what's the craziest thing you've seen there?" I ask with excitement.

He chuckles lowly. Then, he makes a face as if he's thinking hard about it. "Well, we've only been open for three months, but we did have a party of five rent the biggest voyeur room a couple weeks ago."

"Five?"

"Yep. You want to hear the crazy part?"

My eyes widen. "Yes," I reply eagerly.

"There was only one woman."

My jaw hangs down again. "Oh my God! Did you watch them?"

He scratches the back of his neck like he's a little embarrassed. "It was probably the best thing I've ever seen."

I laugh even louder, slapping him on the arm. "You perv!"

"What? It's literally my job! And why am I a perv if they clearly wanted an audience?"

"I can't believe you watched four guys rail one chick. That's crazy!"

"You're just jealous," he replies, and my smile stretches.

"Yeah, you're kinda right," I say with a giggle.

"Sometimes I forget how young you are."

My smile fades a little as I stare at him. "I can handle it. I'm not that young."

He pauses, glancing at me through the darkness. Then he reaches over and curls a lock of my hair behind my ear. "I know you're not, Mia. To be honest, sometimes I'm caught between wanting to keep you innocent and wanting to corrupt you."

My heart dances in my chest at the thought. "What's your plan for the voyeur night?" I ask.

He lets out a heavy sigh. "Three couples and three single female performers."

"But you're just going to have them onstage?"

"Yep."

"Aren't you worried about what people in the audience will be doing?"

He laughs. "Not really. We have rules. If they don't want to stay for the entire performance, they can excuse themselves. That's sort of the idea. We want them to rent out the rooms while they're there to get the full experience."

"It seems weird to me. People screwing onstage like that."

"Says the girl who masturbates on camera for money," he teases, nudging my arm with his.

"I do more than that."

"Sure," he grunts. "Can I go to sleep now?" he asks.

"Yeah," I mumble as I toss and turn again.

"Come here, brat." He reaches over and hooks an arm around my middle, hauling me into his arms, so I can't move anymore. Being wrapped in his warmth is enough to have me falling into the dark abyss of sleep.

The last thought that drifts through my mind before I go under is the reminder that I just lost my virginity...to my stepbrother...in a sex club. This is really not at all how I saw this summer going.

Rule #24: There's only one way to have a truly good morning.

Mia

I wake up to the scent of Garrett and the sensation of something warm and wet against my chest and stomach. Moaning, I peel my eyes open and suddenly everything that happened last night comes crashing to the forefront of my mind.

"Oh my God," I whisper. I'm in Garrett's bed, and he's currently trailing his lips down my body.

"Good morning," he replies.

Lifting my head, I watch as he plants kisses along my thighs before gently tugging my panties down my legs, leaving me in nothing but one of his T-shirts.

"Is this okay?" he asks, and his warm breath kisses the sensitive skin between my legs, goose bumps erupting all over my body.

"Yes," I gasp, my legs falling open for him.

Then his fingers are there, gently pulling my lips apart to get a good look at me. I love the look of appreciation in his eyes, as if he's admiring my sex like it's the best thing he's ever seen. He plants a soft, wet kiss against my clit, and I moan from the contact.

God, I'm so glad I decided to go to his club last night.

And that's the only thought in my head as he runs his tongue from my ass all the way up to my clit. He does that a couple more times, until it becomes too intense. My head falls back with a whimper, my thighs shaking under his strong hold.

"No, no, no." He growls against my sex. "Look at me, Mia. I want you watching me as I make you come."

My breath hitches again, but I don't take my gaze off him as he devours me. He's not rushed or frantic, stroking my clit with slow, soft laps of his tongue. The delicate friction is enough to drive me mad.

When he picks up speed, burying his face between my legs and squeezing my thighs tightly, my body clenches in anticipation of my approaching climax.

Grasping his hair in my hands, I grind myself against his mouth. "Don't stop, Garrett," I cry out. "I'm almost there."

He takes that as his cue to pick up speed and intensity, and the next thing I know, I'm riding a fierce wave of pleasure. My thighs clench around his head, and he growls loudly against me until my body starts tingling and my heart feels like it's going to pound its way out of my chest.

But even as I come down from this high, he doesn't stop. I'm gasping for air and squirming in his grasp while he continues to torture me with his tongue.

"Garrett, it's too much!" I squeal, my clit so sensitive it almost hurts.

When I grab his hair to pull him away, he doesn't budge. Finally, he pulls his mouth off my body and looks up at me. "Listen to me. As long as I'm down here, you won't stop me, understand? This is the only place I want to be. Now, come on. You can give me one more."

With that, he dives back in, assaulting me with his talented tongue and gifted lips. I can hardly breathe as he sucks and licks and nibbles all of my most sensitive spots. But when he slowly slips a finger into my slick heat, I swear I see stars.

The sounds that come out of me while he thrusts his finger in and out are not anything I've ever heard before. Forget watching him at this point—I can barely keep my eyes open. And I'm shocked when another orgasm hits me like a bomb going off between my legs. It's not a slow escalation, but a sudden attack of pleasure, and I let out a scream this time. My back arches and my legs tremble, and when I finally come down, I beg him to stop.

"I can't take it anymore, Garrett! Please!"

He chuckles as he lifts up this time, wiping his mouth. "You can take it."

Before he can drop his mouth back to my clit, I desperately pull at his shirt, bringing him down until he's fully lying on me, and I kiss his mouth with eagerness. My legs wrap around his waist, and although I am entirely spent, I'm still hungry for his touch.

He kisses me back, grinding his hips against me, soaking the front of his pajamas with my arousal. I fumble with the drawstring, trying to get them off of him.

A moment later, he's sliding easily into me, and it's nothing like the climax I just felt from his tongue. It's different and so much better. The impact of his cock pounding inside me, reaching places I didn't know existed, giving me pleasure not even the best toy I own could find.

And I know what it is. Maybe he doesn't want to admit it, but I know that what I'm feeling when Garrett fucks me is a connection you don't get over a webcam or with an object. This is visceral and pure.

Our eyes meet just before he comes, and I squeeze him tighter. As if this one embrace could convey to him that I don't hate him at all. I'm not mad at him and I don't want to fight with him. I wish I could tell him, in more words than I expressed last night, just how much he means to me.

If he knew, if he *really* knew, would it change anything? Would he give us a real shot, or would he keep me as just a plaything? A fuck buddy? A stepsister with benefits?

Before he pulls out, I drag his face down to press my lips to his again, tasting myself on his mouth. And all the things I want to say are on my lips, but I leave them unspoken. If I admit my feelings to him, I'm the vulnerable one, and then what? Face the humiliation of being rejected…again.

Instead, I whisper against his mouth, "You were right."

Confusion colors his expression. "About what?"

"Sex is relaxing," I reply as every muscle in my body melts into the bed.

A smile tugs at the corners of his mouth as he rests his weight on me.

Eventually, he does pull out. Then he's climbing off the bed, getting dressed, and driving me home. And just like that, things between us feel no better than they were yesterday.

"So…if I did need some help with the event," he says before I can climb out of the car at the house. I turn back and wait for him to finish his request.

"Yes?"

"You'll help me?"

"How are you going to pay me?" I ask in a teasing tone.

"Come back to the club. Just give me some warning this time."

With an eye roll, I open my car door. "Fine. I'll text you later."

"Fine," he replies, smacking my ass as I climb out.

The moment I'm alone in my house, I think about Drake, and I have a strange urge to talk to him. To tell him everything, which is *insane*, but he knows I have feelings for Garrett. He doesn't seem so possessive that I can't tell him about my sex life.

I mean, he knows I can't save myself for him. He won't even show me his face.

Then I remember how I left things yesterday, and I guess the least I can do is apologize for the weird way I acted.

Pulling up the messages, I type one out.

I'm sorry about the weird way I acted yesterday.

He responds right away.

Don't apologize. You were right. Are you feeling better now?

I bite my lip as I think about just how much better I'm feeling.

Yes. Much better.

Any specific reason you're feeling so good? he asks.

We had sex last night. My stepbrother and me.

God, please don't be mad, I pray.

I'm happy for you. How was it?

I laugh.

It was amazing. Three times and once this morning.

Is it weird that I tell you this stuff?

No. I like when you tell me this stuff. I can't explain why.

Good, I reply. **I like telling you.**

Then, I put together my next text carefully, biting my bottom lip between my teeth as I do. At some point in the last few days, the scales have tipped in Garrett's favor. Even as he dismissed me as just being something physical and tried to cut me off completely after the lake house, I still knew that it would be him over Drake.

I hope you know this means that you and I can't really do what we used to do.

A few long minutes go by while I wait for his response. When the typing bubbles pop up, I struggle to breathe.

I'm proud of you for that decision. And I understand.

I was thinking I'd still like to send you a gift. Can I do that?

I smile at the screen, but then my smile falters. Is this wrong? To accept gifts from another man after sleeping with Garrett? I mean, in his own words, we're just playing. It's just physical. As long as he's not going to commit to me, I guess that means I can still do whatever I want.

Plus, this still sort of counts as work.

Yeah. I have a PO box.

Will you send it to me, please?

So I do. And I bite back the guilt that follows. I should really tell Garrett about this, but then I remember he never told me he owned a sex club, so fuck him. He can get over me having one pen pal. Who sends me gifts. And sometimes sees me naked.

Okay, he would be pissed, but still…he owes me. And it's not like we're dating for real.

Don't worry, he says. What I'm sending you, you can use with him.

Now that has my curiosity piqued.

Rule #25: It's the thought that counts.

Mia

GARRETT DIDN'T TEXT ME LAST NIGHT. AND WHEN I MESSAGED him, he gave me a generic excuse about being busy, and it was starting to worry me. So here I stand, on his doorstep with donuts and coffee.

"Morning!" I chirp as his door opens.

"What are you doing here?" he asks, looking confused. He's in his running shorts and a tight T-shirt, looking too fucking good.

"You asked me to help with the event, so here I am." I smile, holding up a dozen donuts.

"You're annoying, you know that?"

"Yep," I reply with a smile as I push past him.

His dining room table is scattered with papers and notes, and it looks like the dishes desperately need to be done. I set the box down on the table, finding an empty space, and start tidying up the mess he's made.

"Stop it," he mutters stubbornly.

"Come on, Garrett. I'm just trying to help, so let me help. I've got nothing better to do."

"You're not working?" he asks, and it's the first time he's brought up my job, so I spin on him, not quite sure how to answer that. I'm not going to tell him about Drake, since he's not really a patron anymore anyway. I don't charge him.

"Not at the moment. Why? Are you jealous?"

"No," he mutters. He can't exactly keep me from working as long as he's not going to make us official. Rounding the kitchen island, I help myself to napkins, and when I turn around to get a donut, I catch him watching me.

"Stop staring, you creep," I tease him. He finally lets out a smile as he drops into his chair in front of his laptop.

"Okay, what are you stuck on?"

"I don't know." He groans. "Nothing feels right. These girls are all great, but it's not right for Salacious."

"Let me see," I reply, bringing over another chair and sitting next to him. The girl on screen is beautiful, but she's all plastic and he's right—it's not right for Salacious.

"Not her," I say, shaking my head at the girl on his screen.

"Why not?"

"She relies too much on her body and big tits. You need someone with a more genuine personality. A real performer."

He groans again, slumping against the back of his chair. "We only have two weeks to figure this out. I'm just going to cancel."

"Don't say that. We'll figure it out."

"Emerson says we need an event to bring more attention to the voyeur hall, but nothing about this is going to bring in more members if it doesn't match the tone of the club."

Turning toward him, I lean back in my chair.

"Garrett, most of these girls perform just for men. Just like I do, but that's not what your club is about. Salacious is for everyone, men and women."

"So what do we do?" he asks, and I chew on the inside of my lip as I think. And I try to imagine what I would like, not as a camgirl, but as just a girl.

"You're trying to bring in more clientele, but you're catering this event for the wrong audience."

How do we make this event more inviting for the women and not just the men? Naturally, wherever the women go, the men will follow anyway. And then it dawns on me. In a rush, I sit up, excited with my idea.

"What?" he asks, sitting up straighter too.

"Don't invite their fans… Invite the performers."

"I thought that's what we were doing," he replies, looking confused.

"No, I mean…invite the performers to be members, Garrett. You can make it a big event just for them and invite them to use the rooms, but treat *them* like your VIPs."

His shoulders relax as he stares at me, and I see the stress melting off his face as the idea sinks in. "Holy shit. You're right. That's fucking genius. The event won't be a performance by them. It'll be a performance *for* them."

"And when they love it there, they'll become members and tell their fans."

"Oh my God, I could kiss you," he says, bursting from his chair. Suddenly, he's hoisting me off the chair and carrying me to the bedroom.

"We still have so much work to do!" I shout in a fit of giggles, but he's not hearing a word of it.

When I open my PO box that afternoon, I find a discreet black package waiting for me. It's rectangular and about the size of a box a cell phone might come in, but I already know before even opening it that that's not what's inside.

I got your gift, I text Drake in the car before heading for home.

Good, he replies instantly. Take it home and show it to me.

"Oh God," I groan without responding. I don't open the box until I get back to the house. Slipping into the basement when I get there, I close the door behind me and drop the black box on the coffee table and pull out my phone to message Drake.

Okay, I'm home.

Video on, he replies.

Propping my phone up on the stand, I take a deep breath as I hit the video call button. He answers right away, but he keeps his video off.

Through the chat, he says, I'm at work and can't show my video right now, but I want to see you open it.

"Okay," I reply, curling my hair behind my ear. "I'm nervous."

Don't be. I think you're going to love it.

First, I tear the tape, keeping the box closed, and pull out a prettier box inside. This one has a black ribbon that I pull to open the lid. As I peel it open, my breath catches on the glass dome, shaped with a bright gem on one end and pointed at the other.

It's a...

"Oh my God," I stammer, closing the box. "Are you serious?"

Yes, he replies without hesitation.

"I can't put this is in. Drake...I just started having sex and now you want me to do anal. I can't."

It's just a plug, kitten. It can't hurt you.

Plus, I'm not asking you to do anal. I'm just showing you something else that will feel good.

"How do you know? Have *you* tried it?" I ask with sarcasm.

Can't say that I have.

Now listen, he says. There's lube in the box too. You need to use that.

"Oh my God." I groan again. "Then what? Just wear it for fun?"

Put it in before you see him again. Surprise him with it.

"Because it's hot?"

Yes. Very, he replies.

"I'm nervous," I say hesitantly.

Don't be. It's just a toy. Have a little fun with it.

I am going to the club in a couple hours to meet Garrett and go over the plans with Emerson. But can I really wear this the whole time?

Of course I can. I am not the same girl I was three weeks ago. Being with Garrett, letting him watch me and finding my voice to really ask for what I want with him, has changed me. I used to be so afraid of being physically vulnerable with men, but I'm not afraid anymore.

Rule #26: When you're on top, you're in control.

Garrett

"Was Mia at the club the other day?"

I look up from my laptop to see Emerson leaning against the doorframe. "Um…maybe. Who told you that?"

"I heard it from Charlotte who heard it from Eden." There is a smug grin threatening to show itself on his face, so I focus back on the contracts for the event, instead of leveling him with a petty glare.

"Well, go ahead," I mutter.

"Go ahead what?"

"Say you told me so."

He laughs. "I'm not sure it's something I should rub in your face. I'm glad you two have made up, that's all."

"Well, she still hates me," I reply, leaning back in my chair and looking up at him.

"Even after five hours in room twelve?"

"Yep. Turns out sex is better that way. When we hate each other."

"Hmm," he replies, deliberating this idea, and I can tell he doesn't believe me.

Not that he should. The hate part isn't real. It's just the convenient lie I tell myself to avoid what's really going on...which is that I'm getting in too deep.

"How is the event planning going?" he asks, noticing the contract on my computer.

"I wanted to talk to you about that, actually. Mia had a fantastic idea that I want to run by you."

As I detail everything Mia and I discussed, he looks impressed.

"I think that's fucking genius," he replies. "I told you it would be smart to bring her on."

"You said you weren't going to say 'I told you so,'" I reply with a crooked smile.

"Couldn't help myself." He lingers in the doorway before adding, "You should get a room with her."

My head turns in his direction. "Excuse me?"

"You said it yourself, we need something fresh in the hall, so get a room with her. Or put her in one alone. Or with Eden."

"Let me stop you right there," I interrupt him.

"What? She's a sex worker herself. Why are you—"

"Please don't say that," I reply, rubbing my forehead.

"What? Call her a sex worker? That's what she is. There's no shame in it."

"I know there's no shame, but I mean...how would you feel if it was Charlie? Flashing her puss—"

"Watch it," he barks.

"My point exactly."

He rolls his eyes before nodding. "Well, there's a difference. You just said things between you and Mia are casual. Unless it's not..."

I don't reply as I stare at the computer screen, not focusing on anything, allowing that thought to permeate. I know why it bothers me, and he knows too. I just don't know if I'm ready to admit it yet.

"Speaking of," he says, and I glance up at the security camera on the wall that shows the front desk, and there she is. Unmistakable silvery-blond hair styled perfectly to hang around her shoulders. She's in a snug dress that accentuates her curves and makes my mouth water because I can already feel her full breasts in my hands and picture how her ass moves when I pound into her from behind.

And I know exactly what she's hiding under that dress. Am I a devious asshole for doing this? Encouraging her to wear that plug as Drake, so I can see it for myself as Garrett? Probably.

"Finish event planning later," Emerson says with a subtle laugh.

I pop out of my office chair, practically ready to sprint to the front of the club to catch her before she accidentally falls into the wrong hands or *someone* talks to her.

But as I make my way down the hall toward the main room entrance, I feel Emerson on my heels.

"Where the fuck are you going?" I ask.

"To say hello," he replies.

"Fuck off. No, you're not."

He's wearing a wicked grin as he pulls open the main room door. "Will you calm down? Charlotte's at the bar, and I want to introduce her."

My heels practically skid against the floor as I stop him and press a hand to his chest. "No. You can't."

"What? Why?"

"Because Mia is not my girlfriend. I've made that very clear. We don't need to introduce them or act like they can be close friends now." Besides, I know my stepsister, and for as long as I can remember, she's been wary of making female friends, stemming from the way those catty bitches treated her on her gymnastics team.

"Too late," he replies, nodding toward the bar across the room, where Little Miss Social-and-Outgoing Charlie and Eden are already chatting it up with my fucking stepsister. And to my surprise, Mia looks...okay. She's smiling at the bartender, laughing with the other women, and not looking as uncomfortable as I expected her to be.

I watch her for a moment before crossing the room to greet her, and I watch the way her expression changes when she notices me coming. The way her eyes graze over my body, admiring my suit. And if I'm not mistaken, there's something else there too… almost like she's glad to see me.

"Hi." I greet her, but I don't touch her, not yet.

"Hi," she replies, sticking to the rules.

"You ready?" I ask, and she doesn't even look uncomfortable as she nods at me.

"Yep." Of course, Mia wouldn't even be bothered by people knowing she's about to have sex with her stepbrother.

"Wait, you're taking her already? I just got to meet her!" Charlie whines as she weaves her arm through Mia's.

"I'm taking her," I state, pulling her away.

"Fine. Have fun," Charlie jokes with sarcasm. "And I'm sure I'll see you again."

"It was nice to meet you," Mia replies, waving back at the group as I drag her across the room.

We don't speak as I guide her to room twenty-two, and even before I unlock the door, my spine is buzzing with excitement, my cock swelling in my pants, ready to see her expression when we enter.

Standing in the doorway, she gasps as she sees what I consider the most physically adventurous room we have. In the corner, a swing hangs from the ceiling. The bed is more of a platform, firmer than the rest, to allow for more controlled movement while still being comfortable. There are pillows, but no blankets, and the restraints aren't discreet on this one. Above the platform are bars and handles built strong enough to withhold a person's weight.

Along the side of the room are more pieces of sex furniture, some that take a good deal of imagination to figure out, but I watch Mia's eyes dance around the room, her pupils dilating with anticipation as she does.

"I was afraid we were just going to rent another bedroom tonight," she mutters quietly.

Leaning over her from behind, I grind my already stiff length into her back. "If we're just fucking, then we're going to fuck our way through this entire club."

She shivers, leaning against me, and I press my nose into her neck, inhaling her scent. My cock twitches again. I try to remember the moment when everything changed for me and Mia—when the smell of her skin alone started sending my heart racing and my dick throbbing. Was it the video chat? Or was it before that?

Neither of us are patient tonight. The second she spins toward me and kisses my mouth, we're tearing at our clothes and moving with haste toward the platform bed. As I lean down to slide her panties to the floor, she squeezes my shoulder and moves away. I almost forget what's waiting for me.

"What's wrong?" I ask.

"I have something to show you," she mumbles, biting her lip. I'm on my knees in front of her as she delicately spins and bends at the waist, completely naked and revealing a teal gem wedged between her porcelain cheeks.

The growl that climbs its way out of my chest is feral. I grip Mia's hips tightly as I pull her closer, placing a warm kiss on the right cheek and brushing my thumb over the toy.

"Oh, baby," I say, my voice muffled against her skin. "Is this for me?"

"I heard that it makes sex even better."

I moan again. My hands cascade across her flesh, down her gentle spine, and around her soft, pillowy thighs. My lips trail behind my fingers, and when she moves to lie down first, I flip her on top of me as I recline my head on one of the pillows.

"I want you to ride my cock."

Her high-pitched moan against my lips sounds a hell of a lot like yes to me. And she's already moving her hips down toward my waiting cock.

"Slow down," I say with a laugh as I kiss her neck. "You're so eager for my cock, aren't you?"

"Yes," she replies with a pant.

"But don't you want to ride my face first?"

"Yes," she cries out again, and I shift her upward. If I thought the scent of her skin turned me on, this one makes me downright savage. I run my ravenous tongue along the warm folds of her cunt.

Her high-pitched mewls fill the room as I hook my arms around her thighs and dive in. She's squirming in my hold, but at this point, I can't keep my mouth off of her. My lips wrap around her clit as I suck and flick it with my tongue. "Oh my God," she moans.

When I gaze up at her, I'm pleasantly surprised to find her staring back down at me, a twinkle of excitement in her eyes as her legs start to tremble. I want to feel her come on my tongue, just like she did the other day. I *need* it. I am an addict for Mia, hooked on the way she looks as she climaxes, and I crave her orgasms even more than I crave my own.

Her hips start to grind, and I notice the way she keeps lifting herself up, only to have my arms pull her back down.

I lift her up long enough to give myself enough room to talk. "Mia, when I said sit on my face, I meant *sit on my fucking face.*"

She grips the headboard as her weight settles, and I lap hungrily at her delicious pussy, watching her various expressions with each suck, nibble, and lick, until all the telltale signs of her impending orgasm are obvious. Then, I go in for the kill, sucking on her clit so hard, she's screaming as her body is locked in multiple tremors of pleasure.

She's barely regained the ability to breathe before sliding down my body and settling her weight on my cock. So goddamn eager.

But no matter how excited she is, she still has to move slowly. She still has to stretch to accommodate me, her face wincing from the burn. Finally, her tight pussy swallows my cock when she sets herself completely on my lap.

I can't help myself as I grab her face and pull it down for a rough kiss. She moans into my mouth when she starts moving on her own, chasing her pleasure once more as she grinds her hips on top of me.

"Oh, I like this position," she says with a sweet hum as she sits back up straight.

"Use those bars," I say, gesturing toward the handles over her head. With some hesitation, she reaches up and takes hold, immediately noticing the way it gives her more leverage.

"Yes," she cries out sweetly.

"Good girl. Now, make yourself come again. Use my cock, Mia."

Her movements pick up speed as she slides up and down my shaft, and it's the most beautiful fucking sight in the world. Her eyes closed and her bottom lip pinched between her teeth as she bounces her body on mine, finding what feels good and using the friction we're creating to get there.

"How does this feel?" I ask, sliding my hands back to the plug, giving it a little nudge. She hums in response.

"So good," she replies. "It's so…tight."

Reaching over, I find my pants strewn across the platform, and I fish my phone out of the pocket. "Mia, I need to record this. Can I?"

Her eyes pop open, and she pauses when she notices the phone in my hand. With a brave look on her face, she nods. "Yes."

Without hesitation, I open the camera app and aim it at her. With her eyes dancing back and forth from my face to the phone, she starts moving again.

"Eyes on me, Mia."

The expression on her face is intense. I watch her features change as she finds something that feels good, going harder, faster, deeper until she's trembling and holding her breath and gripping the bar so tight, her knuckles turn white. Her tits bounce and the soft flesh of her hips dance with every pounding drop on my cock.

I struggle to keep her in the frame of the video as she moves, but it's not her body I want on camera—it's her face. I keep the shaky recording on her upper half, so her strong arms gripping the bars and the euphoria on her face are the stars of the show.

"I'm coming, Garrett," she pants, before giving out one long sexy cry and seizing up in a look that screams ecstasy. And I catch every moment of it on camera, which I'll sure as fuck enjoy watching later.

When I know she's done, ready to collapse on my chest, I put my phone down. Then, I pull her mouth to mine again, kissing her while she's still trying to catch her breath.

"Lift up for me," I tell her, and when she does, I thrust my hips upward, impaling her hard. She yelps, latching her lips on mine in a deep kiss. Our tongues tangle as I fuck her, our bodies slapping together and creating the most carnal, dirty sound this room has ever heard.

"Fuck, fuck, fuck," I mutter as I slam home one more time before I come hard, spilling inside her.

For a moment, she stays on top of me, resting her face against my chest, and I stroke her sweat-damp back, feeling her heart pound through her rib cage. It's intimate and quiet for a moment. My hand slides down her spine, making her flinch when I reach her ass.

"I want to fuck you here someday. I want every part of you to be mine." I press gently on the plug, and she whimpers as I do.

Lifting up, she stares down at me. "If I was going to trust anyone to do that, it would be you."

The word *trust* sends a shock wave of shame through my heart. I'm lying to her. I'm the last person she should trust. But she does anyway.

"Why do you have such issues trusting men?" I ask.

Heaving a sigh, she settles herself on my chest, my cock pulling out as she drapes a leg over mine and cuddles into my arm.

"You might not remember too well, but I developed at a young age, Garrett. Before I was even through puberty, I could feel the way men would gawk at me. The vulgar catcalls boys shouted at me. All the things they wanted to do to me or have me do to them, and it made me feel so cheap. Like I was worth nothing but entertainment for them. I felt like something for them to use, and it made me feel so gross."

"And how the hell did that lead to being a camgirl?"

"Because it puts me in control. I'm the one taking something from them. And it gives me back a little of that power, so I don't feel so used."

I brush her hair out of her eyes, my heart galloping in my chest at the thought of anyone hurting her or taking anything from her she doesn't want to give.

"You know I'm not like them, right? This might just be sex, but—"

"Garrett, stop," she says, sitting up and pressing her fingers to my lips. "You are *nothing* like them. When I'm with you, I feel like you actually see me. Not just my body. Not my big tits or round ass. But me. I'm not a piece of meat to you. I can see that."

"You're not a piece of meat, Mia. And no one should make you feel that way."

The moment stretches between us, growing heavy as we stare at each other. And I can't tell if we're still talking as friends, stepsiblings, or something more, but we're treading into dangerous territory. I can't help it. Mia has wound her way into my life, and for the first time, I'm not in any rush to get her out of it.

Rule #27: Love isn't shit.

Mia

IT WENT WELL. HE LOVED IT.

I type into the chat box while sitting at the bar in the club. Garrett had some work to do, and I wasn't quite ready to leave. So even though I told him I was catching an Uber and going home, I detoured to the bar instead. He doesn't like it when I linger around the club long or go anywhere alone, but I am my own person, and he doesn't own me.

So here I sit, sometime past two in the morning, texting a stranger on the internet who gave me a butt plug that I just wore while having sex with my stepbrother.

Can we say…what the fuck?

Did *you* like it? he asks.

Yes, I reply. It made everything feel even better.

Good.

I'm sipping on a glass of white wine while I ready myself to type this next part. Truth be told, I knew this was coming. These feelings for Garrett are real, and I see him slowly opening up to me. Even if he wants to deny it or claim that he doesn't want a girlfriend, there's something real between us. And I can't ruin that by talking to someone else.

I have bad news, I say.

I'm listening.

We have to stop talking. Things with him are just getting good, and I don't want to risk it.

What about your job? Are you still going to be a camgirl? he asks.

I don't know, I reply.

Do you want to?

Honestly, yes. I loved it and sometimes, I miss it. Feeling sexy and strong and desired.

He doesn't make you feel those things?

Hmm. Does he? Garrett puts my pleasure first, I can see that, but there's something only I can give myself. And I don't just mean pleasure...but power.

I don't want to get that from him. Does that make sense?

Yes, it does.

Well, I think you're sexy and strong and desired.

But you don't think I should be a camgirl anymore, I reply, finishing his statement.

Of course I don't. He probably doesn't want you to either.

My mouth twists as I read the messages, an uneasy feeling settling in my gut. It's like they both want to own a part of me but that doesn't leave much of me to own for myself. I don't want to feel like property, like I can't do what I want.

On their terms, no less.

And Drake is right—Garrett would definitely not want me performing anymore.

"Can I buy you a drink?" a dark voice says from three seats away. Turning toward him, I pause, staring at the definition of a silver fox: broad, sharp features in an expensive-looking suit with a thick white beard and a smile that nearly knocks me off my barstool.

"Um...I—"

"Back off, Ronan. She's with Garrett," the cute bartender says to the man as he passes him gold liquor in a glass tumbler.

"Garrett?" the man replies as he rakes his eyes over my body. "I didn't know Garrett had a girl."

"He didn't—doesn't," I stammer. "But yeah…we are sort of…"

He laughs, deep and sexy. I never considered myself into older men, but holy hell…that could change. "It's okay. I get it. I'm not going to piss off one of the owners. Especially not Garrett."

"Why do you say that? 'Especially not Garrett.'"

He scoots onto one of the closer barstools as he leans toward me. He smells delicious, like rich cologne and aged bourbon.

"Because I like Garrett. He makes me laugh. Always smiling, making sure everyone is having a good time. I like that about him. He's a businessman but also a people person. Not something we come across very often."

I nod, taking the last sip of my wine. Geo is refilling it before I can even set it down. My last drink of the night before I have to either call a ride, for real this time, or drag Garrett out of here. Will we sleep at his apartment again? It's become a habit lately. Something that makes me *feel* like this is more than sex.

"Does he treat you right?" Ronan asks.

I swallow. Does he? I think back to the conversation with Drake and the reminder that they both want things for me that I'm not sure I want for myself. Does Garrett even know how to treat a girl right? He's great in bed, and like he said earlier tonight, he doesn't treat me like a thing to fuck or claim or just enjoy. I'm more than that to him.

But when it comes to commitment and relationships, I feel like I'm giving more than I'm getting.

"You're thinking about that question far too long," Ronan continues.

"I care about Garrett very much," I reply. "And I know he cares about me too."

He leans in with a crooked grin. "That didn't answer my question."

Pressing my lips together, I nod. "I know, but that's all I've got right now."

Heaving a long sigh, he lifts his glass to his lips and swallows it down in one gulp. Then he drops the glass on the bar and turns toward me. "I've been married twice and in love more times than I can count, so here's my advice for you."

I straighten my spine and turn toward him.

"Love isn't shit. It's not worth a damn thing. But time, attention, priority…those things are real, and until a man gives you those, don't give him the time of day, beautiful. Now, don't tell Garrett I said that. Like I said…I like him. Hold him to it, though."

I feel myself tensing, forcing down a gulp as his words hit hard.

"Thank you," I reply softly.

He smiles as he rises from his barstool and waves to the bartender. Then his hand brushes my back as he leaves, and I'm left staring into the half-empty wineglass in my hands. Time, attention, priority. The three things I've always wanted from my stepbrother. For him to notice me. For him to care and let me into his life. I just want to matter enough to him.

Even when I was too stubborn to show it or ask for it.

I suddenly realize just how accommodating I've been. How easy I've made this for him and how little I ask for. And if I don't start asking for more, for what I really want, I'm never going to get it.

"All done?" Geo asks as I finish my wine.

"Yes," I reply, and maybe it's the two glasses of wine or the pep talk from the silver-haired sex machine that just left, but I'm feeling bold. Empowered. And ready to show Garrett that I'm not some lovestruck virgin who will wait around forever.

"Geo, how do I go about renting a room?"

His perfectly shaped eyebrows shoot up to his forehead as he stares at me. "You want to rent a room…with someone?"

"No. Alone. A voyeur room."

That makes the look of surprise in his expression melt into a mischievous smile. "I can help you with that."

———————

I learned a long time ago that basing your decisions on the standard of what normal people would do leads to a very boring life. The first time I ever went into a private chat on the cam, I was terrified, but I didn't show it.

So what if other people think it's crazy? Why would I deny myself something I wanted to do because other people thought it was weird? People who weren't even involved.

Getting a voyeur room in a sex club by myself is crazy, but it's been on my mind since the first time Eden led me down here. An idea I brushed away a hundred times because of how *weird* other people might think it is.

Well, fuck that. I don't play by anyone else's rules.

Geo was able to rent me the key card for the room and showed me where to enter and how to adjust the lights if I want it darker or brighter. Brighter makes it harder to see the people on the other side, so I decide to leave it dark. I want to see them watching me.

Naturally, I chose a room with toys.

Once I enter, the door closing behind me, I walk up to the glass facing the hall. There are about six people I can see from here. And they're all watching other rooms, paying no attention to me.

I imagine at any moment Garrett is going to find out I'm in here, and it will be over before it even began. So I might as well make the most of it while I can.

Staring at the window in front of me, barely able to see the people on the other side, I slip my light blue dress off my shoulders, one side at a time, letting it fall to the floor. Underneath, I have on a white bra and purple silk panties. Being half-naked in the window draws the attention of one of the women staring into the room next to me. I have no idea what's going on in there; I can't hear or see it.

As she steps up to my room's window, the tingle of excitement I was anticipating skates down my spine, landing between my legs in warm arousal. While she watches, I explore the room slowly, browsing the clear shelves against the wall. There is an assortment of vibrators and dildos, among other things.

As my fingers brush each item, deliberating my decision, I notice the woman moving in the corner of my eye. Turning toward her, I notice her pointing to an item high on the shelf.

With a twinkle in my eye, I pick up a pink silicone wand vibrator. Looking back at her, I gesture toward the vibrator to be sure this is what she was pointing to.

With a smile, she nods.

Behind her, a man approaches, watching me too. That tingle down my spine hits harder.

Biting my lip, I press the power button on the vibrator. It's a quiet buzz, subtle and soft enough to make my body light up with excitement.

On the lowest setting, I graze the vibration over my right breast, letting the hum wake up my bloodstream, causing my thighs to clench. Letting my head hang back, I slide the silicone down, over my belly, and just tease my clit with a delicate touch.

Even on the lowest setting, this toy is effective.

It's definitely right for my first time in the room. I don't really want to go overboard.

So with the couple still watching, I carry the vibrator over to the bed. But she's pointing at something again, grabbing my attention. This time, she's gesturing at something hanging from the wall. Turning toward the black clamps hanging from silver chains, I grin.

"This?" I ask, picking up one of the nipple clamps.

With a lustful gaze, she nods again. Her boyfriend is stroking her arm and then her neck, but she's still watching me.

Sitting on the edge of the bed, facing the window, I unclasp my bra, letting the fabric fall away as I touch the vibrator to my nipples again, causing them to harden with arousal. Once they are stiff peaks, I take the clamps and watch the window as I slip the first one on.

With the low light outside the room, I can see both the faint outlines of the people on the other side and my own subtle reflection. And I watch myself as I clamp the second one in place, the pain sending flames of excitement to my panties. I'm wet and ready to touch myself.

Leaning one hand back on the bed, I pick up the vibrator and stare at my own faint reflection as I press the buzz to my clit. I look amazing in the window, metal clasps hanging from my breasts, and my thighs clenched together. The woman I see in that reflection is strong and empowering and beautiful, regardless of how thick her thighs are or how round her belly is.

When I feel the first wave of pleasure, easing off so I don't come too soon, I notice more than just the four original eyes. There is a crowd now.

I feel them watching. I feel their arousal from watching me. And it spurs on my own.

My panties stay on as I increase the intensity of the vibrator, pressing it harder against my clit and falling back onto the mattress. My back arches and my hair hangs over the black cotton of the sheets as I grind myself against the humming silicone between my legs.

The sensation of the clamps and the eyes and the vibration quickly becomes too much and soon, I'm soaring through clouds of euphoria. My orgasm carries me away, so intense I have to clench the sheets tight in my fist, letting out a guttural cry so loud, I know they can hear me on the other side of the glass.

When I finally pull the vibrator away from my body, I have to lie still on the bed and wait for my heartbeat to slow down before I stand. When I finally rise from the bed, I'm practically on top of the world, buzzing with excitement and pride.

Then, without warning, the door to the room swings open, and I'm left staring at a furious-looking Garrett.

Rule #28: Let your inner caveman out.

Garrett

MY COCK HAS NEVER BEEN SO HARD IN ALL MY LIFE.

Hunter was the one to sprint into the office while I was on a call with the talent agent to tell me that there was something in the hall I needed to see. I assumed it was a group or someone getting out of hand. I did not in a million years expect to see *my* Mia alone in room three, her nipples in clamps and a pink vibrator between her legs.

It was like the first time I saw her on my phone all over again.

And just like that night, she was beautiful beyond compare. So gorgeous up there, it almost hurt to watch. The other people in the hall could feel it too, their eyes glued to her quivering body and the arch of her spine as she made herself climax.

I didn't even know this was a gift, but here she is. Somehow making something normally perceived as awkward and vulgar look like a fucking art form. This isn't a grotesque display of her pussy or something meant to make us feel dirty for watching. Not a single person in the room can look away.

I should be furious. I should rush in there, shut the curtain, and carry her out, but I can't move. My body is frozen in place, and I'd kill anyone who tried to stop her now.

When she finally does reach her orgasm, her moan barely making it through the glass between us, not a single person in this hallway even breathes. It's as if she takes us with her, like we can feel what she's feeling. The vision of her, white-blond hair splayed, tan skin against the black fabric, and pert breasts shuddering with her climax, will forever be etched in my mind. A stunning mental photograph I'll have until the day I die.

When she finally sits up, I snap into motion. This caveman-like rage courses through me and everything becomes a blur. Before she can even rise off the bed, I'm in the room. I want to grab her, shake her, kiss her, but I'm too afraid to touch her out of fear of hurting her.

I love the way she stands up, chin high and mouth set. There's not a hint of an apology on her lips, and I'm glad. I don't want her to be sorry. I just want her to be *mine*.

The clamps are still tight around her nipples as I cross the room and crash my mouth against hers, the metal digging into my chest. My hands bury themselves in her hair as I hold her face against mine, breathing in the air she exhales and devouring the softness of her lips.

I want to tell her how beautiful she is, how perfect and amazing and wonderful, but my stupid fucking brain holds the praise in silence, keeping me from expressing everything I'm feeling. If there was ever a perfect time to say it, this is it. But I'm too paralyzed by fear, afraid that the moment I express just how much Mia means to me, she'll break my heart. Let me down. Kill my spirit. So I keep my feelings guarded and my words silent… deciding to use my body instead.

I'm willing to tell her just how much I want to fuck her, just not how much I want to keep her.

"Turn the fuck around," I mutter against her mouth. And when movement catches my eye, I remember we're in a voyeur room, and there are almost a dozen people watching. Panic courses through my veins as I rush to the window to snap the curtain closed, hiding us from their view.

"Keep it open," she cries.

"Oh no, Mia. You're mine. All fucking mine." I growl as I unfasten my belt, stalking back to her. I've never felt so carnal and possessive. But this need isn't just in my cock. It's in my blood, pumping in my veins, this feral urgency to be inside her and make her mine.

I don't bother with any more kissing or foreplay. She's already wet and ready for me. Mine to take.

That public display awoke something in me that I don't want to subside. I've never felt so alive or connected to another person in my life.

"Garrett," she whimpers as I spin her around and shove her top half against the bed. Her panties come off in a rough swipe and I press my eager cock against her cunt, already wet with her own orgasm, making it easy to thrust inside her. The moment her heat swallows my cock, I let out a deep groan of satisfaction.

"I don't like you flashing your pussy for everyone to see, Mia, but fuck—" I growl with need as I slam into her again. "It made me want to claim you that much more."

"Yes!" she cries out. Her fingers dig into the sheets of the bed as she shifts her hips back against me.

"This pussy is mine, Mia. All fucking mine. You should see how well it takes my cock."

"Yes," she says again.

"I don't want anyone looking at it, touching it, or even fucking thinking about it, understand?"

"Yes!" She screams for a third time as I thrust so hard, the bed shifts. I'm pounding relentlessly, our bodies slapping in a quick, rough cadence. I'm not fucking her to savor it or prolong it. I'm fucking her to claim her.

"Say it," I command. "Say you're mine."

"I'm yours," she murmurs against the bed.

I slam into her harder. "Louder."

"I'm yours," she cries.

"I want to hear you scream it, Mia. Tell every single fucking person in this club who you belong to."

"Garrett, I'm yours!" she screams.

"Is this too hard for you, Mia?"

She shakes her head, and she's shoving her hips back again. "Harder."

With that, I reach around, snatching the chain of the nipple clamps and yanking them off in a quick swipe. She screams, but I know, at that very second, her body is overwhelmed with adrenaline, making the sensation that much more intense.

I can't hold on anymore. With three more bruising thrusts, my orgasm violently slams into me at full speed, and my cock unloads inside her. Before I'm done, I wrap my hand around her throat and hoist her up, so I can take her lips with mine. We are both wearing a sheen of sweat from the exertion, and our hearts are beating so wildly I can feel the quick *thump-thump-thump* of the pulse in her neck.

"I want to fill you up," I mumble against her mouth. "I want you so full of my cum, it drips out of you forever."

"Garrett," she whimpers as I kiss her again.

"I want to fuck you whenever I want and I want you to take that fucking IUD out so I can really pump you full, Mia."

"I want that too," she whispers in a pleading cry. I'm holding her so tight to my body, she's barely standing on her own. And when I finally blink my eyes open, I feel like I've woken up from a dream.

Jesus, did I really just say that? Fuck…what am I thinking?

Releasing her, I pull out and turn away, quickly shoving my cock back in my pants and refastening the button. Did I basically just imply that I want to get her pregnant? Am I going fucking crazy?

It's just sex talk, I tell myself. She knows that. I'm not being serious. I don't *really* want Mia to have my baby… I mean, during sex I do. Naturally. The image of her on the bed like she was a few minutes ago was hot, but add a swollen belly to that image and yeah, any man would have said what I did. It was my cock talking.

We don't say a word as she puts her clothes back on. In fact, we don't bring up the whole thing for the rest of the night. Not during the drive to my place and not when she crawls into my bed, cuddling up to my chest.

I have a feeling that what I said after we had sex has completely eclipsed the entire incident anyway.

Rule #29: Everything will be okay.

Garrett

SWEAT DRIPS DOWN MY SPINE AS I LET THE EVENTS OF LAST NIGHT replay in my head. And the last ten nights before that. A dangerous thing to do on a public running trail around the city.

But it wasn't just about the sex last night. What we did and what we said made it more than that, and how can I really be surprised? In the last two weeks, my stepsister has gone from being the pesky little girl I watched grow up into the only person on the earth that I want to see when I open my eyes in the morning.

But how long can this really go on? How long can I keep up this charade and be two men at once? She loves Drake for entirely different reasons than she loves me. If she even does. If I don't figure out how to open up as myself the way he does, then I'm going to really lose her forever.

I'm at the start of my third mile when my phone rings. I answer it using the earbuds I'm wearing and assume it's Emerson or Maggie with work news about the event.

But the moment the call goes through, I hear sobbing. I stop in my tracks on the jogging trail.

"Garrett," she cries.

"Mia," I stammer. "What is it? What's wrong?" Ice floods my veins at the sound of her voice, the pain of her sobs lancing my heart like a knife.

"He collapsed at work," she bellows through her tears. "He was taken in an ambulance and now he's in surgery and I don't know what's going on."

I know immediately it's Paul.

"Where are you?"

"At St. Francis. By the harbor," she wails.

"Listen to me, Mia. He's going to be okay. Calm down, okay?"

"I'm scared." And I hear it in her voice, the fear and panic. He better be okay because I can't bear the thought of what his death would do to her.

The thought has me tensing up like a time bomb ready to explode. I'm frantic as I pull out my phone and check the location. It's only a couple miles away, just along the oceanfront. And that's the last thought in my head before I tell her, "I'm on my way. Mia, I'm coming."

Then, I hit the End button and I fucking run.

When I reach the hospital, I practically collapse onto the reception desk as I ask for Paul Harris. And the lady typing away at the computer is way too fucking slow as she looks him up.

"It says here he's still in surgery, but family members are waiting on the third floor, east wing."

I'm halfway to the elevator by the time she finishes her sentence. An elevator door is opening right on time, and I squeeze in with a group of nurses, punching the third-floor button in a panic. Sweat is pouring down my face and back, but I don't care. She won't care.

The elevator chimes as it reaches my floor, and as the doors open, I see her. Standing in the maroon-and-gray waiting room, her face beet red and covered in tears as she chews on her nails. She spins to see me and I'm across the hall and gathering her into my arms before the doors are even fully opened.

And that's when she really loses it. Clutching on to me like she needs me to stand, I hold her tight in my arms, letting her sob into my shirt. Out of the corner of my eye, I see my mom watching us, and I glance at her with an apology on my face. I should be hugging her too. Her husband's life is in jeopardy, but right now, there's only one person on this earth who matters. I don't make the rules and I certainly didn't see this coming, but as long as Mia needs my arms to wrap around her and my chest to cry into, that's exactly what she's going to fucking get.

Paul is going to be okay. He had an abscess that ruptured and nearly led to sepsis. A side effect of the cancer and treatment, but luckily, not the return of another tumor. No more chemo. No more radiation. Just surgery and one hell of a scare.

They keep him back there for most of the day. I'm able to get Mia to calm down enough to sit in the waiting room and eat a little something, but she doesn't leave my side and she never once lets me go. The entire time we're in the waiting area, I notice my mother's nervous eyes landing on us more than once.

She glances down at where our hands are linked or where I accidentally touch Mia's bare leg. I keep correcting myself, but Mia is too stressed to care, resting her hand on my shoulder or stroking my arm like no one is watching.

After an almost six-hour surgery, Paul is finally in recovery. When I take the girls in to see him, he's just waking up. My mother runs to his side first, touching his arm delicately as she perches herself on the side of his bed.

Mia goes to the other side, finally letting me go for the first time today. I watch from the foot of his bed as he wakes up.

"We were so worried about you, Dad," Mia cries, fresh tears spilling down her cheeks.

"Oh, Mia. I'm sorry. I'm okay," he says in a raspy, pained tone.

"The doctor said you should be able to go home tomorrow," my mother replies.

As I stand there and watch the three of them, both women fawning over him and him comforting them in return, my heart aches for something it's never ached for before. Growing up, it was always just me and my mother—the best mother, really. She was devoted to me, and I never once felt alone or obligated to another person. But she loved me so selflessly that I never realized until just now that that love cost her something. She never remarried until I was older. Never dated. Never dared to want more.

And that entire time I was ignorant of what I was missing…or making her miss. A family. People on both sides of your hospital bed.

I'm glad she found Paul and Mia and finally has the family she always deserved. As if she can read my mind, my mother looks my way and reaches out a hand to me. I put my fingers in hers and the four of us sit here in comfortable silence, no one speaking or needing anything more than what we have in this space.

Mia glances my way for only a split second and the ache in my heart grows.

Fuck.

Suddenly, I know what this ache is. I know what it is I want. And it's not her body or sex. It's knowing that one day when I'm in this hospital bed that she'll be at my side. And she won't be alone.

My hand slips from my mother's as I mentally panic.

"I'm going to go grab some air. Paul, do you need anything?"

He shakes his head, and I feel their three gazes on me as I quickly move toward the door. "I'll be back."

I can't do this. I can't keep going down this path, especially not with Mia. I'm not that guy. I'm not family-man material, and I never will be. Not only do I own a fucking sex club, but I'm not equipped to be supportive and confident the way Paul is. I'm a mess. I seem fine to Mia now, but at some point, she's going to learn the truth and see me at my lowest. Then what?

It's fine. She knows this is just sex. We're not attached like that. Pretty soon, this will be a thing of the past and she'll move on with someone better for her.

"Garrett," she calls when I reach the hospital exit.

I spin and find her jogging my way. Regardless of the fact that her eyes are swollen from crying and there isn't a shred of makeup on her face, she still looks ridiculously beautiful.

"Are you okay?" she asks. When she reaches me, her fingers glide across the skin of my forearms and I want to flinch from her touch.

"Yeah. I just needed air. Are you okay?"

"I am now," she replies solemnly. "Your mom said we should go home and rest."

"What about her?"

"She's not leaving his side." When her hands reach for me again, I let her wind them around my waist, pulling her body close.

This is the final surrender. I've realized my mistake too late. I can't avoid where this thing is going with Mia. We're already there. And I don't hate it as much as I expected to.

We both desperately need showers, me more than her. So when we reach my place, I pull her into the master bathroom. I have a very solid plan for this girl. Shower, food, sleep. And that's it. No sex. How very gentlemanly of me.

Turning the water on, I undress her first, which she lets me do. I said no sex, but I can't help but steal a quick kiss after tugging her shirt over her head. She's already shampooing her hair when I climb in after her, and I'm finding it hard not to let my fingers graze over her soft, soapy flesh.

"You okay?" I ask, checking in with her again.

She nods. I don't know why I keep asking that, waiting for her to open up and spill whatever's on her mind. As if I would even be equipped to handle that if she does. I'm really not one to talk. I literally never open up the way she wants me to.

After our quick shower, I find her something comfortable to wear before I head to the kitchen to make her some food. Moments later, she walks out of the bedroom in my gray sweatpants and a T-shirt that fits tight over her breasts. She gives me a warm smile, and I pause, staring at her.

"I look like a boy," she complains.

"The hottest boy I've ever seen," I reply as I pull the carton of eggs out of the fridge.

She giggles as she climbs onto one of the stools around the island. Pulling her knees up to her chest, curled up in my pajamas, she looks so young. Glancing back at her as I crack eggs into a bowl, I try to pinpoint the moment when Mia stopped feeling too young for me. And I realize that our age difference was never my problem. It was how I thought it would be perceived. How people would look at me or, more importantly, at her. But from the minute Mia could hold a conversation with me, I saw her as my equal. Like we were always kindred spirits, two halves of one whole.

"Did you run to the hospital?" she asks while I'm whisking the eggs.

"Yes."

"How far?"

I shrug. "A couple miles. I was already near the bay on my jog."

"You could have taken a cab or gone home to change first. Why did you have to get there so fast?"

My movement stops as I stare at her. "Because you needed me. Because I wanted...to be there with you."

Solemnly, she nods as if she's pleased with that answer. "Garrett...what are we?"

Taking a deep breath, I ready myself for the answer. The one I already know.

"Because I know that when I found out about my dad, there's only one person I wanted to call. One person I needed at that moment. So I think you're my person, but I don't want you to be mine if I'm not yours."

"Mia…" I mutter, questions and doubt swimming around in my head.

"Last night you said I was yours. I just want to know…if any of that was real."

"It was real," I mumble, like an idiot who doesn't have the vocabulary to properly string together a full sentence to express just how I feel.

She's staring at me with a nervous expression, and I set the bowl in my hand down and press my palms against the cool granite of the counter. I want to go to her, but it's not the time for touching. It's time for talking. And I suck at it enough as it is, so it's best to keep some distance to keep from getting distracted.

"Mia, I haven't been in a relationship in a really long time, and I'm a mess. You'd be signing yourself up for—"

"I'm a mess too, Garrett. But if you're going to call me yours, I need to know that I am."

In the back of my mind, I distantly recognize that this is the time to come clean. I need to fess up to being Drake and the camgirl thing, so we can put it behind us. But I'm still a fucking coward.

It's ironic to me that I hid behind the Drake profile because it was my barrier so I could have Mia without letting her see the real me. Now it's a wall, keeping me from everything I want. Do I want Mia if it means having this lie between us forever, or do I risk losing her and tell her the truth?

Moving to her side of the island, I step up to her, eager to touch her face as I pull her in for a kiss.

I can't risk it.

"I am yours, and I'll give this a shot if you will."

"I promise," she whispers in return, a gentle smile lifting the corners of her mouth as she leans in for another kiss. I notice the way her hands hold me a little tighter and her lips hold mine a little longer, as if she's showing just how much she wants this, and the guilt assaults me again.

"We should probably wait until my dad gets out of the hospital before we tell him," she mumbles against my lips.

I wince. "No, I think the hospital might be a convenient location for my sake."

She laughs. "He'll get over it."

"Well, yeah. Neither of them is the type to hold grudges. And I think it would be really fucking weird for a long time, but they'd eventually get used to it. We're still us."

Leaving her arms, I return to the eggs, grabbing some cheese and ham out of the fridge before I resume scrambling. Glancing up at her, I feel a sense of peace for the moment as the guilt fades.

She's here in my apartment in the middle of the afternoon and I'm cooking for her, and nothing feels weird or wrong, and it's become obvious to me that while I tried to say I didn't want a girlfriend, that seems to be what I got anyway.

Moments later, I scoop her omelet onto the plate and carry it to the table for her. She must have worked up an appetite because she eats every bite, and I watch her, a feeling of pride washing over me as she does.

She yawns while I'm cleaning up the kitchen, and the next time I turn around, she's gone. I find her curled up in my bed, already asleep by the time I enter the room. Standing in the doorway, I watch her sleep, replaying every moment of the last month that led to this.

For fifteen years, I've known Mia. And while I loved her in my own weird way the entire time, there was never anything more. For so long, nothing. Then suddenly, there was everything.

Just like that.

Standing there watching her, so peaceful and content, I tell myself that I can really do this for her. I can keep it together. I can be good—be happy. Shield her from the darkness until it all fades away. People have overcome worse.

With that, I crawl into bed next to her. As I pull the covers up, she turns, nuzzling her body against my chest. She's breathing heavily as I press a kiss to her forehead.

"Love you, kitten," I whisper, but she doesn't respond, already too deep in her dreams.

Rule #30: Moms know everything.

Garrett

My mom is sleeping in a chair next to Paul's bed when I deliver her dinner. It's almost nine, and since Mia was still sleeping, I figured it would be safe to step out for a little bit, just to check on things at the hospital.

"Hey, Mom." I gently nudge her shoulder after setting down the sub sandwich I picked up at the deli for her. She stirs awake and glances at Paul in a panic, but he's still sleeping soundly.

"He's fine. I just brought you something to eat."

"Oh…thanks, sweetie. How's Mia?"

"She's good. Napping at my place. What did the doctor say?"

"Oh, he's recovering well. They want to keep an eye on him for another day, so it doesn't look like he'll be going home tomorrow."

"Oh, damn. I'm sorry," I reply. I sit in the empty chair near the foot of his bed. She pats my leg as I do.

"It's okay. At least he's okay. Have to look on the bright side."

"Yeah…" I didn't really intend to stick around long. I'm eager to get back to Mia, but I also can't leave my mom here.

"Mom, do you want to go home and get some sleep or a shower or something? I can stay with him."

"No. I'm fine," she replies with dark circles under her eyes. Then her gaze lands on my face, and I can tell she's about to say something serious. I tense up with anticipation. "Mia was so upset. So scared."

"I know."

"And she called you. Before I even thought to call you, she did."

"I'm glad I was nearby," I reply, waiting for her to get to the point.

"I know Mia's been seeing someone. Ever since we got back from the lake, she's been gone almost every night. Giggling like a schoolgirl. Always on her phone."

I wait in silence, watching her face as she speaks quietly enough not to wake Paul. And I have to force myself to breathe.

What am I going to say if she asks? The shame and guilt for what I've done with Mia suddenly come crashing to the forefront of my mind. This is their little Mia, the girl my own mother adopted as her own. The golden child. The innocent, sweet daughter who I've recently defiled in numerous ways in the past two weeks.

I know I said they would get used to the idea of us together, but what if they don't? Not that I could blame them. I'm the club-owning bachelor and party animal who's thirteen years older than her, and that's not even accounting for my other issues.

My mother reaches out and touches my hand, quieting the manic voices in my head.

"I wouldn't have guessed in a hundred years it was you, Garrett." And there it is. Like a lightning strike, it hits with pinpoint precision, changing everything. There's no point denying it now. When moms know, they just know.

"Mom—"

"Once I saw it, I felt like such a fool for not noticing sooner. I don't think she even tried to hide it. I realized how natural you two look together."

"Jesus," I mutter as I drop my face into my hands.

"Oh, relax," she replies. "It's not like she's your actual sister. And you were already twenty-one by the time you met, so it's not like you grew up with her around. I just thought…you didn't like her."

"I don't know if I'm ready to have this conversation," I reply, not looking up from the floor.

"Well, you better get ready because I'm not going to lie for you. If Paul sees what I saw today, he's going to know too."

I glance up at him to see him still snoring peacefully. I feel like I've betrayed his trust somehow.

"Mia is so loyal, Garrett. To a fault. And she's stubborn. I know she will stick by your side through anything, but I just need you to think carefully about this before you embark on something that could break this family."

My head falls, staring at my clasped hands as her words settle in.

"I don't want to hurt her."

"Then don't. Be honest and up-front with her. But if you lead her on or lie to her, that will be on you. And she will never forgive you for it." There's that lightning strike again, this time getting me right where it hurts.

"Why do you assume I'll hurt her? Do you have so little faith in me?"

"I know you, Garrett. I know you have your own battles and demons, and I'm telling you not to hide those things from her because she will weather any storm with you, but if you keep it hidden and deceive her, you *will* lose her."

It's quiet as I run my fingers through my hair, remembering the conversation we had before I left. How good it felt with her in my arms this morning.

I gaze up into her eyes. "You're not mad?"

"I'm not her father." Her eyes skate over to the man sleeping between us. "If I were you, I'd come forward before he finds out like I did. He won't like that."

"We will," I reply with a nod.

"Is it serious?" she asks, and I don't answer right away. There are very few things I take seriously, and I honestly never thought Mia would be one of them.

"Yeah, I think it is."

She inhales and lets it out in a big sigh. "It'll take some getting used to. It is a little weird. But you two could be really good for each other. I've never seen you like that with anyone, the way you were with her today. She brings out something in you."

"Like what?" I ask, glancing up into my mother's eyes. There's a slight tremor in my voice, smothered emotion threatening to leak out.

She swallows and stares at me as she answers, "Peace."

Peace? That's what my mother saw today while Mia sobbed hysterically into my chest and I was a sweaty, red, heaving mess?

Before I can even ask her to elaborate, she continues, "Sometimes I think I failed you, Garrett."

My eyes dance up to her face in surprise. Like mothers often do, she doesn't stifle the emotion but lets it pool at the surface and spill into her words and tears.

"Because I never understood you. I couldn't help you. I just wanted to love you and give you all of my attention, hoping it was enough, but there always seemed to be a disconnect between us. I was afraid you'd feel that disconnect with everyone in your life."

My mother has *never* spoken like this and never about this. We don't talk about my issues. The conversation was always about *me* and *my* behavior and *my* problems, so that this illness and I were the same.

I didn't just have a disease—I *was* the disease. Or at least that's how it felt, and I never realized that until this very moment when my mother is finally talking about the elephant that has been in the room with us my entire life. One big manic-depressive elephant.

I don't speak. I don't know what the fuck I would say if I could. But she continues, talking in a low whisper, so we don't wake Paul.

"I realize now that I failed you, Garrett. I kept you so close to me your entire life because I thought that I could love you enough to make up for all of my mistakes."

"Mom, you didn't—" My voice is stern and serious because I'd like to end this awkward conversation right now, but she doesn't let me.

"I'm sorry, Garrett." Tears stream down her face, and I promptly shut up. I lock down the emotions rising in my throat, and I hold her hand instead. Like I did for Mia today, I try to be the rock my mother needs now. Even if I'm the one she's claiming to have hurt.

Although I never saw it that way. My mother tried. I was the one who caused the problems and made it so fucking hard for her. I'm the one who should be apologizing, but I'm still not very good at expressing that shit.

"So when I say that Mia brings out the peace in you, Garrett, I mean that the connection I see between you two keeps you grounded like I've never seen before. Like the storm inside you has subsided. And that's what I wanted for you all along. And I don't care that I'm not the one who can help you or that she's your stepsister or that Paul might hate it. You're at peace, and that's all I've ever wanted for you."

With that, she snatches a tissue from the box next to her chair and wipes her eyes. The elephant disappears and the mood lightens.

But I'm still speechless.

As the nurses come in and my mother talks with them, I don't move or say a word. Mentally, I keep replaying every moment with Mia at the lake house and the club, realizing that my mother is right. When I'm with Mia, I don't feel alone or like I'm battling the heavy winds of my own emotions. I'm so focused on her, and even when we were fighting or teasing each other, with one look, she kept me tethered.

It hits me that the girl I never thought I could be with might have been made for me all along.

Rule #31: Don't let him make a fool out of you.

Mia

IT'S DARK WHEN I WAKE UP, AND NEXT TO ME THE BED IS EMPTY, BUT there's a buzzing coming from somewhere in the apartment. I stretch as I roll out of his bed, stumbling to the door. It's a good thing he gave me his sweats, and I'm not stuck walking around naked.

"Garrett," I call, but there's no answer. Where the hell did he go? Maybe he had to go to work.

The door buzzes again, and I jog over to answer it.

"Coming!" I call, and when I pull it open, I'm struck speechless by the six-foot blond masterpiece I've seen walking around the club once or twice. "Hi," I stammer awkwardly.

"Hi." He grins. "You must be Mia. Isabel and Hunter sent me over with dinner and flowers for Garrett. Is he here?"

"Um…no."

"We heard your dad was in the hospital, so we just wanted to do what we could."

"Oh," I reply, stepping out of the way to let him in. "That's really nice of you. I don't know where Garrett went, but you can put it in the kitchen."

As he brushes past me, I get a whiff of his cologne, subtle and masculine at the same time.

"How is your dad?" he asks after setting a pasta dish and a bottle of wine on the counter.

"He's recovering. Should be home tomorrow," I say with a smile.

"Good. I'll let the others know." He leans against the counter casually, looking far too handsome as he smiles at me.

"I'm sorry. I don't think we've met," I say. "Are you one of the owners?"

He laughs. "Oh, fuck. That was rude of me." As he puts out his hand, I reach for it. "I'm Drake, a friend of Hunter's and the general contract—"

My hand pauses before it reaches his. "Drake?" I ask, interrupting him.

"Yeah. God, you haven't heard of me already, have you? If so, what did you hear?"

The tunnel vision sets in and nothing makes any sense. It's a different Drake. It has to be. This isn't *my* Drake. At the very least he'd recognize me and say something, but still…just the mention of his name tilts my world off its axis.

"No, I haven't…I mean," I stammer. "Did you say you're the contractor?"

"Yeah," he replies with a smile. "We did the building renovations for Salacious."

"Construction," I mumble. It's a coincidence. It has to be. There could be a million Drakes who work in construction.

"And we definitely haven't met?" I ask, feeling like an idiot. I just need to be sure and other than outright asking *Have you ever watched me get naked on your phone screen?* there's really no way to be sure.

He chuckles, sounding uncomfortable. "Not officially, but I've seen you around the club, and Garrett's talked about you. A lot."

When I don't respond, staring blankly at the window across the room, Drake steps closer. "Are you sure you're okay?"

"Yeah," I quickly reply, shaking my head. "I just woke up and it's been a long day."

"Of course. Do you need anything before I go? Isabel said to just put the lasagna in the oven for about thirty minutes to warm it up."

"Thank you," I say, forcing a smile.

Behind him, the front door opens, and I watch as Garrett steps into the apartment. His eyes latch immediately onto the tall construction worker standing in his kitchen.

"Drake..." he mutters nervously, his eyes dancing between me and him.

As the man turns to greet Garrett and explain why he's here, I feel a slow tingle of dread coursing up my spine. Like a fear I've had for longer than I care to admit. A fear that I've been tricked again.

Duped. Played.

No. I shake the thought away. He wouldn't do that. We're good now. He's finally opening up and committing. We made promises to each other. I finally have everything I've ever wanted.

When I look up, Drake is waving goodbye from the front door and I shoot him a fake smile and a curt wave. Then, Garrett and I are alone, and the tension is thick. So thick it presses on my chest, making it hard to breathe. Hard to be normal and look at him and smile.

Is it just me? Can he feel it too?

I'm overthinking this, aren't I?

"You okay?" he asks, and I glance up into his face. It's the same face I've kissed a hundred times in the past two weeks. But it's also the face of the man who used to find my misery amusing. Who I was sure would never truly love anyone because he was too caught up in himself. It's like I've started to see him through a new lens, and I'm just now remembering who he truly is.

"Yeah," I mutter, turning toward the bedroom to get my phone. "Where did you go?"

"To take my mom something to eat."

"How is she?" I ask, making small talk as I retrieve my phone from the nightstand.

"Good. They're keeping your dad for an extra day, just to keep an eye on him."

Shit, my dad. I should really be focusing on him, not panicking about something like this. Because I'm probably wrong anyway.

Garrett isn't pretending to be Drake. I'm being delusional.

But I have to know for sure.

So, as I walk back out to the living room, where he's standing and staring at me with a hint of worry in his eyes, I pull up the app. Seeing Drake's username sends a wave of anxiety through me.

I'm the one talking to two men at once. If I text Drake right now and it's *not* Garrett, then how am I any better? I've been lying too, haven't I?

Hi, I type into the box, my thumb shaking before I hit Send.

Please don't be him. Please don't be him. Please don't be him.

From across the room, I hear the unmistakable sound of his phone chiming with a notification.

And everything stops. The tension is now suffocating. My cheeks grow hot with rage, and my breath trembles as my gaze lifts to his face, but he doesn't move.

"Mia," he whispers, a pleading sound, and tears spring to my eyes.

I resist the urge to throw my phone at him, squeezing it so hard in my hand, it hurts.

"No," I mutter as I turn away from him, "no, you would not do that to me."

"Please listen to me," he begs again, this time stepping closer, but I quickly put up a hand to stop him.

"No," I say again, repeating myself because it's the only word that I can muster at the moment.

No, no, no, no, no.

"It started as a mistake, and I just couldn't stop…"

My mouth falls open as I glare at him. "A mistake? You watched me… I heard your voice!"

"I know it was wrong, but everything I told you was real. You have to believe me."

Suddenly, my mind goes back to that night. The first time Drake and I chatted, and I remember everything. "That's why you came to the lake." It all makes sense now.

"I had to see you."

"Was this just one big joke to you?"

"No, Mia. Please listen to me…"

"I can't!" I yell. "I can't even look at you. The whole time you were just lying to me…manipulating me…making me fall in love with you."

He reaches for me, and I act on instinct, my hand flying and landing hard against the side of his face. It feels good, the burning sting against my palm and the anguish on his face. I want him to hurt and feel half of what I feel right now.

"I feel like a fool. *You* made me feel like a fool. You were just *using* me."

Suddenly, he crowds me toward the wall, his face close to mine as he whispers, "I'm the fool. I was never supposed to find your camgirl video, but you were so beautiful, I couldn't help myself. Then, I fell in love with you, and I'm so sorry, kitten."

"No!" I scream, struggling against his arms. "Don't call me that."

Storming across the room, I snatch my purse off the counter and fish my keys out as I rush toward the door.

"Please don't leave," he begs, the emotion thick in his voice, and when I get to the door, I almost falter. For one split second, I almost stay.

But I can't. Instead, I turn toward him, tears streaking down my face as I look him in the eyes. "I always wanted you more."

When I close the door behind me, I take the expression on his face with me. I couldn't forget that look if I tried.

Rule #32: Don't forgive him until he earns it.

Mia

DAD GOT OUT OF THE HOSPITAL TWO WEEKS AGO, AND I HAVE thrown myself into taking care of him. It's a decent distraction and a hell of a lot better than crying in the basement. I've already used binge drinking and emotional support shopping to cope, but I'm running out of money, so I need a better distraction.

He's doing better than I expected, able to walk around the house and eat small meals unassisted, which I find annoying, because I desperately need something more time-consuming. So now I'm being bothersome, constantly by his side, begging him for tasks and trying to do absolutely anything that will keep my mind off the fact that I miss Garrett.

Laura can tell something is up. You can only use the "he must be busy with work" excuse so many times. Especially for a guy who ran three miles in the middle of summer to be with me at the hospital.

It's been two full weeks since I spoke to him, and I'm still livid, but the worry is setting in too. I was too hurt that night to be angry, and I've managed to keep myself from calling him just to yell and tell him how mad I am at him. But also, to check on him.

The voyeur event is this weekend, and I had enough of a hand in it to feel invested. I should be there, but I can't risk being around Garrett yet. I need more time to think and be angry.

When I go in to check on my dad, he's not in bed like he should be. Instead, he's on the back patio, enjoying the sunshine.

"You're supposed to be sleeping," I say as I join him in the opposite chair.

"I'm tired of sleeping." Then he glances in my direction with a harsh expression. "Besides, you're one to talk. You look like you could use some sleep yourself."

"Ouch."

"Why are you sitting around here taking care of me? We've hardly seen you all summer and now you won't leave."

"You just had surgery and you scared the shit out of me. Is it so bad that I want to make sure you're okay and spend some time with you?"

"I'm fine," he says with a roll of his eyes. "Stop hanging around here. Go to the beach or go hang out with Garrett."

His name instantly makes me clam up.

"Oh, you two are fighting, aren't you?" he asks, obviously noticing the way my mood sours at the mention of his name.

"Yeah," I reply.

"What did he do this time?"

I don't look at my dad as I chew on my lower lip. I can't even scratch the surface of this conversation without it getting very awkward and inappropriate. So I stay quiet.

"Laura told me what happened when I was in surgery."

My head snaps up as I stare at him. "What happened?"

"She said you called him, which in itself is a surprise. But then she said you two hardly separated for hours while you waited."

I have to force myself to swallow down the uncomfortable lump building in my throat. "We were just scared."

"Yeah..." he replies, not sounding too convinced.

"Later that night, he came back to the hospital and told

his mother everything. He told her it was serious. That he was nervous how everyone would react but that he loved you."

What? He said that?

"Dad—" It's on the tip of my tongue to deny it or to apologize, but I don't exactly know why.

He holds up his hand to stop me. "I don't need details, but I also don't want you to lie about it."

"Are you mad?"

"A little…but you're twenty-three. And I didn't raise a girl who couldn't stand up for herself. I know if he does ever hurt you, you'll give him hell."

My chest aches with the reminder that he did, in fact, hurt me. A self-fulfilling prophecy since Garrett did, in some sense, try to warn me.

"I don't know what to say…"

"Tell me why you're here and not with him," he says with a furrowed brow.

"Because he fucked it up already. Sorry," I stammer, covering my mouth after cussing in front of my dad.

He just laughs but immediately winces from the pain. "Hmm…" he replies, and I wait for him to continue. "Is it something you can forgive him for? Something you can work out?"

"I don't know. He humiliated me."

My dad laughs again, but cuts it short when he realizes he can't even chuckle without paying for it.

"Will you stop it?" I say, jumping up to tend to him. "If you pop a stitch, Laura is going to kill you."

"Well, come on. That's funny."

"What's so funny about Garrett humiliating me?"

"It's Garrett," he says, as if it shouldn't be surprising at all. "You two have been picking on each other for fifteen years. Now you want to have a relationship with him and you think things will be different. Honey, people don't change just because your relationship has."

"Well, he lied to me, and it's way more than a prank or a joke."

"I'm sorry," he says, his stoic eyes set on me. "Don't forgive him until he earns it."

"But...?" I reply because I can feel him wanting to continue.

"But...I hope he earns it. You're still family and you've been happy lately. I'm your dad, so as much as I hate to think about you having a boyfriend, I do like to see you happy."

My throat begins to sting with emotion. What is it about a heart-to-heart with your dad that makes you want to start crying immediately?

"I know Laura wants to see him happy too."

Just the mention of Garrett being happy sets my jaw, and I look up at my dad. But he doesn't continue, and I'm left to worry even more.

I'm cleaning up the kitchen with Laura when my phone rings. I don't recognize the number, but it's local and for some reason, I feel compelled to hit the green button.

"Hello?"

"I heard about you," a sweet voice replies.

"Eden?"

"You remember me," she says with a laugh. "I didn't know if you would. Charlie gave me your number. I hope you don't mind me calling."

I almost forgot that I gave Charlotte my number in the midst of the event planning.

"Of course not," I say, glancing at Laura as I sneak out of the kitchen to talk in private. "But what exactly did you hear?"

"I heard you blew away the voyeur hall with a little solo performance."

Oh. That. Inwardly, I groan. "You heard about that, huh?"

"Honey, everyone heard about that."

"Well, that's a little embarrassing," I say as I disappear down into the basement.

"Embarrassing? From what I heard it was hot as fuck. I've always wanted to take a room alone but never had the guts to do it. You're amazing."

I laugh. "How is that amazing?"

"Because you don't give a fuck. You're hot and you know it and you own it and make people look at you. I wish I could be you."

This time, I laugh a little louder. "Please."

"I'm serious! That kind of confidence is so hot. You have to perform this weekend."

This weekend…the event. "I can't do that."

"Why not?"

"Because I'm not talking to Garrett right now."

"Well, he hasn't even been in all week, so you probably don't need to worry about him anyway. Plus, what better way to show that you don't need him than to show up and blow the roof off this place."

But I do need him. And I do care that he hasn't shown up to work. But I don't say that. I'm still angry at him, but the worry is there too.

"I don't know…"

"Well, think about it. I'd love to help you plan your set. We could get you on a rotating platform. I'm thinking all white on a black bed…maybe even get you some toys to play with. The crowd would eat it up."

The idea is enticing, and if it weren't for Garrett, I wouldn't hesitate to say yes.

"I'll think about it, okay?"

"That's a yes."

Laughter bubbles out of me. "No, it's not. It means I'll think about it."

"I'll see you tonight at ten so we can talk about it."

"Eden!"

"Charlotte is sitting next to me. She said it sounds good."

"Stop," I reply with a laugh.

"Okay, see you soon!" they both say in unison before the line goes dead.

I try to wipe the smile off my face as I start the shower. I guess Eden doesn't leave me much choice, but I think it's really about more than that. There's a chance he will be there. A chance I'll see him and know that he's okay. Even if I am mad at him. Even if I'm definitely *not* going to forgive him.

Rule #33: Beware of black hair ties.

Garrett

I SHOULD BE ABLE TO BOUNCE BACK FROM THIS. GO TO THE CLUB. Go for a run. It's *one* girl. One mistake. It shouldn't be this hard.

For the past decade, I could do what needed to be done to shake an episode. Maybe hide under the covers for a day or two and then bounce back. I don't do meds or therapy, and I've gotten through every single one of these nasty bouts of depression without any help.

Except for *one fucking time.*

And I am not repeating that episode again. I'm not.

But no matter what I tell myself, everything right now is hard. It's like a sickness oozing through my veins. This slimy, sick feeling penetrates my mood, turning everything sour and heavy and *wrong.* It shouldn't be this fucking *hard.*

This whole spell was triggered by her leaving, but it's just a fucking breakup. *Get your head together, Garrett. And kick this mood already.*

I should be relieved she dumped me. It's better this way. The whole thing with Mia is over; she's free to move on and find someone better. And I can get back to the life I love, the one where I can focus on the shit that really matters to me. Like work.

So why do I suddenly feel like a giant piece of shit?

Rolling out of bed, I walk to the window. Replaying the events of that night, the part I hate the most is the good mood I was in walking up to my apartment door, on a high after confessing everything to my mom, ready to confess it all to Mia. I was in love. I was ready to commit. I was ready to be in a relationship and keep the promises I made, even though the very idea terrified the living fuck out of me.

And then I saw Drake standing in my kitchen, and I knew it was over.

I had so many chances to come clean, but I blew every single one. Maybe I didn't want to. Maybe, deep down, I knew that there was no hope, and I self-sabotaged...again. Shocker.

Oh well, I tell myself for the hundredth time in the last fourteen days. *Oh* fucking *well*.

This is better for Mia. In fact, it's the best damn thing I could do for her. She's free to find someone who deserves her. Someone hotter, like Drake. Or smarter, like Hunter. Or more confident, like Emerson.

I'm a mess, and I tried to tell her that. So now I've done her the courtesy of saving her months or even years of trouble. A girl like her can do a fuck-ton better than be with a mess like me.

Goddammit. I need to get out of my head. Muttering a curse to myself, I head toward the bathroom. I have to get back to the club today. The event is tomorrow night, and if I don't make an appearance, they're going to cancel it.

Maybe they should.

I should go for a run. A run would be good. But all I do is stare at myself in the mirror and try to muster an ounce of the energy it would take to even put on my fucking shoes. It's just not there. It's nowhere to be found.

"Fuck," I mutter again, slamming my palm against the

countertop. I stare into my reflection and berate the man looking back for being the lazy, crazy, broken piece of garbage he is.

I'm not doing this again. I'm not going to spiral down again. It took me too goddamn long to pull myself out of it last time, and I've worked too fucking hard to keep this *thing*, this emotional parasite that gnaws and consumes and rots, hidden from everyone. If I let this out now, then it wins.

And I'm not going to let that happen.

I talk a big game for a guy who is defeated only moments later by a hair tie. One single black elastic hair tie, sitting on the back of the toilet where she left it two weeks ago before she climbed into my shower with me.

That's my trigger. The thing that sends me back into the dark, safe confines of my bed for the fourteenth day in a row. A black rubber band.

A solitary reminder that she was here, she was happy, she was mine…and I ruined it.

Ten years ago
Garrett

I pull up to my mom's house two hours late, still wearing last night's suit, with the remnants of a twenty-four-hour tequila buzz, about four hours of sleep, and an energy drink in my hand. I probably should have just gone home to sleep it off, but fuck it. I'm in a good mood. Before jogging into the house, I quickly glance in the rearview mirror to fix my hair. There's not much I can do about the circles under my eyes at this point.

As I step out of the car, my mother is waiting for me.

"You're late," she says from the front porch, standing with her arms crossed and glaring at me angrily. Fuck.

"I had to work," I say as I paste a fake smile on my face and jog up to the house.

"Work? It's two in the afternoon, Garrett. You work at a nightclub, so tell me why the hell you're just now getting here?"

I laugh instead of answering her. My mother doesn't want me to actually fill her in on my last twenty-four hours, the two girls I woke up next to…whose names I don't even remember. Yeah, I was working—about ten hours ago. We'll just call the rest *networking*.

"Would you rather I just didn't come?" I joke, but she doesn't laugh.

"It's her birthday, Garrett. Don't walk in the house if you're going to be like this."

"Like what?" I snap.

"You smell like alcohol. Your suit is wrinkled, and you look like you haven't slept in days."

"Thanks, Mom," I say with a laugh as I lean in to plant a kiss on her cheek, but she pulls away. "I have slept. In fact, I just woke up."

She stops me, putting a firm hand on my chest.

"I'm serious, Garrett. Talk to me."

"I'm fine," I reply, trying to make it sound convincing enough.

"You're not fine."

"Mom, I promise. I'm just working a lot, okay? I'm fine."

She heaves a sigh as I open the door and walk into her house—her new house. The one three sizes bigger than the one I grew up in. There's laughter coming from the backyard and a spread of food on the dining room table. Passing by, I grab a chip and scoop up some dip before heading out to the back patio where Paul is sitting with some of their new friends and their kids are splashing around in the pool.

I am severely overdressed, and the laughter dies as everyone glares up at me. I don't belong here. They might as well paint it on my forehead, but fuck it. I'm here, and I'm not going to just bounce now.

"Hey, Garrett," Paul says, breaking the silence with a cordial greeting.

"Hey, Paul," I reply. His friends are all still staring at me uncomfortably.

Then, I spot the bright-eyed blond with freckles and braces in the pool. Previously giggling with her friends, she instantly pauses and frowns in my direction when she sees me.

"Happy birthday, brat," I call toward her, but she doesn't respond. Just stares at me with a cool expression. Then her eyes dance over to the woman standing beside me, and I see her share a look with my mother. A tight-lipped smile.

And that feeling of being unwanted is no longer subtle or quiet. It's loud and humiliating. Turning my back on the uncomfortable eyes, I go back into the house. At least the spread of party food won't judge me. And I only have to root around in the cooler to find an ice-cold beer—the expensive brand too.

"Thanks, Paul," I mumble quietly to myself as I crack it open. They continue their conversation outside, and I shrug out of my jacket.

I'm eating alone in the kitchen when Paul's thirteen-year-old brat of a daughter finds me. "What happened to you?" she asks in a snotty, sarcastic tone. She's wrapped in a tropical flower beach towel, her dirty blond hair still wet and stuck to her head.

"What happened to you?" I reply with a sneer.

"You didn't even wear your swimsuit to a pool party."

"I don't plan on swimming, and I'm not a kid."

"Well, you act like one," she snaps back, and I know she's just being a brat. It's what she always does when we're together, and I can dish out the attitude too, but today, I'm just feeling tired. And bitter. And empty.

"Easy on the chips," I reply, watching her hand as it reaches for another handful of Doritos. That was a dick thing to say because I am a dick. I'm an asshole, and she's just a sweet kid whose mom died when she was a baby and who certainly didn't ask for such a dickhead of a stepbrother.

But deep down, I hate Mia for really stupid reasons. Reasons that only a self-absorbed, chemically imbalanced man-child would hate a little girl. I'm not proud of it, and I'm not denying the fact that I am a grade-A asshole.

"Fuck you, Garrett," she mutters in return, tossing a handful of chips at me.

I deserved that. Then she storms out of the house, and my mom is rushing in, obviously overhearing her little princess getting upset.

"What was that all about?" she asks.

"She was being a little bitch," I reply.

"Garrett!" My mother's voice is piercing, too loud and harsh to feel like a warning. I've gone too far. I've pushed too hard. Everyone is at their limit, and I know by the way she's looking at me now, the limit has been passed.

"Why don't you just leave?" my mother says, unable to look me in the eye. "The party's just about over anyway."

The party doesn't look over. But it sure as fuck looks like I'm killing the mood. Without a word, I spin on my heels and bolt out of the kitchen. "It's all right, Mom. I won't interrupt your new family's perfect day."

"Stop it," she snaps. "That's not fair."

I catch a glimpse of my reflection in the black screen of the television as I pass, and I realize just how wrong I look here. I'm a mess. My whole life is a mess. Every single decision I've made has led me to this mess.

"You're clearly in a bad mood," she says with a little more care as I make my way to the front door.

I scoff. "A bad mood?"

A bad mood. Fuck, I wish I knew what a bad mood felt like. I wish my bad moods weren't like tornado-sized spirals. I wish I could brush off a bad mood with some sleep and a warm meal.

"Your life is so perfect now, and you don't want me around. I get it."

"Stop it," she mutters. "That's not fair."

"No, it's not," I reply.

"You need to grow up, Garrett. You're twenty-six. It's not fair to Mia to have you show up like this."

"Probably better if I didn't come at all, right?"

"I would never say that," my mother argues. "I just want you to be happy, Garrett."

I throw my arms in the air. "I wish I knew how, Mom."

Out of the corner of my eye, I see the blond standing in the doorway, tears streaking down her face with a frown as she stares at me. She wants me to leave, I can tell. She'd rather I wasn't in her life at all, and I'm more than happy to satisfy her wishes.

"Sorry to ruin your birthday, brat," I mutter before disappearing through the front door.

The rest of the day I'm numb, and I feel like I'm silently sinking into mud.

I go to my apartment. I drink a little more. I replay everything that happened, letting the harshness of their looks dig a little deeper each time.

Replaying today funnels into replaying last night, then the last week, then the last month, until I realize that my life is shit. My job is shit. My friends are shit, and every good feeling I had when I woke up today is stained black.

When eight o'clock rolls around, I don't leave for work like I'm supposed to. I don't even call in. They don't need me there. They probably don't even want me there.

I dig out an old bottle of benzos from the back of my closet because I just need to quiet the voices. I haven't taken them in years, but I haven't had a real attack since high school either. But I remember liking the way they drowned out the noise, and I'm just thinking that they will help me sleep. Maybe two will help take the edge off. Maybe three will make the vodka hit a little harder.

Before I know it, I'm in a bad-decision spiral, and the rest is an accident. It really is. They'll say it wasn't an accident, but it was. Because I don't want to die. I just don't want to live like this anymore.

Rule #34: Quitting is not an option.

Garrett

I DON'T KNOW WHAT TIME IT WAS WHEN MY PHONE DIED, BUT WHEN I wake up the next morning, the screen is black, so I toss it across the room. It doesn't matter; she's not calling, and I'm pretty sure the incessant banging sound in the distance isn't from my phone anyway.

"Garrett, open up or I'm calling 9-1-1."

Emerson? What the fuck?

"I'm coming…" I groan as I roll out of bed. When my feet hit the floor, the room tilts a little and I stumble. Probably more from the fifth of vodka I put away last night and not an actual trick of physics.

He bangs again.

"I'm coming!" I yell. I look like shit, smell like shit, and feel like shit, but it's a little late to fix it now. Emerson Grant is about to unhinge my front door.

When I pull it open, he stares at me, nostrils flared and panic in his eyes. "Jesus," he mutters.

"Good morning to you too," I reply. I must look better than I thought.

"It's two in the afternoon."

I reply with a shrug while he stands on the welcome mat, just looking at me, probably wondering what the fuck he's supposed to say now. So I start for him, since I assume he's here to see why I haven't come into the club all week.

"Sorry I haven't been in…just feeling under the weather."

He glances down at my clothes and then into my apartment. I squeeze the door closed a little to keep him from seeing the mess I'm hiding behind me.

"You're sick?" he asks.

"Yeah. Must have caught something," I lie.

"Huh," he replies, pulling his phone out of his pocket. "Is that why you sent me these messages last night?"

When he holds up his phone, I wince, my text messages from last night staring back at me.

I quit.
I'm sorry.
I'll sell you my portion of the company.

Oh, vodka. I grimace as I clutch onto the door, faintly remembering sending those texts. The idea about quitting isn't as faint, though. I've been thinking about that for more than a few days. Guess I just needed some alcohol and a serotonin deficiency to finally send it.

"Garrett, what's going on?"

Fuck it. "Yeah, I just think it's time for me to move on from Salacious. It does fine without me—"

"No."

"What do you mean no?" I laugh.

"I mean no."

"Emerson, you can't stop me from—"

"What happened with Mia?" He tries to peek around me again.

"Nothing. We're not…together. We were just fucking."

"Bullshit. What happened?"

I scoff. "You're being an asshole today," I joke, but my head is splitting, and the sooner I get rid of him, the sooner I can go back to bed, where it's dark and quiet. And there are no friends invading my privacy and bossing me around.

"Why don't you get showered and come into the club with me?"

"I told you I'm not feeling well," I mutter, not hiding the irritation in my voice anymore.

"Yeah, well, I think getting out of here might help."

"Tomorrow."

He's staring at me, his brow furrowed, and for a moment, I almost hate him. Because he has no fucking idea.

And just when I think he's about to give up and walk away, he shoves past me and mutters, "I'm not leaving." Then, he marches right into my messy apartment.

"Emerson, what the fuck?" The door closes behind me as I follow him into my kitchen, grimacing at the pile of dishes in the sink and the barely touched spoiled lasagna on the counter.

"You don't want to go to work, that's fine. But at least go take a shower. I'll wait." I'm mortified as he picks up a bag of two-day-old takeout and tosses it in the garbage. Anger boils in my veins as I glare at him. The fucking audacity of this guy.

"Get the fuck out of my apartment," I bark.

Turning toward me, he replies, "No. You want me out, you'll have to throw me out." As he crosses his arms and glares at me, I realize this motherfucker is serious. I'm not a goddamn idiot; I know why he's doing this, why he won't leave, and it's humiliating. He's treating me like a child, so I heave a sigh before I actually consider trying to wrestle this well-dressed millionaire out of my apartment.

"Emerson, I'm fine, okay? You don't have to babysit me."

"Well, I'm not leaving."

"I'm telling you I'm fine, dammit." My voice comes out louder than I wanted it to, but he doesn't even flinch.

"I'm sorry, Garrett. But I can't leave."

"I'm not a fucking child. And I don't want you to see me like this. So please, just fucking go." I'm putting up a good fight, but the spiral is too strong—definitely stronger than me.

The asshole in the suit standing in my kitchen doesn't even budge. Okay, now I really do hate him. A lot.

I hate the fact that for ten years, he's been too nice to me. Always checking in when I'd ghost for a day or two, always asking too many questions or trying to care when I clearly didn't want him to. But he's never done this. Then again…it's been a long time since I was *this* far gone.

And as much as I hate him, I hate letting him down even more. Which is the only reason I give in to his annoying fucking request.

"You want me to go shower? Fine!" Spinning toward my bedroom, I slam the door so hard a picture falls off the wall in my room. Great, now I'm throwing a tantrum like a child. On the bright side, this is the most energy I've used in the last two weeks. But it does nothing for my splitting headache.

The shower just makes me tired again, and I avoid the temptation to crawl back into bed. When I do finally come out of the bedroom in a clean pair of jeans and a semi-clean T-shirt, Emerson *fucking* Grant is standing at my kitchen sink with his shirtsleeves rolled to the elbows as he loads my dishwasher.

"You've got to be fucking kidding me," I mutter, rubbing my temple.

"Feel better?"

"Not even a little bit," I reply coldly. "Will you please, for the love of God, stop cleaning my kitchen?"

"No. Now tell me about Mia."

When I smell the aroma of coffee, I cross the room and pour myself a cup. It's not vodka, but it's the second-best thing.

"I'll give you one guess," I grumble.

"She figured out you were the man behind the profile."

"Yep," I reply with a sarcastic grin, holding up my coffee cup.

"Have you apologized?"

"I tried, but come on...I don't deserve her forgiveness. It's over. I let it go, and so should you." Taking my coffee cup over to the barstool, I sit in the same spot she sat in that night. The memory of the promises we made hits like a tidal wave.

"I'm sorry," he says, and when he looks at me this time, it doesn't feel so much like he's angry or disappointed anymore. He does look sorry. I think that might be worse.

"Don't pity me, Emerson. I'll be fine. I fucked up, but it doesn't change anything. I still think I should just back off at Salacious."

"Why?" he asks.

"Look at me."

"I am. I've worked with you for ten years, Garrett. Salacious was a great app because of your ideas, and now it's a great fucking club because of you. And tonight, we have an epic fucking event happening that *you* put together, so get out of this apartment with me and come see it."

"I can't."

"Yes, you can."

"You don't understand," I mutter darkly into my steaming cup of coffee.

"I don't have to understand, and I never will if you don't fucking talk to me. Talk to Mia. Talk to a therapist, just fucking talk to someone. But you're not giving up. That's not an option."

I breathe heavily, forcing back the stinging emotion rising to the top, making everything behind my eyes and in my throat ache with the need to just let it out. And after a long, torturous silence, the dam breaks. Tears leak across my face, and I quickly wipe them away before he can see them. This fucking sucks. Then a box of tissues appears in front of me, and I glare up at him with anger.

"I hate you."

He laughs, a large hand landing on my shoulder. "That's fine. You can hate me."

"I spent the last ten years keeping my shit together, and now you just want me to lose it."

"Eh, you didn't keep it that hidden, Garrett. I saw it."

"Lovely," I reply.

"I tried to help, but you never let me."

"I told you," I reply, glaring up at him, "I didn't want you to see me like this."

"You think depression is something to be ashamed of, Garrett? You didn't choose this any more than Mia's dad chose to have cancer. If he were my best friend, what kind of man would I be if I left him alone in his apartment when he was sick?"

For once, I don't respond right away. I don't have a quippy comeback or a sarcastic reply. The emotion is so thick in my throat that I can't seem to form words anyway. It's a long time before I'm able to clear it and mutter, "Thank you."

"You don't have to thank me. I'm just sorry I didn't force myself into your apartment sooner."

I let out a small chuckle, and he laughs a little too. The heavy weight of sadness seems to have evaporated a little, leaving us both feeling a little lighter.

"Don't you have an event to get to?" I ask.

"I'm not going," he replies as he leans his broad arms on the granite countertop.

"Bullshit. Yes, you are."

"Not if you're not." The look on his face is stoic and unforgiving, and I know that he's got me. The master manipulator that he is has to just control everything and everyone, and now he has me right where he wants me. Even after that touching moment we just had, I'd still like to punch him in the jaw.

My teeth clench as I squeeze the coffee cup tighter in my fingers. "You're the world's worst business partner," I mutter.

"Well, then I guess it's a good thing I'm not here as your business partner."

Rule #35: Payback is a bitch.

Garrett

THE CLUB IS ALMOST UNRECOGNIZABLE. IT'S EVEN BETTER THAN I imagined. There's a low, false ceiling created from thick, black velvet curtains, to give the room a more intimate vibe. The lights are so low it's almost impossible to see another person, but low LED lights run along the length of the floor, guiding patrons through the main room, which has been transformed so that the voyeur hall is no longer a hall; it's the entire club.

There's a sultry beat, louder than normal, mingled with the low hush of whispers in the crowd. And when I glance around, I see so many new faces. People I remember sending invitations to. Performers and agents and then our regulars too.

Ronan Kade tips his glass toward me when I notice him at the bar with a beautiful woman on his lap. A new one, of course. I spot Eden and Charlotte near the front, looking busy, and I feel a pang of regret for a moment that Mia isn't here. She should see this, but the odds of her stepping foot in this building again are pretty slim.

Emerson and I stroll through the space, each room occupied.

And it makes me laugh as I think about Mia comparing the voyeur hall to a museum, and when I look at it like this, she's right. It does look like people are admiring art in a museum. Suddenly, I feel a tap on my shoulder, and I turn to find Isabel, Hunter's wife, throwing her arms around my neck.

"It's so good to see you," she whispers. "You look great!" She rakes her eyes admiringly over my suit, the black embossed velvet Tom Ford jacket, one I picked especially for this occasion.

"Thanks," I stammer uncomfortably as I smile back at the stunning redhead. This woman has to be the kindest person on the planet, soft-spoken and generous. Almost makes you wonder how she ended up with a foul-mouthed guy like Hunter.

He shows up at her side a moment later and shakes my hand with a tense smile. "Good to see you," he mutters, because that's about as much general emotion as Hunter ever shows.

"Are you going to the main stage?" Isabel asks, clasping her hands together.

"The main stage?" I reply.

"Yeah, she looks *so* beautiful."

"Who?" I ask, but Emerson grabs my shoulder and steers me away from the conversation. "What is she talking about?"

We make our way through the hallway toward the main room, where one room is set up onstage. It's black on black with a platform bed on a round dais and against the wall are cuffs, hanging from a single point in the back. It's simple and classy, and I remember the design being Mia's idea.

"Don't be mad at me," Emerson says quietly.

"What?" I ask, feeling the blood drain from my face.

"Remember when I said Mia wasn't going to be here tonight?"

Just then, the lights go down, so it's almost pitch-black and the music gets louder, drowning out all the noise in the sex-filled club. A small spotlight shines on the stage. A moment later, she walks into it, a subtle gleam glistening in her pearly-white hair. And my jaw nearly hits the floor.

I glare back at Emerson with my teeth clenched. He avoids my gaze as he quickly replies, "I lied."

"What the…" I mumble, but she draws my gaze again.

In flowing white silk draped over her shoulders and literally *nothing else*, she looks ethereal and angelic. I'm speechless as I watch her glide gracefully across the stage, her body in sync with the beat of the music.

She crawls sensually onto the bed, and it starts to rotate slowly. After picking up a piece of black silk off the bed, she ties it around her head, blindfolding herself.

The way she commands the crowd reminds me of the girl in the bar, onstage, gyrating to the music during her terribly sung karaoke, but this is different. The sexuality she exudes is amazing to me, and I can't take my eyes off her.

When I glance to the side, I see Emerson watching her too, and I punch his shoulder hard, but he only laughs as he puts his hands up. "I'm leaving," he whispers, "but you should stay."

With that, he slinks through the crowd and leaves the main room. I'm left alone with her and about thirty other people as she touches herself, twisting her nipples in a sensual tease that has my mouth watering.

When she rolls back to her knees, the bed rotates until we are all waiting with anticipation for the view we want so badly. She's running her fingers through her folds, touching herself with long, delicate fingers, her hips writhing as she does.

And I snap. Like that night in the hallway when I caught her in the room, and I feel a carnal urge to claim her for myself. My dick wants that too.

Bolting up to the stage, I don't even care that people are watching me. In fact, I don't even see them as I climb onto the bed behind her. Immediately, she tenses with a gasp. I pull her upright, tearing the blindfold off her face, and make her look me in the eye.

"What are you doing?" she asks in surprise with a quiver in her voice.

"Reminding you who you belong to." My hands stroke over her breasts as I bring her mouth to mine, kissing her hard. She falls into the kiss for a moment, her lips melting softly between mine before finally pushing away.

"No," she whispers, "I'm still mad at you."

In a rush, she climbs off the bed, bolting offstage. I barely manage to cut her off in time, putting my body in front of hers before she can leave. I notice her eyes glance toward the audience once, but I still don't care about them. I only see her.

"Let me make it up to you," I say, lifting her chin up to me, but she jerks it out of my grasp. When she tries to move around me, I stop her again. Then, with my hands on her hips, I lower myself to my knees in front of her. Gazing up at her, I touch her body, my hands gliding softly over her waist and down to her thighs, then up the middle. She trembles when my fingers reach the tender skin where her legs touch.

"Please, kitten," I whisper. "Let me show you how sorry I am." My touch grazes the moist skin of her cunt, and she exhales slowly as her eyes drift closed. With my eyes on her face, I stroke her clit and watch her reaction.

"Here?" she replies in a breathy moan.

"Yes, here."

I press my lips against her stomach, tasting the sweetness of her skin as I move my face downward, sliding my tongue into her heat, and she grabs my head, grinding herself against me.

"Garrett, wait," she pleads.

Reluctantly, I pull my mouth away and stare up at her. "Yes, kitten?"

A wicked smile pulls one corner of her mouth upward. "Stand up." I do as she says, rising to my feet. "Take your clothes off."

With my eyes on her, I peel my jacket off, throwing it on the bed, before unbuttoning my shirt as she peels open my buckle. My cock twitches in my pants from her touch, and while I slip my shoes off, she slides my pants down.

Distantly, I feel them watching, but I block them out. I keep my focus on her as I take off my boxers, letting them slide down my legs, my stiff cock bouncing up as it's freed from its confines.

When I reach for her, she stops me, holding my wrists in her hands. And I cock my head to the side, waiting for her to explain why I can't touch her.

"You want to make it up to me?"

"Of course," I reply.

With a gentle nudge, she pushes me backward until my back hits the black wall at the back of the room. She has to rise to her tiptoes to reach the cuffs. And my eyes go wide when I realize she wants to bind me to the wall. Giving her all of my trust, I lift my hands for her, so she can wrap the black Velcro around each wrist. Soon, I'm standing with my arms lifted, bound to the wall, completely at her mercy.

Now, I really feel them watching. My heart pounds rapidly in my chest as I glance out at the crowd, their hungry gazes on my naked body and jutting cock, hard and ready for Mia's touch. I have never felt so vulnerable in my life. And while it's fucking terrifying, it numbs the voices and thoughts in my head.

"Do your worst," I whisper to her, and as her hands slide down my body, she smiles.

"Oh, I plan on it. Why don't we show them how bad you are?" she says in a sultry whisper.

My breath hitches as she lowers to her knees in front of me, kissing her way down my chest as she goes. When her face reaches the height of my cock, goose bumps erupt along my skin. I watch with a hooded gaze as her tongue reaches for my shaft, licking a small circle around the swollen head.

"Oh, Mia," I growl, struggling against the restraints as she teases me. When she swallows my cock into her mouth, I'm distantly wondering how *this* is my punishment. Mia would never let me off the hook that easy. And I wish I could think of something, but she's currently sucking every thought out of my head.

The crowd in the room has grown. I can barely see with the light in my eyes, but I can tell the empty spaces have been filled, and they are all watching me. The closer I get to my climax, the more I want to hide. For so long, I was the one watching, the one on the sidelines, and now I'm here, front and center, and it feels all wrong, but then I look down at her, and she silences all of those voices again.

"I'm gonna come, kitten," I growl, and just before the climax takes over, she pulls her mouth off my cock and scratches her nails across my abs. I squirm against the holds again, the orgasm fading as the pain of her scratches scares it away.

Then with that mischievous look on her face, she stares up at me, and I watch her reach for something hidden behind the bed, where the audience can't see.

"Do you remember what you bought me?" she asks in a wicked, teasing tone.

My mind scrambles. What did I buy her?

When the light catches the metal in her hand, my mouth goes dry. Oh, fuck.

"I was going to use this in my performance, but now that you're here…it seems like such a terrible opportunity to waste."

I take a deep breath, watching her twirl the metal plug around in her fingers. It's not something I've ever tried before, but it's also not something I'm entirely against either. I mean…I made her try it.

"Like I said, do your worst." With my eyes squeezed shut, I let my head fall back and rest against the wall.

Then her hand glides carefully up my leg as she whispers sweetly, "Are you sure? You don't have to."

"I'm sure, kitten. I trust you."

"Okay, good," she replies wickedly. "Turn around."

With my hands still bound above my head, she spins me so now my backside is exposed to the audience. It's not as humiliating as I thought it would be. More…exciting and intense, but

I have her hands sliding up my back, tracing her fingers over my thighs and then up my spine as her breath grazes my skin.

"Are you okay?"

"Yes," I reply, and then her hand wraps around my front, taking my stiff length in her hands and making me cry out from the sensation.

"It's not about humiliation, Garrett. It's about vulnerability." She lets go of my cock, and I hear the snap of her opening the bottle of lube. I wait with anticipation as she continues, "It's liberating, isn't it? Knowing that they want you. That they want to see you feel good. That they want your pleasure as much as you do."

She's right. It is exhilarating, and my cock is throbbing just from the thought of being watched. Then, I feel her press the warm metal between my cheeks, slowly easing it into place, and a guttural moan escapes my body. My mind goes blank as the plug nudges my prostate.

"Oh fuck, oh fuck, oh fuck, Mia," I growl, her name drawing itself out of my mouth and turning into a long, hungry groan of pleasure.

Her nails drag delicately against my back as she hums in approval. "So dirty, Garrett. They love it. You should see the way they're looking at you."

"Suck me off. Now," I bark, my hands shaking against the holds. "Ride my dick or something, kitten. I swear I'm gonna fucking lose it."

She laughs, teasing me, and I struggle some more. When her fingers dig into the cheeks of my ass, I want to scream.

"I like watching you squirm," she replies cruelly.

"Oh, kitten. You're gonna pay for this. I'm gonna fuck you so hard when I get out of these."

I quickly learn the more I struggle, the more the plug pokes and teases my prostate, making my cock ache and leak at the tip.

"I look forward to it." She hums.

"Please, baby. Wrap those pretty lips around me. I'm begging you."

"Tell me you're sorry," she whispers against my back.

"I'm sorry, Mia. I swear to God, I'm so sorry. You know I'm sorry." I've resorted to groveling, and I'm not ashamed of it.

"And you'll talk to me from now on instead of hiding behind a stupid fake profile…"

"Yes, of course. I promise."

"And you'll let me do this to you again?"

Even through my pain, I can't resist smiling as I reply, "You sadistic bitch."

"Is that a yes?"

"Fuck yes."

Then she spins me around so my back hits the wall as she drops to her knees again, and when her eager lips wrap around my cock, I let out a sound so loud, it rattles my bones. I can feel her humming around me as she works my shaft with her lips and lots of saliva. With the added pressure of the plug, I'm not just soaring toward my climax, I'm careening toward it, head-on like a violent collision.

I come and come and come for so long, it feels like she's draining me of everything I have. Sweat drips down my temple as I gaze down at her, those beautiful blue eyes gazing back up at me, and when my cock is spent and my body goes limp, she pulls her perfect mouth off my cock, closes her lips, and swallows.

Rule #36: What comes around goes around.

Mia

He's gone wild—and I love it. Unhinged and free Garrett is my favorite version of him. After relieving him of the pressure on his prostate and reaching up to undo the Velcro straps holding him against the wall, I feel his feral gaze on me. It's a little like unleashing a wild animal.

The moment he's free, I'm hoisted off the floor, his arms under my legs as I land hard against the platform bed.

"You're gonna pay for that, kitten." Then he dives headfirst between my legs, the soft skin of his freshly shaven face against my sex. I let out a loud cry of pleasure as he licks and sucks on every inch of me, rounding his lips on my clit and sucking so hard, I stop breathing. Coming up for air, he stares at me with a hungry gaze. "Now, purr for me."

And he's back to devouring me like he can't make me come fast enough. And I need it. The act of tying him up, sucking him off, and seeing just how crazy that little backdoor play made him, I'm more turned on and ready to explode than I've ever been in my life.

Not to mention the added effect of dramatic lighting, sexy beats, and the horny watchful eyes in the crowd… I think I died and went to sex heaven.

My fingers dig into his hair as my climax teases me, nearly cresting three times, only to evade me at the last moment. I glance up at him each time that he eases up, wondering why he's teasing me so much. I guess I already know. I teased him pretty mercilessly when he was strapped to the wall, so I should have seen this coming. I guess it's only fair.

"Garrett, please," I beg when he takes his mouth away again.

"What's wrong? Am I torturing you?"

"Just make me come," I plead.

"I'm drawing this out for as long as I can because as soon as I'm done, you're taking my cum again."

Oh God. My toes curl and my spine tingles just from the sexy, enticing filth of his words.

He's pushed me so far, my head is hanging off the edge of the bed as we continue to slowly rotate, giving the audience a three-sixty view of him eating me out like his lips were made for my pussy.

Finally, he plunges two fingers in, curling them at just the right angle that they finally send me flying. My thighs squeeze hard around him, and I'm practically levitating off the bed as I come. Pleasure ignites through every inch of my body, from my head down to my toes. His growl vibrates through me, but he doesn't let up.

I hope he doesn't try to get another one out of me right away like he did that day. I didn't even know orgasms could be a form of torture until Garrett tried wringing them out of me one after the other.

But when I glance up at him, I see that he has very quickly recovered from his own orgasm and is currently at full mast again, slowly stroking himself as he prowls toward me. Grabbing my legs, he jerks me to the edge of the bed. He's standing on the rotating platform as he impales me abruptly on his cock.

Still sensitive in my post-orgasm state, everything is so intense and satisfying. Hooking my legs over his forearms, he pounds into me.

Our gazes are locked as we collide, but when the sensation gets so good, I feel my toes curling again, my eyes drift close and my head hangs backward. Suddenly, he stops thrusting.

My eyes pop open, and I stare at him in confusion.

"When you look away, I stop."

I bite my lip and keep eye contact with him as he starts moving again, slamming harder and harder until it becomes almost impossible to keep my eyes from closing. I've completely forgotten about the crowd and the stage and all of the reasons why I'm mad at him. I'm not saying I've forgiven him already, but the things he did wrong don't exist at this moment. There's just him and me and the intensity between us.

"Touch yourself," he mutters breathlessly, and I know he's close. "Come with me, kitten."

Reaching down, I strum at my clit, already so sensitive and at the precipice, so it doesn't take much before I'm trembling through another orgasm. He's slamming in slower, his thrusts less controlled now, his cock jerking inside me as he comes. I am consumed by him, not quite knowing where his pleasure ends and mine begins. And through more than just our eye contact, we feel so entirely unified that my heart throbs with this reminder that there is another heart out there that beats as one with mine.

Garrett and I aren't alike or compatible or kindred spirits—we are one. It's why the boundaries in our relationship were so confusing. Because I never hated him, and he never hated me, but the fire burned between us regardless. It was easier to pretend we were nothing more than stepsiblings when we didn't know how to label what this thing between us was. Now, we know it's love, and it was always meant to be.

His chest is heaving as he begins to slump, dropping my legs and climbing over me, so his body is a warm layer covering me. Then, he kisses me. It's a soft, tender movement of lips and tongues.

Suddenly, the light above us goes out, and we are bathed in darkness. It's instantly cooler and all the chatter from the crowd comes back, reminding me that we just fucked like crazy in front of what looks like a hundred people.

My legs are wobbling under me as I walk out of the bathroom behind the stage. I'm cleaned up and in fresh clothes, and suddenly, it makes sense to me why Salacious has locker-room style bathrooms with showers and dressing rooms. Sex is a workout.

The crowd has dwindled and most of the rooms are empty now, and I'm surprised to see it's almost three in the morning. My eyes feel instantly heavy at that realization. When I find Garrett by the bar, he's with the rest of the owners and their girlfriends.

When I spot the tall blond, real Drake, I awkwardly avoid his eye contact. It's just another reminder of what this month has been like, something I don't need at the moment.

"There she is!" Charlie announces as she slings an arm around my shoulder. "You were freaking amazing." I like Charlie. She's the right mix of crass and classy, and she never fails to make me laugh. And being here this week with her and Eden has me thinking that I might have actually found a group of female friends that don't treat me like competition and don't judge me because I'm not a size two and still choose to dress the way I do. They just accept me, no conditions.

"Thank you," I reply, wrapping her up in a hug.

Does it feel weird to be complimented for how well I had sex? I mean…yeah, a little. It feels like something that *should* feel weird, but not here.

I yawn against my will.

Garrett sees it and steps up. "Let me take you home. It's late."

"I drove myself here," I argue, but as he gazes down at me, a soft, knowing expression on his face; I know what he means. He doesn't want to drop me off at home. He wants to take me to his home.

"Your car will be safe here."

"Okay," I reply, and it's not because I forgive him for that apology during sex. It's because I want to forgive him, and in order to do that I need an apology and some answers.

We say goodbye to everyone and don't speak much on our way to the car. Once I slide in next to him, he reaches a hand toward me, clasping our hands over the console.

"You really were beautiful up there tonight."

"Thank you," I reply in a whisper.

"And I meant every word. I am sorry, Mia."

"I know you are."

"Can we start over?" he asks, and I feel the tremble in his hands.

So I reach across and pull his face up to mine for a kiss. With our lips still touching, I reply, "Garrett, you let me stick a butt plug up your ass in front of a hundred people. The least I can do is hear you out."

He laughs, a full grin pulling across his lips, as he kisses me back, and it warms my heart to see that smile. So much that I lean in to kiss it again.

Rule #37: Love the mess too.

Mia

HE'S INSISTENT ON FEEDING ME, SO I'M SITTING ON THE BARSTOOL again in the middle of the night, while he toasts a grilled cheese on the stove like I'm a child. Once he places the plate in front of me, he starts talking before I can even ask.

"Emerson cleaned my kitchen," he says, and it's a weird place to start, but Garrett isn't used to opening up, so I'll take whatever I can get.

"I'm having a hard time picturing that," I reply.

"He doesn't even clean his own kitchen," he jokes. "But mine was a mess, and he gave me no choice. It was a nonconsensual kitchen cleaning."

"He's a good friend," I reply before taking a bite.

"Infuriatingly so."

It's quiet for a moment as he retrieves a bottle of water for me from the fridge. Before opening it, I ask, "So why was your kitchen such a mess?" Although, I already know.

He lets out a heavy sigh. Then he looks me in the eye, those fierce blue irises staring into my soul. "A two-week-long depressive episode."

Tears prick the backs of my eyes, and I resist the urge to hold him as a reward for finally being brave enough to utter those words to me. But we need this conversation not to be muddled by physical touch. "That was hard to say out loud, wasn't it?"

He nods. "It wasn't the first time. Probably won't be the last either."

This new Garrett, the one finally opening his heart and letting me see the real him, is so exhilarating, I almost can't eat. But he points at my plate before ordering me to finish it.

"When did it start?" I ask, eager to know more, to *see* more of him.

"As long as I can remember. It felt like a dark voice in my head, always telling me how bad I was, how hopeless everything was, and I had no choice but to believe it. I was the laid-back, easygoing guy. I wasn't supposed to be *depressed*. So I did everything I could to hide it."

"Weren't you ever prescribed anything to help?"

His head hangs, and a look of discomfort colors his expression. "Baby, I was never diagnosed."

"But your mom…knew, didn't she?"

"She knew I was a pain in the ass. She knew I was difficult and unpredictable and hard to connect with. But she didn't know the first thing about raising a depressed kid."

I lean forward, resting my forearms against the counter. The urge to hold him now is getting harder to fight. The pain and guilt he's been carrying for so long has etched its way into his very identity. Garrett sees himself as the problem and not this illness that plagues him.

"But it wasn't your fault," I say, and his eyes lift up to my face. Quickly, he swallows and forces a tense smile.

"I know…or at least I'm starting to figure that out. And it wasn't hers either. She tried… I really do believe that."

"So do I," I reply, biting my lip. "I'm just sorry you had to hide it for so long. I mean, you hid it from me for fifteen years."

"Mia…" he says delicately, drawing out my name, and I tilt my head and wait. "I hid it *especially* from you. I did everything I could to keep people from seeing it. But then after a while, it felt like…no one really saw *me* anymore. It was easier to stay alone, watch from the sidelines, and never put myself in the position to be vulnerable. Ten years went by like that."

"I'm sorry," I whisper. I'm heartbroken, knowing that Garrett has spent so much of his life alone and not because he wanted to be, but because it was the only way to keep his dark secrets hidden.

"When Paul was in the hospital, my mom said something to me about you. About how you brought me peace, settled all the mania a little bit."

"Do you think that's true?" I ask, secretly praying he does. I want to bring him every ounce of peace I possibly can.

"Yes. I think I still need actual help—help I probably should have gotten a long time ago, but I do think you make it better. Because I can be myself around you, Mia. I can show you my sometimes ugly mess of a life and you can show me yours, and it doesn't scare us away."

Biting my lip, I hold back my smile. When I came to the lake house this summer, my life was at peak messiness. I was holding power over men because I was too eager to be sexual and too scared to be vulnerable. I wanted a life I was too timid to ask for. But in just over a month, I've gotten to a stage in my life where I can wear my sexuality on my sleeve without shame or fear.

A place I got to with Garrett because he never once made me feel used or naive.

"And everything you told me on the app…was true?"

He gives me a pained smile. "You mean the ten years without sex? Yep."

"How?" I ask, tears pooling in my eyes again.

"How can such a smoke show like me keep it in my pants for so long? I had to beat the ladies off with a stick," he jokes, and I blink away my tears, shaking my head as I ball up my napkin and throw it at his head.

"I'm being serious, Garrett."

"Sorry. I'm being serious too. The truth is that I didn't miss sex. Because all of the sex I'd had up until that point was meaningless. Nameless connections that were unfulfilling and forgettable. I could get more satisfaction with my own hand and my imagination."

"Do you still feel that way?" I ask, painfully aware that if Garrett still doesn't feel fulfilled by sex, it could be a bad sign for us.

He tilts his head down and glares at me. "Obviously not. I already told you...you're mine now. And I'm not giving you up that easily."

"Good," I reply.

"Now, eat," he commands again, and this time, I listen.

Once my sandwich is nothing but crumbs on the tiny white plate, he takes me to bed. The hint of sunrise is apparent through the window, which he quickly closes with thick blackout curtains. Then we climb into bed together, half-naked and with no intention to have sex. But I curl up onto the pillow next to him, and we face each other.

And although there's no heat between us at the moment, I still revel in the feel of his gentle hands roaming my body appreciatively. He strokes my soft rib cage and dances his fingers along the ridges of my spine. He glides his fingers over my ass and back up to caress my belly in a way that makes me lightheaded. I've always loved my own body, but it's an entirely different thing to be with a man who appreciates it just as much, if not more.

As we lie here, I realize there are so many conversations ahead of us. Stories and secrets to be told and more than enough time to get through them all. And I do forgive him. Honestly, I probably forgave him even before he apologized. I just needed time to process my anger. Because deep down, if I'm being honest with myself...I wanted Drake to be Garrett. In my mind, he always was. There was no *real* Drake.

There always has been and only ever will be Garrett for me. My life has been a mess of failed attempts and indecision, but he is the one thing I can be sure of.

"Was that night you saw me on the app the first time you saw me like that? Attracted to me, I mean."

"Yes," he replies without hesitation. "I hope that doesn't hurt your feelings, but before that night, you were too young or too *my stepsister* to be anything else."

"It doesn't hurt my feelings," I whisper through the darkness. "Although I've been crushing on you since I was old enough to start crushing on boys."

He laughs. "Well, obviously." He drags me closer, wrapping his arms around my waist and bringing me to his chest, so there's not an inch of space between us. "I'm sorry I was such an asshole all those years. You didn't deserve that."

"Why *were* you so mean to me?" I ask, tracing patterns over the skin of his chest.

"Because that's how I protected you, Mia."

With that, I freeze and glance up at him. "Protected me from what?"

"Me. Don't you remember what a mess I was?"

"No," I reply honestly. "I don't remember you being a mess. I remember you being outgoing and fun and spontaneous. But I didn't see the mess."

"That's because I hid it from you. I wanted you to see the good stuff. Not the weaknesses."

Perching up on my forearms, I glare at him. "It's not a weakness, Garrett. And I didn't see the mess because I love the mess. I love you for the good and the bad. Plus, I have messes too."

He lets out a heavy breath, his blue eyes mirroring mine. And suddenly, I completely understand why he lied for so long, why he kept the fake profile as Drake. Because that was the only way for him to open up without putting himself at risk. But now, without that fake profile, he has nothing protecting him. And yet, he's still here. He still trusts me enough to let me in.

Brushing my hair out of my face, he pulls my face down to his and kisses my lips with tenderness.

"You know how much you mean to me, right?"

Tears prick my eyes again as I nod. "Yes."

"I really did try to hide for so long, but you…"

With a smile on my face and his eyes on mine, I reply, "I see you."

Rule #38: Some things do last forever.

Garrett's epilogue

THERE ARE THREE THINGS I'M SERIOUS ABOUT: RUNNING, A GOOD suit, and the bombshell blond drawing a crowd in room four. This shit never gets old. Tonight, she's in a short school-girl skirt, her tits hanging out of the front of her unbuttoned blouse, bouncing beautifully as she humps her pillow like it's a damn rodeo bull. *God damn, she's good at this.*

Every night, she takes a room, and I swear people show up at the club just for this. And while that caveman urge to go in there and take her for myself is still there, the sense of pride I feel watching her is unmatched. When I take her home later, I'll get it all out of my system anyway.

When her set comes to an end, she stands with her cheeks flushed and her hair a mess, and her gaze finds me through the window, shooting me a devious smile before she pulls the curtain closed.

The hall is at max capacity, as is our VIP membership. Turns out there are a lot of rich people in Briar Point who like to watch other people fuck. Color me shocked.

Does it bother me that most of these people have seen me naked and fucking like an animal onstage after having my prostate publicly prodded? No. Not anymore. In the three months since that night at the club, I've even been dragged into the voyeur rooms a time or two.

I mean, don't get me wrong, I still like to watch. I'm still a voyeur, and that will never change. My therapist likes to use big words like *self-inflicted disassociation*, but we both agree that there isn't a damn thing wrong with liking to watch people fuck—consensually, of course.

It really is about the most interesting thing two people can do…or more than two people, as I'm reminded by the energetic threesome taking place in the room next to Mia. It's when I spot Drake's tall form and light hair that I immediately look away and continue down the hall toward the exit where Mia will come out after she gets changed.

It's early, a lot earlier than we normally leave the club, but we have plans, and we can't be late. Although if I'm honest, I'd like to skip the whole thing entirely. But I'm not a fucking coward, and I said we were going to do this. So here we go.

"Ready?" she asks as she loops her arm through mine.

Leaning down, I kiss her forehead. "Not even a little bit."

She laughs. "You big baby. Come on. It'll be fun."

"You and I have very different definitions of fun."

On the drive, we listen to music and she sings along while I hold her left hand in mine, my thumb rolling the gold band back and forth to try and calm my nerves.

Are we moving a little fast? I don't think so. I've known Mia since I was twenty-one, and considering that I've basically grown into a new person since then, I feel like I've known her all my life. There isn't a person on this planet more suitable for me or for her.

It's not like Mom and Paul don't know we're together. It's made family dinners only slightly awkward. It was one thing to tell them we were a couple, but it was an entirely other thing to show affection in front of them. The first time Mia held my hand in front of her dad, I wanted to jump out the window to escape his furious stare.

But this is big news.

Nothing in my life has ever felt so serious, but the day I realized I wanted to marry Mia, I didn't hesitate. We had woken up one day last week, and when she climbed out of bed to open the window and let the sun in, I realized I wanted this to last forever. Ten years ago, I couldn't imagine wanting something forever. Now, I want everything good in my life to last. Slowly over the last decade, since we started Salacious, my life has started to take on some permanence. My friends feel like forever. This company feels like forever. And for a guy who never saw a forever kind of life in his cards, at the exact moment I realized I wanted Mia forever, I let the words slip out.

I wasn't on my knee. I didn't have a ring. And it wasn't some elaborate show of commitment.

I just looked at her from my pillow and said, "Marry me."

The way she gasped, the tender expression on her face, and the tremble of her lips are images that will remain stored in my memory until the day I die. To be honest, I don't even care much about the wedding, because it couldn't possibly compare to the way she looked at me in that moment before tearfully nodding and whispering, "Yes."

As we pull up to the bar downtown, where we're meeting our parents for drinks, I squeeze the steering wheel and take a few minutes to breathe before getting out of the car.

"Whenever you're ready," she says patiently from the passenger seat. Pulling her face to mine, I kiss her fiercely.

Then with a deep sigh, I look at her. "I'm ready."

My mom and Paul already have a table in the back. They wave us over with big smiles, and I'm relieved to see how much better her dad looks since his surgery. He's put on quite a bit of weight, which after the last year, is a good thing.

As Mia greets them, I keep her hand in mine, making the hugs a little awkward, but I don't need that hunk of gold on her hand to give away the news before we're ready. Sitting down, we order drinks, and while I've cut way back on the alcohol these past few months, I'm not going to turn down a Jack and Coke to calm my nerves tonight.

When Mia orders herself a spiked seltzer, my mother reacts with a loud, "Oh, dammit!"

We look at her with furrowed brows, and she quickly replies, "I was hoping you were gonna tell us you're pregnant."

"Mom!" I shout, the shock making my jaw drop.

Mia bursts out laughing, her bright smile making her dimples even deeper and those round cheeks of hers look so fucking kissable. "Not yet!" she squeals.

And I squeeze her fingers under the table. Not yet.

Not never...just not yet.

My heart pounds a little faster as I stare at her, the insane vision I had a few months ago seeming like a reality almost within my reach. How had it seemed so impossible back then, but now…

Unable to keep in her excitement, Mia tears her hand out of my grasp and displays the diamond studded band on her finger. "We're engaged!"

The shriek that comes out of my mother's mouth nearly silences the whole bar. Paul is smiling next to her, so that's a good sign. I find myself searching his reaction for any indication that he's disappointed, that I'm not good enough for his only daughter, that she could find someone better, but it's not there. Instead, he stands up and takes my hand, yanking me into an almost violent bear hug.

"I'm proud of you," he mutters, and it silences the intrusive thoughts.

There's an obnoxious exchange of hugs and questions and showing off the ring a hundred more times, and I don't even finish my drink by the time the excitement has died down. We start talking about dates and venues, and the girls get excited about the idea of having it at the lake house, a conversation I sit back for, simply basking in Mia's joy.

It's almost peaceful and relaxing, and I think everything might be all right. That is until the karaoke menu is placed on our table and my fiancée beams at it with mischievous excitement. And I have to bite back my laughter because I know exactly what she's thinking.

Pulling her close, I mutter low in her ear, "Don't even think about it, kitten." But she's an obstinate brat, and there's no stopping her.

As she grabs the pencil from the cup, she laughs. "Oh, come on, Garrett. You've done crazier things onstage."

Rule #39: What goes around, comes around.

Almost two years later
Mia's epilogue

"NOT AGAIN!" I SHRIEK AS HE PRESSES THE BUTTON ON THE PINK vibrator. It buzzes to life, and the moment it touches my clit, even on the lowest setting, I melt into the mattress.

"One more, kitten," he murmurs against my thigh as he forces me to yet another climax, *almost* against my will. "Just give me one more."

This is the fourth one tonight. That's not counting the morning orgasms or the one he gave me while we were in the hotel elevator—with security cameras watching. It's a miracle we haven't been kicked out of this hotel yet.

But this isn't just an anniversary vacation. It's a mission.

He climbs over my body, quieting my rambling thoughts with a harsh kiss. "I told you I had a surprise for you, didn't I?"

"Mm-hm," I reply, so tired I can barely keep my eyes open.

"Look at me, kitten," he commands as he leans back into a kneeling position between my legs. Sneaking a peek at him, I spot the tiny clear bottle of lube in his hands and my eyes pop open.

Lifting up to my elbows, my mouth goes dry and my heart picks up speed.

"Now?"

He nods.

"That's not how babies are made, Garrett," I say as I stare up at him with lust and excitement in my eyes.

"I think we've had enough baby-making sex this week, kitten. I've pumped you so full of cum, there's not a chance in hell you're not pregnant."

I swallow, my belly assaulted with butterflies from his words. Not just the idea of being pumped full of his cum—which I am—but the idea of a baby growing inside.

With a click, the top of the bottle flips open, and he gently drops two beads of lube onto his fingers. "Remember voyeur night at the club?" he asks as he eases my legs apart and delicately rubs at the tight hole. My mouth falls open, and I collapse onto the mattress.

"How could I forget?" I reply with a breathy whimper. "The sight of that cute butt of yours with the pretty teal gem squeezed between your cheeks. Everyone in Briar Point remembers that night."

With that, he slips his finger inside me and I gasp. Slowly, he strokes in and out, adding a second finger until I'm a squirming, panting mess of need.

"Just fuck me already, Garrett," I beg, and he replies with a low chuckle.

"But I like teasing you so much."

"You're an asshole," I murmur playfully. Then, there's another click of the bottle and I glance up to see him coating his cock with lube.

When I feel the head of his cock on my back entrance, I tense. My eyes clench shut, and instead of pushing forward, he pulls away.

"You know the rules, kitten."

My lids fly open and I stare up at him, the mischievous blue eyes looking back so full of love and happiness that I feel mine start to sting with the threat of tears. Doing anal is really a strange time for happy tears, but nothing with Garrett is ever conventional.

"Kiss me," I whisper, and he quickly answers my request, laying his body over me and pressing his soft lips to mine. It's a familiar kiss by this point, but it still makes my heart skip a beat every time.

"Ready?" he asks.

Eagerly, I nod.

Sitting back up, he hooks my legs over his arms and presses his cock into me, sliding past the ring of muscle until I am overwhelmed by this new feeling of fullness.

"You okay?" he asks, pausing once he's seated all the way in.

"Yes," I groan, my back arching and my legs starting to tremble.

And when he starts to move, a low growl emits from his chest as he stares down at the place where he's fucking me.

"Fuck, baby. I wish you could see this. It's so fucking hot. My filthy little kitten."

His thrusts are slow, but he goes so deep each time, I feel as if our bodies are one, more so than during regular sex. One of his hands finds mine, clutching our fingers together in a tight grasp while the other reaches for something on the bed. My mind is already so sidetracked by sensation that I don't register what he's doing until the vibration lands directly on my clit.

The scream that comes out of me will definitely get us kicked out of the hotel—for sure, this time.

My knees part even more, his cock picking up speed, and I practically levitate off the bed. This feels like nothing we've ever done before. Even with the plug, which we've *both* used since that first time. This is like all of the best sensations rolled into one. Forget fireworks and climaxes, my body is one giant explosion of pleasure.

Our hands are holding each other so tight, my nails are

digging into the skin of his palm. He's fucking me hard now, grunting with each violent thrust of his cock. Until finally, we both come undone. My body is deep in the throes of my orgasm when he quickly pulls out, spilling his cum all over my belly. The tingles across every square inch of my flesh are so intense I can't even feel the warm jets he's expelling.

It feels like hours go by as we both gasp for air. I don't fall asleep, but I'm definitely not entirely awake when I feel him delicately wiping my skin clean. After tossing the washcloth into the bathroom, he collapses next to me on the bed, his hand resting on the softness of my belly, the exact spot he just cleaned for me.

He's been doing this a lot lately. He always seems to be thinking about what our future might hold. The man who was once perfectly content with bachelorhood—or so he said—has been the most eager for each forward step in our relationship. Moving in together, getting married, buying our first house, and then this.

As badly as he wanted to, we didn't jump right into the baby making after the wedding. He wanted to be ready, at least as much as he could be. For him, that meant at least one solid year of therapy and antidepressants, and a solid three hundred and sixty-five days of proving to himself that he had everything under control. My faith in him never wavered, not once.

The episodes haven't gone away completely, and they never will. But at least he's able to get through them now and still be a loving husband and hardworking club owner. And hopefully soon, a devoted father.

I was actually happy we took this time for ourselves. As badly as I craved carrying a little blue-eyed bundle of joy, I really wanted some alone time with Garrett first. I had just started having sex and working at the club. There were so many kinky things I wanted to do and explore before a big belly got in the way.

"Are you asleep already?" he whispers against my forehead.

"Almost," I reply. As I curl into his arms, every muscle in my body cries in pain. We've fucked more in this hotel than we have in the past two years, and that's saying a lot, considering where we work.

It was his idea to come to Japan for our anniversary this year, and I have a suspicion he brought me just for the karaoke experience, which has been the second-best thing we've done all week. Last night, we rented a room and he got drunk for the first time in over a year, just watching me sing my heart out until I almost lost my voice.

Then, he made me sing the entirety of Fiona Apple's "Criminal" while I sat on his lap, his hand up my dress. Getting through the last chorus was nearly impossible. As it turns out, singing during an orgasm isn't easy.

"What are you thinking about?" he asks.

"Fiona Apple," I mutter sleepily.

"Oh yeah, that was fun. Hey, we should have a karaoke night at the club. People can sing while they fuck," he says with far too much energy for a man who just came so hard he nearly broke the bed.

"That's a terrible idea, babe."

"If anyone could pull it off, it'd be you," he says, kissing my cheek.

"Emerson would never go for it."

"Probably not." He yawns, pulling me against his chest.

"Besides, I'm about to be too busy to take on new projects at the club," I murmur. "Assuming this trip worked."

"Well, if it doesn't, we'll have to keep trying."

"Good plan."

Our voices are barely whispers at this point, sleepy mumbles through the darkness. But before I drift off to dream about sex-club karaoke, I softly say, "I love you."

His arms squeeze around my shoulders. "I love you too, brat."

Rule #40: Don't blink.

Bonus epilogue
Garrett

"HE'S ASLEEP."

Mia hurries through the door, shutting it quietly behind her while also trying to tear her clothes off at the same time.

I let out a soft chuckle as I close my laptop and set it on the nightstand next to the bed. The new club acquisition paperwork will have to wait because my wife is getting naked and that always takes priority.

"He's with my mom and Paul. What's the rush?"

She tears her oversized T-shirt over her head, revealing her beautifully engorged breasts and soft belly, making my cock twitch with need.

"Because," she says with a sigh, "the moment he wakes up he's going to want my tits again, and I just need a break."

"Come here, brat," I reply with a smile. "Let me look at you."

With a wicked smile, she crawls over me, completely naked, and I let out a hungry moan as she settles her weight on my lap. My fingers knead the pale flesh of her hips before running up her waist and cupping her full tits in each hand. She hums with pleasure as I do.

"You are so fucking sexy," I say in a low growl. My hands continue their trail upward until I'm burying them in her hair and tugging her down toward me to capture her lips in a kiss.

This woman is my home. I have laid claim on every piece of her perfect body. And she has given me everything I've ever needed—love, support, space when I need it, and confidence where it was lacking. Nothing could ever turn me on quite as much as that.

Now adding on the fact that she's carried and birthed my son, I'm in heaven.

Liam was born six months ago, and I'm still amazed and shocked by how love can feel so overwhelming.

"Hurry up, take your pants off. I need to see your cock."

"You don't have to tell me twice," I reply as I shimmy out of my sweats. The moment they're down to my knees, she's digging my hard shaft out of my boxers and stroking it relentlessly.

"Baby, what is the rush?" I say breathlessly. The feel of her hand around me steals the air from my lungs.

With a tight grip of my length, she looks me straight in the eyes. "Ever since I squeezed that baby out of my body, I have felt like Mommy, and I love it, I do. But right now, I desperately need to feel like the dick-hungry woman I am. So let me have this, okay? I want to feel like a filthy slut. I want to be your dirty, nasty, sex crazed little girl. Can you please just give me what I want?"

Jesus Christ.

I nearly come in her hand from the words alone. I don't deserve this woman. I don't. No one does. She's beyond the worthiness of men. She's God-tier perfect. But somehow I ended up the luckiest man on earth, and you will never find me complaining.

"Oh, Mia," I groan as I tighten my grip on her scalp and tug her back down toward me. When our mouths are just inches apart, I whisper, "You will always be my dirty little cock slut.

Always. Now put it in your mouth, but don't you dare suck. Not yet."

Her mouth turns up into a sly smile, and the moment I let go of her head, she slides down toward my waiting cock. Just like I told her to, she closes her lips around my stiff length. Her mouth is warm and inviting, and I resist the urge to thrust.

"Look at you, kitten. My dick is in your mouth. Do you like it?"

She gently nods.

"I remember the first time I watched you suck my dick. We were just a few miles from here, hiding in the woods. Remember that, baby?"

She nods again.

"Alright, now suck."

Desperate for it, she tightens her lips and sucks in, bobbing her head just a little as I dig my fingers in her short blond hair.

The tight heaven of her wet mouth drags a long, growling moan out of my body.

"God...damn...Mia," I stammer. The rest of the noises I make are indecipherable gibberish. Her lips close around the head as her tongue flicks the underside, making my body jolt and my balls draw up tight. She's going to have me shooting my load in record time.

Before she gets the chance, I force her mouth off of me and flip her onto her back. After devouring her soft lips, I work my way down, kissing a trail over her plush breasts and stomach until I'm dragging my tongue through her wet cunt. She cries out and arches her back in response, and it spurs me on. I suck harder, rubbing my facial hair over her sensitive skin like this is a competition to see who can make the other come faster.

I win.

Within about five minutes of sucking and nibbling her clit, she finally screams into a pillow while her thighs tremble around my ears.

Before she's even recovered, I'm sinking deep into her body, watching my cock as it disappears into her. Warm legs wrap around my waist as I lay my body over her. This feeling, the familiar embrace, is what heaven must feel like.

With my lips against hers and our hands entwined, I fuck her until I feel her tremble again. Then I'm shooting my own orgasm deep inside her.

We lie there for a while, each of us catching our breath. I bury my face in her neck, her hair tickling my face as I breathe in her intoxicating scent. Her fingers dance delicately along the backs of my arms. When I lift up, staring down at her, I notice all the ways she's subtly changed in the last three years. Her hair is a lot shorter now, cropped just above her shoulders. She wears far less makeup than she used to, letting me gaze into her eyes without all the thick black lashes in the way.

She's truly perfect in every single way.

"What are you thinking?" she whispers.

"Nothing," I reply before pressing my lips to hers. "Just that I love you."

"I love you too," she says with a soft smile.

We lay that way for a while before I eventually pull out of her and roll onto my back. Mia is asleep in minutes, so I press my lips to her forehead and climb out of bed.

After washing up in the downstairs bathroom, I head up to the main level of the house. It's raining, which explains why we're spending our third day at the lake house inside. We still enjoy our yearly summer retreats at the lake, and even though we could easily buy our own house in town, I sort of enjoy sleeping in the basement like old times. It reminds me of how Mia and I started. Now, married with a kid of our own.

My step-dad, Paul, is snoring peacefully on the recliner in the living room while my mom sits on the covered patio watching the rain fall with a mug in her hand. I blush at the thought of what Mia and I were just doing downstairs, but it's not like it's the first time we fucked down there, hoping the walls were soundproof enough.

Just then, I hear a familiar cooing sound coming from the travel crib in the living room. When I peer over the top, I see my bald-headed, blue-eyed son holding his feet in his hands, sucking one toe into his mouth. When he sees me, he lets out a squeal of delight, kicking wildly.

"Shh…" I say with a finger over my lips. I look up at Paul to see if Liam woke him, but he's still snoozing. His cancer has been in remission for over a year now, so it's good to see him packing on weight and getting back to his old self.

"You're supposed to be sleeping too," I whisper. When Liam squeals again, I lean down and scoop him up into my arms.

He gnaws on his fist and drools all over the front of his onesie while gazing up at me. I love that he is an absolute spitting image of Mia. Those big cheeks and pouty-lip smile. She says he'll start to resemble me as he gets older, but I don't care. I don't need him to look like me when I can stare into his eyes and see a piece of myself there.

Holding him in one arm, I take him to the kitchen to prepare him a bottle from the milk Mia left in the fridge. He watches, still chewing on his fingers, while I put it in the bottle warmer and turn the knob to warm it.

When he starts gabbing impatiently, I give him a little bounce.

Then I catch a glimpse of myself in the reflection from the window. A little heavier than I was five years ago, but in a good way. Soft facial hair from lack of interest in shaving. Hair in desperate need of a cut. I look like a mess and nothing like the man I was before. A very happy mess, though. If you had told me five years ago I'd be married with a kid (let alone with my step-sister) I would have called you crazy. But this feels so right.

Mia and Liam fill this place in my heart that used to ache from emptiness. I never once let myself believe that these two could cure the chemical imbalance that has plagued me for so long, and they don't, but they do give me something more to fight for. Something to live for.

They remind me that I matter. That my life and existence are important. That being depressed can't keep me from the fulfilling life I deserve.

Fatherhood is still terrifying, but it's nowhere near as scary as what I faced before when I was alone and hopeless.

Liam coos again, and I squeeze him a little tighter, bringing him up to my face so I can squish a big kiss on his soft, pudgy cheeks. He immediately tries to eat me when I do, and I let out a laugh.

A moment later the bottle warmer chimes, so I take the bottle out and give it a shake before bringing it to his mouth. He latches on with a ravenous hunger. I swear this kid could eat every second of the day if we let him.

"I know it's not the nipple you want, but Mommy is sleeping, so it'll have to do." When I smile down at him, he takes a break from drinking to smile back. Then he's suckling again like he hasn't eaten in days.

I carry him downstairs to the basement where Mia is still sleeping. I settle onto the bed next to her and place Liam between us, propped up on a pillow, his chubby little fingers holding the bottle in place.

Then I cuddle down next to him, holding him close and thanking my lucky stars that I was given a second chance in life. That somehow I ended up with the two most perfect people on earth as my family.

I could stare at these two for hours.

And that's exactly what I do.

KEEP READING FOR AN EXCERPT OF THE THIRD BOOK
IN THE RED-HOT SALACIOUS PLAYERS' CLUB SERIES
BY *USA TODAY* BESTSELLING AUTHOR SARA CATE

Give Me
More

Rule #1: When you can't be the third wheel, have a threesome instead.

Drake

I'M A FUCKING SCOUNDREL. I GUESS THAT'S AN OLD-FASHIONED term, but I don't really like the modern-day translation as much. Playboy. Man whore. Fuck boy.

I get around. I don't do relationships, and I can't stand the idea of commitment. The only people I've been with for any amount of time, I cheated on—multiple times. The first one being my high school girlfriend, whose name I can't even remember, and I didn't just cheat on her, I cheated on her with her best friend... only hours after taking her virginity.

I told you, scoundrel.

I'm not proud of it. I don't think it makes me a good guy and I'm not the kind of douchebag to flaunt it, but that's just who I am. I like to fuck, and while I respect every single person I'm with, it's not really a priority to me to learn shit about them. We can have a good time together and part ways, and no one gets hurt.

So it comes as a shock to no one that when my best friend offered me a job as head of renovations at his new sex club, I said, sign me the fuck up. I paved the bricks of my own paradise. Finally

SARA CATE

in the prime of my life, I should be set to live out my days exactly like this. At Salacious, I don't have to worry about sex partners who want tomorrows and forevers. I get to fuck as much as I want. Be as kinky as I want. With whoever I want—girls or guys.

Which leads me here. With one beautiful set of lips around my cock while another petite brunette rides my face. She's howling like she's been possessed by the devil as her clit grinds against my tongue. I'm about two seconds away from yanking my cock out of her friend's mouth and shoving it down her throat, just to shut her up.

I was going to let her come first, but she's getting out of hand, so I toss her off of me and pull her friend's lips off my cock to replace one mouth with the other. This isn't their first rodeo... that much is obvious.

Sometimes when it's their first threesome, you can tell by the way they stumble through the transitions, not quite knowing where to go when we change positions or where their parts belong, but these girls are seasoned. I can tell when the quiet one starts going to town on the other girl like she's in a pie-eating contest.

How exactly did I get here?

Well, technically, I got to this Phoenix rental house with Hunter and Isabel yesterday afternoon.

But more specifically, I landed here in pussy heaven after my aforementioned best friends decided to ditch me to celebrate their anniversary with a night on the town, leaving me to hunt down some mattress ornaments at the local nightclub. Obviously, it worked like a charm.

I mean...it's not like I wanted to celebrate their anniversary with them. Not even their wedding anniversary, but their ten-year *dating* anniversary. Who even celebrates those after getting married?

I don't know why I sound bitter because I'm definitely not. I mean...I'm about to shoot my load down a twenty-two-year-old's throat. Why would I complain?

Being the third wheel with those two is getting old anyway. I've been the third wheel for the entire decade of their relationship. Fuck, I was there the day they met too. I remember the look on my best friend's lovestruck face when he locked eyes with the demure four-eyed redhead carrying her books across the street.

I was there for everything after too. Hunter cleaning up his act. Getting a job for her. Climbing his way up the corporate ladder *for her*. Making himself the owner of a club *for her*.

Maybe if I had been the kind of guy to settle down with a beautiful girl of my own, I would have flown a little farther from their nest, but since I'm not, they practically treat me like their thirty-four-year-old love child, keeping me around for their holidays and birthdays, and as you can see, vacations.

It's not like I insert myself in their lives, but they are the only family I have. They're *all* I have.

And on that thought—not exactly sure why—I come, shooting straight down the loud girl's throat, and she swallows it down like a good little girl. I'm not sure either of them has come yet, so after my dick is spent, I collapse onto the mattress and let them finish each other.

In my post-orgasm state, I'm drifting off as I hear the front door open in the distance. There's some low chatter and movement across the small house until I hear their door close down the hall.

Something heavy weighs on my chest at the thought.

"You're not done yet, are you?" the quiet girl asks.

"Give me a minute, darlin'." Heaving a sigh, I relax flat on my back as the one with the nose ring—I think her name starts with a K—starts kissing her way up my body. She's already stroking my cock, trying to bring it back to life. Kristy, Kelsey, Kyla?

Seriously, woman. It's been like five minutes. Ever heard of a refractory period?

Then, there's a high-pitched moan in the distance, and I tense up. There's only some drywall between my room and theirs, and it's abundantly clear just how thin it is when I hear Isabel cry out again.

"Here he comes," the girl says as my dick thickens under her eager tugs. The other girl is in her own post-orgasm recovery next to us.

"Sounds like a party next door," the sleepy one replies as the bed starts thumping against the wall in a slow, rough cadence.

"Maybe we should ask to join them. Make this one *big* party," the girl on my cock adds.

"You talk too much." I flip her over and grab a rubber off the nightstand. Sheathing my already hard cock, I listen to the sound of my best friends fucking as I slam into the girl on her knees in front of me. She lets out a husky cry, so I grab her by the hair, pulling her up so her ear is next to my mouth as I mutter, "Louder."

And she does, but it's not enough to drown out the sounds of the woman in the next room. The one I should not be hearing, thinking about, or getting off to.

Rule #2: A little competition never hurt anybody.

Isabel

MY HUSBAND LOOKS UNHAPPY. ACTUALLY, I TAKE THAT BACK. HE looks happy because Hunter is good at putting on a smile and faking it for me when he needs to, but I can tell these things. I can see the subtle glances of regret and sorrow on his face.

"Are you sure you like your steak?" I ask.

"Yes, baby. I love it." He reaches across the table and takes my fingers in his hand, stroking my knuckles gently. I smile back at him.

I'm not the kind of woman to devote myself to being what society would consider *a good wife*. I don't even know what that means. In my younger days, I was so opposed to marriage. The idea of devoting my life to one relationship seemed irrational and daunting. How could I promise one person that I would love *only* them for the rest of my life? How on earth could anyone make that promise? Like we can see the future. Like any of us knows what's waiting around the corner.

But then I met Hunter Scott.

Hunter makes loving him easy. He worships me, makes me

better in every way, encourages me, inspires me, and makes me fall in love with him a little more each day.

So, naturally, I want him to feel that same radiating happiness he makes me feel, but I can tell by the way he's twisting the wedding ring on his finger and chewing on his lower lip as he stares down at the red wine in his glass that something is up.

"Should we have invited him?" I ask.

His gaze dances up to mine. "No. It's our anniversary. He understands. Plus, I'm sure he's already shacking up with someone at the rental right now."

I swallow down the unsettling feeling that image brings. Drake is a grown man, single and gorgeous. He can do whatever he wants. But is he really going to screw his way through our cross-country road trip? I'm sure it doesn't help that we are touring four different sex clubs on our business trip-slash-mini-vacation. I feel like we're taking our little boy to Disneyland.

An image of Drake in a hat with black mouse ears and his name embroidered on the back makes me giggle.

"What's so funny?"

"Oh nothing. Just wondering why we brought Drake, of all people, on this trip. There's a good chance we will lose him somewhere along the way."

"He always does this on our vacations," he replies with a laugh.

"We should know by now not to share a rental with him," I reply playfully.

"We really should." His fingers squeeze mine.

"You know…we should have brought him to dinner. Since he was there the day we met."

"Was he?" Hunter replies. "I only remember you."

I roll my eyes as I try to hide my blush. "Stop."

"No. Isabel, that was the best day of my life—the first of many. Seeing you on your way to the library, carrying that stack of books while your glasses started to slip down your nose." He's smiling, and it's infectious.

"You're mocking me," I reply.

"No, I'm not. I remember the exact thought that went through my head at that moment."

"Was it 'who still goes to the library?'"

"No. It was… 'I wish I could get a girl like that.'"

Leaning forward, I meet him halfway before our lips meet. "And somehow you got a girl like that."

When he sits back again, he's wearing another serious expression. "Because I changed."

"No," I argue. "Because I love you unconditionally."

He fidgets with the sleeves of his shirt, tugging them down as a habit to hide his tattoos. They crawl all the way up his arm from his wrist to his neckline. My husband seems to think that making certain choices from sixteen to twenty-three makes him undeserving of love. And I see the self-consciousness.

When I met him, I was a doe-eyed seventeen-year-old virgin. He was a twenty-three-year-old tattoo-covered criminal who did what he had to, to survive. We came from two different sides of town, two different worlds, two different paths. But those paths became one, and although our histories were different, our futures were the same.

Suddenly, Hunter was everywhere I turned. Afraid he would scare me, it took him months to gather up the courage to even talk to me. He figured out pretty fast that I could be found at the public library at least three days a week. And when he finally did approach me, he was so nervous, I could see him trembling. It was adorable.

But Hunter never scared me. Even with the tattoos and the reputation, there was a soft kindness in his eyes. The truth was…I saw him long before he saw me.

Ironically, I always told myself—I could never get a guy like him.

"I love you," I mumble softly as I rest my elbow on the table, placing my chin in my hand like a lovestruck teenager. In some ways, I guess I still am.

He smiles, those bright white teeth making my insides turn all gooey and hot. Why does he have to be so handsome? So charming and fun to look at.

"I love you too, Red."

My cheeks blush, and I know my neck and chest are brighter than my hair. "Hunter…" I say in a low whisper as my foot rubs softly against his leg.

His spine straightens and his head tilts, giving me that lust-filled gaze.

"Let's go back to the rental now."

"Check, please," he calls to the waiter, and I'm smiling so hard, it hurts my cheeks.

———————

We both hear the moaning before the front door even opens. It's just a small two-bedroom condo in downtown Phoenix, near the club we're touring tomorrow night. It was the smartest option since there are three of us. Instead of getting two hotel rooms, for the same price, we could just rent a small place.

But as I set my purse down and hear what sounds like a woman in the throes of a very intense orgasm, I'm starting to reconsider our options.

"Cancel the rest of our reservations," I joke.

"Jesus…I'm sorry."

I laugh. "Hunter…stop apologizing. You own a sex club. Do you really think this even affects me anymore?"

He corners me against the counter, placing both hands on either side of me, blocking me in. "Are you sure it doesn't affect you at all? Not even a little bit?" His lips land gently against the skin of my neck, just under my ear, and I hum in response. He knows all of my weak spots.

"Okay…maybe it does…a little."

His hands wind their way around my waist as he squeezes me closer. Pressing his mouth against my ear, he mutters darkly, "Should we give them a little *stiff* competition?"

"Oh, baby. You know I can do way better than her."

At that moment, another female voice whimpers in the next room, and Hunter pulls back as we stare at each other wide-eyed.

"Them," I correct myself.

With that, Hunter hoists me over his shoulder and carries me squealing into our bedroom. As he slams the door closed behind us, the moaning and groaning in the next room is suddenly louder. I guess we share a wall...wonderful.

Quick to distract me, Hunter drops me onto the bed and yanks me to the edge. My legs quickly wrap around his waist as he pulls his jacket off and then starts unbuttoning his shirt while I watch.

Licking my lips, I feast on the sight of my husband slipping the white cotton from his shoulders, revealing black, white, and red ink covering his skin like a second suit. Then, with a rough jerk, he yanks my dress up to my waist and tears down my panties.

Growling, he drops to his knees and nibbles his way up the insides of my thighs. I'm squirming with anticipation by the time he reaches my center, lapping and licking in fierce strokes as I moan loudly.

"Come on, Red. You can do better than that."

On that note, he plunges two fingers inside me, and my back arches with a guttural cry. His mouth is rough, and his fingers brutal as he sucks and nibbles at my clit.

The blankets are clenched tightly in my fists, and my heels fall with a clunk against the tile floor while my husband wears my thighs like ear muffs, not even coming up for air until I'm screaming.

My orgasm is fast and fierce, but before I've even recovered, he's flipping me onto my knees and crawling onto the bed behind me.

Grabbing onto the headboard, I brace myself for the impact as he slams home.

Hunter is rough in bed. It's probably my second favorite thing about him—just after that kind heart of his. And it's probably the dichotomy of his personality that makes the sex so delectable. He is warm and kind and quiet in person, but in the bedroom, he lets loose. He's wild and rough and almost primal. He growls and commands and dominates in a way that lets me know he wants me and only me. That he *needs* me.

"Louder," he grunts.

I cry out again, our bed smacking against the wall, and I swear I hear the cries on the other side get louder. Then, for some reason, I imagine what he's doing to them in that room. I picture Drake pounding into that girl the way Hunter is me. I picture sweat dripping across his bare pecs and over the ridges of his abs. I picture his dirty blond hair barely touching his shoulders. I picture his face and wonder what it looks like when he comes.

My body is flooded with heat and pleasure as I come again, my fingers straining in their tight grip around the headboard as I scream.

Behind me, Hunter pounds into me two more times before he groans through his own orgasm. And when I open my eyes again, I breathe through a wave of shame with the image of Drake still frozen in the forefront of my mind. And feeling for one second like the hands currently gripping my hips are his.

Quickly, I reach back and latch onto Hunter's hand. Turning toward him, I shake myself out of my imagination and feel relief when I lock eyes with my husband. The *only* man I should be thinking about when I climax.

So…what the hell was that?

Rule #3: Midnight kitchen meetings can be very enlightening.

Hunter

TEN YEARS. *TEN YEARS*.

Still feels like yesterday. I still feel like that drug dealer in the driver's seat of my dad's beat-up SUV. Twenty-three years old and just scrambling to get by.

Ten years in fancy suits and nice cars and a beautiful house I bought and paid for, for my beautiful wife.

I'm not going to spout some bullshit like how I don't deserve this, because I know I fucking do. I worked my ass off to trade a life of selling MDMA for one selling BDSM. I haven't lost touch. Somewhere inside, I'm still that stupid kid who's lucky he never ended up behind bars. But I don't feel bad about that. I did what jail would have done. I rehabilitated myself, and this woman next to me was my sentence.

Isabel is breathing softly, her messy mop of amber hair half-covering her face. Reaching down, I pull back the strands and kiss her forehead as she sleeps. Then, I carefully roll out of bed without waking her.

The red light of the old alarm clock on the nightstand shows

3:22. Life at the club has turned me into a night owl, wide awake all night and falling asleep at dawn. And when I hear a cabinet close in the kitchen, I know I'm not the only one.

"You really keep bad hours for a construction worker." My voice carries across the dark space, and the glass rattles on the counter when Drake hears me.

"Jesus Christ, brother. You scared the shit out of me."

I can't hold in my gravelly chuckle as I reach for a glass just behind him, his bare shoulder brushing mine. "Sorry."

"Couldn't sleep?" he asks.

"You know me," I reply in a lazy mumble. Filling the glass with water, I look over at my best friend bathed only in the light from the tiny bulb above the stovetop. As I set the drink down against the counter, I smile. "I thought for sure you'd be out cold. Sounded like a real workout in there."

He grins wide, leaning back against the marble, his broad hands bracing the surface as he hoists himself on top of it. In nothing but a pair of jeans, his bare feet hanging out of the bottom, he looks almost proud of himself for all the noise he was making tonight.

Technically, it was the girls making all the noise, I guess.

"Oh, you heard that?" he replies with a mischievous smile.

"Come on, Drake. Emerson and Maggie probably heard that back at the club. It's a small miracle the neighbors didn't call the cops. It sounded like you were drowning feral cats in there."

He's chuckling now, his chest rising and falling quickly with each breath. It must be nice to have a manual labor job like construction. Even at thirty-four, he's remained in perfect shape, without having to work out every day. Meanwhile, I had to install a full gym in our basement and live down there, part-time, to keep my physique.

His work on job sites is his weight training and sex is his cardio.

"These Arizona girls are crazy." He laughs. "I was only at the club for an hour before they had me sandwiched in an Uber. Can we stay?" he jokes with a toothy smile like a child.

"*You* can stay. Iz and I have three other clubs in three different states to see between now and next week. A few of them I know for a fact you don't want to miss out on."

"Yeah, that sounds more fun. Besides, the sounds coming from your room weren't much tamer than mine." He raises an eyebrow in my direction.

"Were you listening to my wife's sex sounds?" I reply with a glare in his direction.

"Oh, like it was the first time. Remember when the only place you two had to do it was in the back of the SUV and I had to wait outside? Or when we had that apartment in the city and I worked nights, trying to sleep through your morning sexcapades."

I'm chuckling into my water glass when I hear soft footsteps coming from the bedroom. "What are you boys still doing up?"

Isabel emerges from the hallway in her pajamas, a revealing pair of shorts and a skimpy tank top that shows off her perky nipples through the fabric. By this point, I've gotten over any jealousy where Drake is involved. He's seen Isabel in underwear before. It was a little hard to avoid when we lived together for those few short years before he started construction on our new house.

But when she leans over the counter smiling at us, and her tits are pressed together and practically hanging out of her top, I tense up.

"So you had a fun evening, didn't you?" she teases him. "Was that *two* girls I heard?"

"You heard correctly," he replies with pride in his tone. He's smiling at her, his eyes firmly set on her face. I can only imagine the feat of strength it's taking him not to even glance down at her cleavage.

"And they didn't wear you out?" she asks.

"Isabel...you don't think I can handle a couple twenty-three -year-olds?"

"You're getting up there in age. Can't keep hanging with those sorority girls," she replies with a sarcastic smile.

"Oh, I could handle the *whole* sorority."

She laughs. "I'm sure you could, Drake."

Meanwhile, I'm leaning against the fridge, watching them go back and forth, a subtle smirk tugging at my lips. I could watch these two go on like this forever. Isabel and I can make jokes and laugh together, but we'll never have the playful relationship she has with Drake.

And I'm not jealous of that. Because I know that's all it is. They joke like brother and sister...or at least like best friends.

Which makes sense. The moment she became my girl, he took her on as his friend too. Always looking out for her, treating her like I would, and bringing her right into the fold. As if she always belonged.

But it won't always be like this. That's my pessimistic, grim brain talking, but I know deep down that the clock is ticking on our youth. At some point, Isabel will want kids or Drake will settle down. And this family that I have now will change.

And as much as I do want to start a family with Isabel—and Drake to settle down—I hate change. If things could just stay the way they are between us right now, I'd be happy.

They are still going at it, both laughing and jabbing at each other with sarcastic insults, and through it all, his eyes have stayed on her face, never raking over her body or lingering too long on the parts of her I see other men gawk at. I mean...she's a yoga instructor. She lives in Lycra. And she's a fucking masterpiece. Who wouldn't want to look?

But Drake never does.

It's *her* expressions I'm not quite sure I can read. My wife is more discreet than Drake...or men in general. So when she lets her eyes drift to his pecs or bites her lip as she smiles at him, I start to wonder what is going on in that mind of hers. I'd pay anything to know. Even if it meant she was checking him out.

Again…I'm not sure I could blame her. Drake is as easy on the eyes as Isabel. His chiseled abs, golden sun-bronzed skin, dirty blond chin-length hair, and bright as lightning smile…make it fucking hard not to stare.

And I'm straight.

Isabel yawns as she straightens up and reaches for my hand. "Let's go back to bed. We have a busy day tomorrow."

Technically, today. We're meeting with the owners of a sex club here in the city, and it's the first of four clubs that we'll tour on this trip to collaborate, share ideas, and discuss brand affiliation. I'm not just here to scout for Salacious, but this is really about the opportunity for expansion. Emerson is considering a second location, and buying out a pre-existing club would be easier.

"Come on, Red," I whisper, placing Isabel under my arm and kissing the side of her neck. We wave goodnight to Drake, and just before I disappear down the hallway, I take one last glance backward at him, and I'm surprised to see his smile is gone, and he's watching us leave with an expression of longing on his face.

As Izzy and I crawl back into bed, I ask her, "Does he seem okay to you?"

She laughs. "Is that a serious question?"

"Yeah. I just noticed him looking almost sad."

"I'm sure he's just tired. He looked fine while I was talking to him," she replies, cuddling up on my chest.

"Yeah, that's because he's always smiling with you."

She lifts her head. "What's that supposed to mean?"

"Nothing," I reply. "Just that you two always seem to make each other laugh. But when no one was looking, he seemed a little down."

"So why don't you talk to him tomorrow?" she asks.

"Okay." With that, I plant a kiss on her mouth and squeeze her tighter against my body. With her heart beating softly against my chest, I start to drift off. Her soft hair brushes against my arm and her delicate breath kisses my skin.

Looking down at her, I smile, then kiss her again on the top of the head. How the fuck did I get so lucky? Ten years and I still can't believe it.

I just wish Drake could find someone like Isabel. I know I wasn't imagining that sad look on his face, and it's not the first time I've seen it. He pretends sleeping with random people every night is a dream, but if he could have what I have, I know he'd be happier.

Acknowledgments

Thank you for reading *Eyes on Me*. I really did set out to write a fun, sexy, hot-as-fuck book about the Salacious's biggest goofball, and I really hope I did that, but Garrett clearly had other plans. As so often happens, there was much more to this character than I first thought. Suddenly, what started as the funniest book I could have written quickly became the most important. You know a character means a lot when you find yourself talking about him in more than one therapy session.

If you ever feel the way Garrett did, for even one second, I see you.

If you ever felt the spiral was stronger than you, I see you.

And if you ever once felt like you had to hide the Big Sad because you were too afraid to be vulnerable or appear weak, I see you.

You're not weak. You're a fucking warrior. And you're amazing.

If you gather anything from this book, I hope you know that you can be funny and sometimes a little sad, sexy and emotional, horny and anxious, the life of the party and the one holding the most secrets. Or any combination, really.

The most important thing is that you just keep being.

Never let the storm win. I love you all immensely, and I hope for one second while reading *Eyes on Me* you felt that you are not alone.

Okay, that's enough sad talk. Let's get to these THANKS. Because this was THE hardest book I've ever written, I have sooo many thanks to give. I didn't do this alone, not for one second.

My team.

Amanda Anderson, my right-hand gal. So much more than a publicist, but my friend and biggest cheerleader. Don't believe me? I have voice messages to prove it. The universe brought us together for a reason. I'll say it until I die.

Amanda Kay Anderson, for loving Drake so much. And reading so many wrong versions of his story before I just let him tell it himself. And for being my soul mate.

Adrian Babst, for taking the time to read my stories. I appreciate you so much. I hope you know that. I hope I can offer you half the support you've offered me.

Rachel Leigh. My sister. You've been promoted.

My editor, Rebecca's Fairest Reviews. Your encouragement was great, but your tough edits were even better. I love that you can do both.

My proofreader, Rumi Khan. Your sweet soul makes my life easier. And the fact that you know whether hand job is one word or two.

Misty. Thank you for keeping me smiling through the storm.

My ball-breaker of an assistant, Lori, who works so tirelessly and selflessly behind the scenes. None of these books would have happened without you.

The sweetest reader's group in the world.

And my beautiful Sinners.

To all of the readers, BookTokkers, Bookstagrammers, too many to name, who welcomed me and my books with open arms. Y'all don't receive enough recognition for what you contribute to this community. You reached out after *Praise* to offer your support and well-wishes, and that right there cannot be appreciated enough.

And last, to Garrett for letting me tell his story, even the messy parts.

> If you or someone you know is ever feeling hopeless, please reach out for help. **You're not alone.** U.S. National Suicide Prevention Lifeline: 1-800-273-8255

About the Author

Sara Cate is a *USA Today* bestselling author of contemporary, forbidden romance. Her stories are known for their heart-wrenching plots and toe-curling heat. Living in Arizona with her husband and kids, Sara spends most of her time working in her office with her goldendoodle by her side.

You can find more information about her at saracatebooks.com.

Also by Sara Cate

SALACIOUS PLAYERS' CLUB
Praise
Eyes on Me
Give Me More
Mercy

WILDE BOYS DUET
Gravity
Free Fall

AGE-GAP ROMANCE
Beautiful Monster
Beautiful Sinner

REVERSE AGE GAP ROMANCE
Burn for Me

BLACK HEART DUET (WITH RACHEL LEIGH)
Four
Five

COCKY HERO CLUB
Handsome Devil

WICKED HEARTS
Delicate
Dangerous
Defiant